Learning to Heal

R.D. Cole

Learning to Heal

Book two in the Learning Series

ISBN-10:0-9912894-1-2
ISBN-13: 978-0-9912894-1-7

Published in the United States of America

Editing by Maxann Dobson, The Polished Pen

Cover Art courtesy of Rebecca Berto, Berto Design

Interior Design by Maxann Dobson, The Polished Pen

Table of Contents

Dedication

To all my readers. Thank you for loving Learning to Live and continuing with the series.
Xoxoxo

Prologue
Halloween

Jazz

The elation coursing through my body quickens my pace. I can't wait to tell Ollie the good news so we can start our family. Thinking of us together for the rest of our lives is a dream come true. My cheeks ache from the constant smile that spreads across my face, but it can't be helped. Family is important to me, and over the past two months since we've known each other he's shown me that it's number one for him too.

Walking into his class that first day was so nerve-racking. Sitting around all those strangers and not knowing anyone had me pulling out my bitch card. Of all the things I've learned in life, the most important is confidence. It's what gets you places. You can't let them see you sweat or cower. If they smell fear they will attack, and I've been attacked more times than I want to count. So I took a deep breath, straightened my shoulders, and strutted in like I owned that bitch. But when his eyes met mine I almost stumbled. I'm used to good-looking guys. My brother's best friend David is definite eye candy, but he has a problem keeping his dipstick in his pants. This was different, though. The dusting of grey hair around his temples gave him a distinguished look. Behind his glasses were the sexiest pair of dark blue eyes surrounded by thick lashes that matched his chestnut brown hair. They drew me in from the start, and when I looked into them I felt a shiver as my pulse picked up. It was love at first sight and I was lucky enough to experience it. When I saw the surprise in his eyes, I was bold and winked.

Maybe it was that one action that started our affair. Maybe it was his email asking me to meet him after class a few days later. I don't know or care. All I know is that I've loved him from the first moment I walked into his class.

Continuing into the staff parking lot, I concentrate on my mission. I know he said we can only see each other outside of town, but tonight is different. I continue on my way, wanting to surprise him with the good news. Besides, it's Halloween and I'm dressed up. Nobody will recognize me, and if they do, I'll just act lost or drunk.

I wait until I'm out of sight and quickly punch in the code on the driver's side door of his black Escalade. Thank God for my great memory and the fact that it's already dark out. He should be coming out of his office soon. He had canceled our plans to grade papers. I'm hoping when he hears the news, grading papers will be the last thing on his mind. The buzzing under my skin continues while I crawl in back and wait.

After about twenty minutes I finally hear the beep as he unlocks the doors and then the sound of him sliding across the leather seat as he gets in. I sit patiently, thinking of what our life together will hold while he pulls out of the parking lot. Maybe we can finally go to his place since I'm positive no one saw me get in his car. Maybe he has a few pictures of him as a baby so I can imagine what our little peanut will look like when he or she grows up. Thinking of becoming a mom causes a rush of nervousness. I don't want to be like my birth mom and I hope neglect isn't hereditary.

She was an alcoholic and eventually her cocktails also included anything she could stick into her veins. She was selfish and only interested in her next high or one night stand instead of snapping a photo or two of me, so I don't have any pictures of myself before the age of two. However, she did give me something to always remember her by every time I look in the mirror and see the scar. It's called Tetralogy of Fallot—a congenital heart condition—and after two surgeries I'm able to have a normal life. Well … as normal as it can be.

Shaking those thoughts from my head, I stare at Ollie's profile. He's grown a small beard and even though it scratches when we kiss, it looks really good on his strong jaw. Watching as he loosens his tie, my hands itch to touch him. I take a deep breath. I'm about to surprise him when I hear his phone ring over the car's speakers. Before I can warn him I'm here, he answers and I have no choice but to listen.

"Hello."

I want to purr from the sound of his deep voice. It caresses my skin as it reaches my ears and penetrates my brain. Then I hear the woman on the other line and my heart drops.

"Hey, baby. What time are you going to be here? Addie is dying to hit the streets for her candy fix." I can hear kids in the background screaming, and my eyes start to blur from tears. *Are those his children?*

"I'm headed your way now. Let me talk to her." I hear the rustle and commotion of the phone being passed to someone.

"Daddy, are you coming? All the good candy will be gone soon." The girl sounds so young, but my heart still cracks from the name she calls him. *Daddy.* That is his child. *He lied to me? He fucking lied to me?* I have to take several deep breaths to distract myself from jumping up and strangling him.

"Yeah, sweetness, I'll be there soon. I promise that you won't miss out, okay?" She hollers something playfully, but I can't make it out because of the blood rushing in my head. "Addison? Let me talk to your mom." I hear the girl squeal with laughter. "I love you, Princess."

The affection for this little girl is apparent in his words. Maybe he's divorced. Maybe he just hasn't had the chance to tell me about them. These thoughts continue as I rationalize how and why this happened. I'm starting to rein in my temper and feel better, so I decide to listen instead of jumping to conclusions.

"I love you too, Daddy." The rustling repeats itself and then the woman's voice comes back over the speaker, taking a razor across my already compromised organ.

"Alright, I think she's okay for a few minutes, but please hurry. She already wants to scratch her face paint off."

"I'll be there in ten." His next words just ruin everything we've shared and I want to weep. "I love you."

My heart doesn't just break, it fucking shatters. I feel sick hearing the words he's told me several times directed toward another woman. I let the sadness stay only for another minute before it begins to fester and morph into anger. No, not anger. *Fucking rage*. I want to kill him and cut out his lying tongue. I also want to hit myself a few times for falling for his bullshit. *Ugh! I am so stupid.*

When the phone goes dead and the music comes back on, I slowly sit up and wipe my red, mascara-smeared eyes.

"You're married?" He jumps and the car swerves from his surprise. I don't care, though, because all that I can think about is that he's continuously lied to me for over two months. My fist slams into the seat in front of me, and I ask him again, screaming, "You're married?"

"*Jasmine?* What the hell are you doing?" I see those dark blue eyes stare at me through the rear view mirror, but I feel numb instead of the usual attraction and desire.

"You're married?" I repeat and ignore his question. My question is more fucking important, and I need an answer from his lying mouth. Now!

Hearing a honk from some asshole behind us, I look around and see we're at a gas station. Instantly, I recognize our location. I grab the door handle ready to get away from him even though we're in the middle of the road. He locks it before I can.

"Calm the fuck down and sit still," he commands irritably. Why is he angry when I'm the one who's been lied to constantly?

"Let me out, you lying piece of shit, before I take off this shoe and embed it in your ear." I continuously wipe my face to clear my vision as I yank on the door handle. *Where is the stupid lock?*

Sighing with aggravation, he looks my way and one side of his lip turns up. "Why are you so upset? This doesn't change things for us, baby." He sounds so cocky. I don't even recognize his voice and it causes my skin to crawl.

Shivering from disgust, I try to locate the lock again before I vomit. Where is the sweet guy I fell in love with? What the hell just happened?

Once I notice he's parked the car, the lock releases and I open the door, eager to escape. My non-filtered brain causes word vomit to eject from my mouth.

"You sick bastard. I wonder what your wife will think."

Jumping down, I get ready to slam the heavy door, but he steps out and runs around to my side before I can make my exit.

Invading my space and looking pissed, he stares down at me. He's tall like Jax and compared to my four foot ten frame, it's intimidating. Deciding not to cower, I straighten my shoulders. I have every right to want to kick him in the balls hard enough that they fill his eye sockets. I lean my head back to meet his angry stare with my own.

"Now listen to me. You will not say a fucking thing. Got it?" Seeing the iciness directed my way, I move back and feel my legs hit the step while he continues. "The way you pursued me that first day is evidence enough that you are just a slut. The classroom was filled with other students who watched as you flirted with me. Not the other way around, darling. You are nothing but a freshman looking to pass that will spread her legs for a good grade." He takes a breath and gets in my face, continuing to knock down my confidence. Little by little. Piece by piece. "Plus, my wife is model material. Perfectly made with absolutely no flaws or scars to mar her skin. She's not scared to fuck without a shirt on or with the lights on." He looks from head to toe at me with a sneer on his face. "Not fucked up like you. So remember that before you open that mouth of yours."

As he backs away, I wipe at my tears. His words cut deep and will leave a scar of their own, but this one will be invisible but harder to hide. He knows how the scar between my breasts affects me. I try not to let anyone know how self-conscious I am, but I opened up to him. He was supposed to be my future. How stupid was I to honestly believe the words of affection and love that spewed from his mouth? A mouth that I loved to kiss and would stare at longingly while he lectured the class. Nausea rolls in my belly with the thought of his family at home while we had sex all those times. He kissed me then returned home and kissed his children with those same lips. Kissed his *wife.*

I inhale the night air, trying to breathe while my heart and self-esteem start to crumble and fall away. Even though I'm crying, I fight to remain calm because I refuse to let him know the actual damage his words and actions have caused me. Straightening my spine, I look into his eyes with the last bit of confidence I can scrounge up. "Fuck you."

I shove past him and walk toward Jay Jay's. I hope Mason's there. He always has a way to make me laugh—I sure could use one right now—but I doubt anything will fix the fissure that runs from my heart and collides with my soul.

Chapter One

Thanksgiving

Jazz

Shit, shit, shit! How did I get myself into this? My brain is like a messed up carousel with words continuously spinning around through my head. What am I going to tell them? How are they going to take the news? I don't know but I need to say something clever and possibly funny. Before I have it planned out perfectly, I run out of time. I know it's now or never. I'm woman enough to admit when I'm scared, and right now I'm terrified—not of my parents, but of my brother, who's sitting across from me staring at Tru while he tells us what he's thankful for. Even though I feel like gushing over their cuteness, I remain a nervous wreck. I take a deep breath and act like I'm listening to everyone, but really I'm freaking the hell out. My skin starts breaking into a cold sweat as my turn approaches, and I continuously tap my foot under the table to relieve some of this anxiousness, but it's a useless action. So I try to be positive instead. Maybe Jax won't go apeshit on me because we have Mason and his sister here and they would be witnesses to my murder. God I hope they'd be on my side and not the lynch mob's.

Okay, Jazz, you can do this. Telling them about the baby isn't the end of the world. Right? But it would have been easier with Ollie—excuse me, I mean *asshole*—here. So instead of discussing my future as a wife, I'm going to be discussing how I'm a single mom because I screwed my professor. *Ugh!* Why can't I get over this and just act like it's no big deal? I'm not the only person to get knocked up before I'm out of my teens. They even made a TV show out of kids having babies. I know why it feels like the end of my world. I absolutely hate disappointing people, especially my family. They have sacrificed so much for me my entire life, and I love them and will do just about anything to see them happy. Take college for an example. When they wanted me to go even though my grades sucked in high school, I didn't argue. It was the least I could do after they took me in and saved my life from becoming a dope fiend like my birth mom.

Too soon my thoughts are interrupted and I'm brought back to the here and now. To save face I make a rash decision not to reveal the identity of the father since Tru is the only one who knows about Professor Fuckwad. Let them make their own assumptions. Hopefully Tru won't say anything because she knows how important secrets are. I still don't know all of hers but hopefully she'll continue to keep mine.

I look up and see everyone's eyes on me confirming it's show time. I swallow back down the bile that continuously erodes my esophagus these days and put down the shredded napkin that's in front of me.

"Well, I guess it's my turn." I glance around the table and see Tru's nervous smile, but I can't return it right now. "I'm also thankful for Tru and a wonderful family ..." I feel my stomach starting to churn as I look at Jax. "...which will have a new member in June, because I'm pregnant." Thank God that's over. "Now let's eat." I pick up my fork and start to eat even though food is the last thing on my mind. Twelve pairs of eyes burn a hole in my body, but I continue to shove tasteless forkfuls in my mouth. I swear I'm about to be engulfed by flames and have a heart attack.

"What did you just say, young lady?" Taking a deep breath, I look up from my very interesting plate toward my very pissed off dad.

I give him my sweetest smile. "That you're going to be the sexiest grandpa ever." My voice shakes and my smile falters because his eyes are still hard. I was expecting this reaction from Jax but not daddy.

Hearing a noise, I glance over and see Jax standing, angrily staring in my direction as he leans over the large table and braces his hands flat on the tablecloth-covered surface. Tru just looks at me with pained eyes as I look to her for help. She quickly turns away and I know she's not going to offer any.

Jax moves toward me with his brown eyes narrowed. "Who?" His voice is deep with fury. I've never heard him like this so I'm speechless. When I don't answer, he asks me again—louder this time—and bangs his fist on the table. "Who, Jazz?" The china clatters and I jump. Trying to act unaffected, I shrug my shoulders and look around the table, desperate for an ally. Mom has one hand covering her mouth so I only see her heartrending eyes. David looks pissed with a red tint in his tanned face and ice cold blue eyes. He's like a brother and I've known him since I was fifteen, but he's also a sex-craved manwhore. I avoid my dad's stare, knowing I'll only see disappointment there. Turning to the person who has become a good friend, and the one person who can make me smile, I glance at Mason.

He's staring at me with so much confusion and hurt I try to lighten his mood by giving him a small smile. He doesn't return it like I was hoping, though. I suddenly feel alone and unwelcome in the house where I grew up.

I return my eyes to my brother, "Nobody. Just a guy I've been seeing."

I hear a chair slide back from the table, and I look to see Tru's back as she leaves the room. Jax tears his eyes from me and looks like he's debating on following her or staying. He glances at me once more. "I want a name. And I want it now."

Before I can tell him it doesn't matter because he's not going to be around, I feel Mason's strong, warm hand slide gingerly into mine and squeeze. His support is just what I need to get through the rest of the day, so I hold on tightly and glance his way. I hope my eyes say how much I appreciate his friendship.

He turns toward Jax and says the last thing I would ever expect. "It's mine. I'm the father." My stomach hits my feet and I'm speechless. *What. The. Fuck.*

Before I can find my tongue all hell breaks loose. Jax is across the table and Mason's on the floor under my brother's fist. Mason's little sister Grace, who's autistic and sitting beside him, starts screaming from the commotion. I try to run toward her but Mom's there before I can climb over the bodies rolling around on the dining room floor. Somehow Mason pushes

Jax off, so I step between them as he slowly gets off the floor. Thankfully David's arms are already around Jax to stop him from charging again while he cusses up a storm. I notice Cohen and Kenzie under the archway that separates the kitchen. Kenzie looks like she's in shock while Co looks ready to join in.

"Everybody calm down right now." Mom holds Grace and rubs her back. She looks pointedly at everyone while trying to gain their attention. However, the hostility is so thick a chain saw probably couldn't sever it.

Mason surprises me by facing Jax with a determined look on his face. Dad gets in his line of vision, though, and looks between Mason and me before putting his attention on my brother. He speaks with authority that leaves no room for argument. "Go check on Trudy." He turns back toward us. "You two, in my office."

I watch Jax shake off David's hold before he stomps toward the same direction Tru went. Mason turns and goes to Grace who jumps in his arms as she cries harder from the sight of his busted lip. He looks at my dad without fear or indecision from what he just did. "Sir, can you give me a minute with my sister. I promise, I'll be there, I just need to make sure she's okay."

My dad nods and looks at my mom. After she goes to his side, he pulls her into an embrace before they walk out of the room. Cohen and McKenzie quickly follow, while Drew just shakes his head and walks out in a different direction.

I glance toward Mason, ready to yell at him because of what he did, but my dad bellows, grabbing my attention. "Jasmine Marie Coleman. I mean now."

I turn and see David sitting at the table, eating, with a smirk plastered on his face like Thanksgiving wasn't blown all to Hell and back. I give him the finger because I feel like it. This only causes him to laugh harder of course.

Rolling my eyes, I make my way down the hall and up the stairs with bluster that is totally bogus. In all actuality, I'm really so terrified of what's to come that my heart vibrates my chest. I take a deep breath and start to rationalize with how ridiculous it is to be so scared. My parents love me and only want what's best. I know that. They aren't going to physically harm me. So, why stress? It all comes down to disappointing them, though, and that is something I hate doing, especially after everything they've done for me. My life would be pure shit without them … if I were even alive to experience it.

When I start to calm down, I pass Jax's room and hear Tru's grief stricken cries. My feet stop and the urge to go check on my best friend is so overwhelming I place my shaky hand on the doorknob. I stare at the white bedroom door wanting to make her feel better, but I don't know how or why she's so upset. Regardless of my confusion, the sound of her heartache causes my eyes to burn and my own tears to fall. I change my mind and keep walking, knowing my presence won't be welcome.

I reach my dad's office and knock on the ominous door.

"Come in." My dad's deep baritone voice reaches me through the wood, and I turn the handle. I say a prayer before I walk through, not sure if I'm ready to face my parents.

Once I step inside, my dad walks over and engulfs me in a hug. I let myself relax into his warmth while surrounding me with his familiar smell of Old Spice. Mom soon follows and wraps us both in her slender arms. I feel relief because they still love me. But will they after if they learn about my affair with a married man? Who already has children? We stay wrapped for a few short minutes, and when they both release me I feel bereft. Taking a breath, I go sit on dad's favorite worn, blue couch that's older than me and try to get comfortable. The hug was the last thing I was expecting and it brings more tears to my eyes. "I'm sorry." Just breathing breaches the silence after my sobbing apology escapes my lips.

"How far along are you?" I glance at Dad, so glad for those words instead of him asking me to pack my bags. The man in front of me looks different than he did twenty minutes ago. Older and more tired, not disappointed like I pictured.

Guilt for causing him to age and worry over my selfish actions overtakes me, but I battle it.

"Ten weeks." Pulling out the ultrasound that confirmed my suspicions two weeks ago, I pass it to Mom. I feel an automatic smile lift one corner of my mouth from just looking at the black and white image. I don't know what the hell it all is besides a small lima bean-shaped blob.

"And what's your plan?"

Shaking myself from my thoughts, I turn again and face my dad. When his question registers in my brain, I can't help but look at him like he's lost his flippin' mind. "What do you mean?"

"Jasmine, have you thought about this? And I don't mean about the baby. I mean really, really thought about this and what it means for your health?"

He sits beside me and I turn to face him. He knows all about my heart condition because he's the one that did the second surgery on me since the first one decided to do more harm than good. I was sent in shortly after I landed in the system for having a "tet" episode where I lost oxygen and became cyanotic.

"Yes."

It's all I think about. Instead of speaking my fears out loud, I smile and rush to ease their worries. They need to know or at least think I have everything under control. "But I already spoke to my doctor and they made an appointment with a local specialist to follow my pregnancy." They even have me *on watch.* If I have any issues throughout this pregnancy, they say they'll abort my baby. If it's up to me, though, that will never happen. I plan on taking it easy and after getting today over with, the rest should be a piece of cake. Or at least I hope so. I'll focus on a stress free pregnancy. Maybe do yoga or something like that. Plus, I promised myself I wouldn't worry until after a cause surfaced. Once I go to the specialist, I'll have a better understanding of what the future holds. Besides, every case is different. I've done my research on women with Tetralogy of Fallot who become pregnant and the outcome is usually good. Then again, most were probably able to run outside with other kids or jump in the pool without getting lightheaded and dizzy. Those episodes haven't happened in a while so I hope my heart problem doesn't cause health issues for my unborn child.

I shake these dismal thoughts from my head. I have bigger fish to fry and his name starts with *M.* I plan on frying his ass until he gets some damn sense in his head.

Chapter Two

Mason

Sitting on the dining room floor, I hold Grace in my lap while she cries. I feel like crying myself and not from the pain in my jaw, but from the news Jazz shared. Since that still hurts to think about, I'll concentrate on my throbbing face, but my mind still does a play-by-play of the past five minutes. Well, I think it's been five minutes. Maybe it's been longer. I remember everything happening in slow motion after Jazz announced she was having a baby. Panic set in and my heart broke with every second that passed while I sat there waiting for her to say "just joking" or "not" in her sweet voice. However, she looked uncomfortable and nervous, so I knew it was no joke. Then I felt anger over the bastard abandoning her. No one should raise a child alone. And thinking of Jazz lonely and tired had me grabbing her hand. She has me and it's about time she knows it.

I've known from the moment I saw her picture that she was out of my league. Her vibrant beauty is something only guys like David and Jax attract, not someone who likes to take apart computers or car engines just to put them together again. Studying something slowly to see how I can make it work the same way or differently is what gets my blood pumping, but seeing her caused the same effect and I knew I was in deep shit. I shouldn't have felt any of those things, but I did ... and still do. The more I watched her, the more fascinated I was and it's almost become an obsession. Rash decisions are not in me … or so I thought. Slow is more my speed. I like to study and calculate every possible outcome to all my actions. That way I won't be disappointed when things don't turn out like I thought because I anticipated every possible outcome.

But she always throws me for a loop with everything she says and does. With her confident walk and guarded eyes, she's something else, and I have been building up my courage over the past few months just to touch her. I've been able to a few times and it still amazes me that I even can. Every time I feel her soft skin under my fingertips I get hot and have to pull away before I make a fool out of myself. I'm not like David or Jax when it comes to girls. Sure, I'm not virgin, but I'm no smooth talking playboy either.

My childhood wasn't really a childhood at all. I would stay home most weekends while I was in high school. Mom needed to work a lot so I took care of Grace and still do when she needs to work. Needless to say my social life was nonexistent. I'm not saying I was a leper or some shit like that. I had friends and we'd play video games and go skate at the park, but that was rare. I usually did it if Grace was at therapy. Mom could rarely afford to get off of work to take her so I would study things on the school's internet and print out different pages to take home and work with her. Speech is still not happening, but I believe if she wants to speak, she will.

I shake my head and rub Grace's back as her breathing slows. She's not used to screaming or violence. We try to keep all her surroundings calm because she picks up on every sensation and detail. Today's situation is a lot for her to take in and I'm sure she's feeling an overload of feelings.

"Shhh, baby girl, it's okay." I feel her grip tighten on me and hear her moan as a response to my voice.

Finally after another minute she gets up and walks over to the table like nothing traumatic just happened. I straighten our chairs and make her a plate of sweet potatoes, mac and cheese, and dressing. She still has issues with chewing, so we like to stick to soft foods to prevent her from choking. I kiss the top of her head and notice David watching me while he eats. He doesn't look angry like he did earlier. Jazz has been like a sister to him since they met when she was fifteen. Instead, he's displaying his famous *Mr. Know-it-all* smirk.

"What are you smiling at?"

He leans back in his chair and laughs. "You." He takes a large gulp of his drink before he continues. "I honestly didn't think you had it in you to even touch a girl, but you did. And not just any girl, but your best friend's little sister."

He stands up as I'm about to say something, but I bite my tongue. I led them to believe that I'm the father of Jazz's baby and I won't take it back. I'm desperate to have her in my life and since she obviously doesn't want to acknowledge who the dick head is—no pun intended—I'll try to be good enough for her.

He throws his arm around my shoulder and leads me to the stairs. I'm dreading what waits for me up there, but I need to do this. Also, Jazz is up there alone and I want to be there for her.

Before I can dislodge David's hold, he stops and looks up at the twelve-foot ceiling. "If this has to happen, then I'm glad it happened with you and not some asshole." He releases me and backs away. "Jax will come to realize it too. Just give him time." He walks away whistling while I break out in a sweat.

I take a deep breath with every step. By the time I make it to the top, I'm light-headed. *Way to go, Mason, prove that you're able to make yourself pass out. That'll definitely win her over.*

By the time I reach the office door I start to feel better. My pep talk to myself seemed to help some, but picturing Jazz calms me down even more. Unless I picture her naked … then I really start to get worked up. Shit, the last thing I need is a boner while talking to her parents about getting her pregnant. I imagine the wiring inside my laptop; the low frequency synthesizer and how it sends signals to the phase-frequency detector to help.

I take a deep breath before knocking on the door. Mrs. Coleman immediately opens it and directs me to take a seat. I look around and zero in on Jazz sitting on a worn, blue couch, crying. Taking a seat beside her, I pull her in my arms. I hate it when she's upset because she's not meant to be anything but crazy, confident Jazz. When she hugs me back instead of pushing me away a weight lifts from my shoulders. I know we've become closer over the past few months, but holding her like this is rare. I rub her back softly and feel her tears soak through my nicest shirt. I don't care though, because any part of her is beautiful and welcome.

Too soon, an angry Mr. Coleman breaks the moment as he clears his throat. Looking up at him I realize they've been watching us the whole time. I hope they don't mind me holding their daughter like this, but then again they do think we slept together. I regret my last thought because I don't want Jazz to feel me harden below the waist. The last thing I need is for her to think I'm some kind of sick pervert who gets off on girls crying … or their mothers.

"Son, I can see you care for our daughter. It's very apparent. However, do you realize the responsibility and time it takes to raise a child?"

Jazz lifts her head and turns to face them. "Daddy, I can do this."

"We," I correct her without pause. She turns her glassy blue eyes in my direction for confirmation. Praying she doesn't tell them the truth, I give a subtle nod of my head. I exhale when she turns her attention back to them to continue.

"We can do this. Jax and Tru are getting an apartment and I'll just look for one close by. The campus has a day care, so when I return next fall for classes I'll be able to enroll the baby." She lets go of me and stands up to straighten her spine. I know this means her mind is made up, and I love how stubborn she can be … sometimes. "I've been thinking about this since I found out and I know I … sorry … *we* can and will do this." She scrunches her button nose and nods her head firmly to make her point.

I stand up and grab her hand to show her and them my support. When she smiles at me and squeezes my hand, my heartbeat picks up from the contentment I feel from that small touch.

"I had no idea you two were dating. Do you plan on getting married?" Clara asks this and I don't know how to answer.

The air rushes from my lungs with surprise from the question. As much as I want to be dating Jazz, I don't want her to feel obligated to date me because of the situation. But it would be awesome. Not going to lie.

"No and No. We're just really good friends who let things get out of hand one night," Jazz says in a rush. The kick in my stomach mixed with disappointment has me wanting to bend over. She looks up at me with a small smile. "However, you never know what the future holds."

Mr. Coleman runs his hands through his hair and leaves it in disarray. "I guess we just deal with it and wait." He looks at Jazz and then me with stern eyes. "I know how stubborn my daughter can be. If she's determined to do this all on her own, she will. So if you want to be a part of her life then don't mess up. Got it?"

"Yes, sir."

Her parents hug her before they make their exit. When we're finally left alone I feel at a total loss for my next move. I mean I've barely touched her and now everyone thinks we had sex. I can feel my panic rising with the situation. Wanting to feel calm again, I turn in her direction to gauge her reaction.

After a few seconds of staring at the door and tapping her foot, she finally puts those beautiful sky blue eyes on me. Knowing that I did it for her makes sense. I'd do anything for her. Then I see the anger emanating from their depths and notice her lips press into a thin line.

"What the hell, Mason?" She shoves me back so hard I lose my balance. Luckily, the ugly blue couch is there to save my boney ass.

She stomps her foot and her eyes start to glisten again. I hate that it's me that's causing her to cry. "Are you flippin' crazy? What are you thinking? I thought you were a genius or something. Not a moron."

Anger morphs into sadness and she sits beside me. Her body starts to shake while she cries, so I pull her toward me again. It just seems like she belongs there. That's the only reason I can come up with when I ask myself why I just ruined a good friendship. It's worth it, though, if I can be with her.

How do I explain my actions without sounding like an obsessed psycho? I should just try to come as close to the truth as I can. "Seeing how scared you looked downstairs while everyone just watched ... I just reacted. I don't like seeing you like that. It's not you." That wasn't so bad. Not false but not the whole truth.

Breathing in deep, she pulls away from my body, instantly taking the warmth that flows through me whenever we touch. Geez, I can be such a bitch sometimes. I'm glad the guys can't hear my thoughts. I wonder if Jax has these contemplations of Tru or is it because I grew up in a house full of estrogen that causes me to be a pussy sometimes.

"I just don't get you sometimes." She leans back and sighs while resting her head on the back of the couch. When her head turns to face me, our eyes collide. "One minute you're looking at me like I have two heads and you're going to run. Then you grab my hand and tell everyone that you knocked me up. Who does that Mason?" Silence descends while our thoughts take over. *Did I want to run? No. Not from her, but from the situation.*

"We need to go and straighten this mess out. I can do this on my own, Mason. I have a trust fund and the plan I have is solid." She sits up again and looks at me with her exotic, sky blue eyes that always take me somewhere else. “What you did was amazing and I will always remember it, but I refuse to allow you to go through with it. It’s crazy.” I see the plea in them and feel her hands shake as she reaches out and grabs mine. “Please, Mason. I can handle Jax. He’s my brother and it’s a rule for him to love me regardless of my screw-ups in life, but I can’t handle him being mad at you.”

She straightens her shoulders and gets the determined look back that always makes me smile, like she’s about to pull out her pink cape and save the world. “Now get your ass down there and tell them the truth.”

I sit there watching the sway of her sculpted hips as she heads toward the door. She might be determined to do this on her own, but I’m determined not to let her. Raising a child alone isn’t easy. Just ask my mom. Plus, this is probably my one and only chance to prove to her that I can be good enough. Taking back what I said earlier is definitely not happening, no matter what she says.

She gives me a look that says “get your ass going.” I ignore it, though, and just stare at her, hoping she knows that I’m not backing down. When I finally stand and walk toward her, I’m feeling different … confident even. I smile at her and watch her red-rimmed eyes widen with confusion. She might be stubborn, but so am I when it comes to people I care about. And I more than care for Jazz. I’m totally in love with her.

Chapter Three

Jazz

Mason has lost his damn mind. That's the only reason I can come up with for his actions yesterday. I tried talking to him about it while we were alone, but the idiot wouldn't listen. For someone so smart, he's acting so stupid.

I bang my head on my steering wheel while waiting for the light to turn green. His last word to me before he walked out that door is all I hear in my confused head. *No.* That's it. He just bent down to my level and smiled while that two-letter word rolled off his tongue. Did I argue? Nope. Why? Because I was frozen in place. I didn't recognize this person in my friend's body. Yeah, I was surprised by the confidence I saw in him while he strutted toward me. Yes, people, I said *strutted.* Mason Reed turned into some sexy person I've never met in my life and strutted. His look was suggestive instead of just cute. *Whatever!* I blame his stupidity on the fact he has a penis and my heated libido on hormones. According to the pamphlet my OB gave me they are all over the place.

I hear a horn honk and raise my head noticing traffic is going again. However, before I can push the gas the douche behind me honks again. Why must people mess with me today? I just roll down my window and show them my newly manicured middle finger. I don't feel like wasting my oxygen by telling them to fuck off.

Finally, an hour later, I reach the dorm. The campus is pretty much a ghost town since most people are still on Thanksgiving break. Until classes start back up Monday, I'm hoping to have peace and quiet. And even though I might get bored being alone and away from home, I just had to leave. I couldn't take the looks of disappointment directed toward me any longer. David took Mason and Grace home after he left the office yesterday. Mom, being her sweet self, gave them both a hug and sent them home with plenty of food. Nobody else said a word, though. Well, except David. He was acting like nothing had happened.

Walking in the dorm, I have second thoughts about staying here. I might want some R & R, but being here still brings back horrible memories of last week. I still can see Tru unconscious on the gurney and Jax crying while following behind her limp body. They moved her to a different room due to the crime scene, but we've been staying at the fraternity house with the guys. I'm definitely not going there and taking the chance of running into Mason. I'm hoping in time he'll really think about what I said and stop this ridiculous idea. Idiot.

I decide to just forget the last twenty-four hours and head to my room. I just want to sleep because I'm so tired. After I roll my bag through the doorway, I decide to text Tru one more time. I haven't seen her since I made my announcement and she walked out. I tried to talk to her several times, but Jax was being an ass.

I close my eyes after I fall on my pillow, waiting to see if Tru responds. I hate the silence. I hate being alone like this. I feel more alone right now than I can ever remember. My family is who I've always depended on to pick me up when I'm upset. Not this time, though. This time I have to depend on myself.

After a few minutes I hear banging and jump up with a shrill scream. I quickly look around and notice I'm in the dark and the moonlight is causing creepy ass shadows everywhere. I guess I slept longer than I thought.

The banging continues so I look around for something to use as a weapon, just in case. I don't own a gun like Jax, but I do own some candy apple red, platform stilettos that I'm sure can cause major damage to someone's eye. I rush to the closet and grab one before I slowly creep to the door, holding it up. I'm scared to death, but I think of Charlie's Angels and know if they can do it then I can do it.

When the banging happens a third time I yell, "Who's there?"

"Mason." I pray he's here to tell me he's changed his mind.

After unlocking the door, I crack it open with my shoe still gripped firmly in my hand. I lower it when I see it's truly the idiot himself and not an imposter. Of course I might still kill him if he wants to continue with his stupid idea.

I study him for a second to make sure my hormones are in check and I'm not seeing the sexy Mason I did yesterday. He's still cute with his clean, baby face that hides his dimples. His dark green eyes look almost brown unless he's in the sun. Then they transform into the same green as the leaves that grow on the ancient oak trees.

When I'm satisfied I allow him in. Holding a brown paper bag, he smiles softly when he passes me. I smell the greasy food emanating from its contents and my mouth fills with saliva. Realizing that I haven't eaten since before I left Pensacola, I shut the door and grab the bag from his hands. I don't care if it's rude. I'm still upset with him and I'm starving.

He laughs while I shove a few fries in my mouth. "Hungry?"

I just shrug my shoulders and grab a water from my mini fridge. After I sit on my bed, he follows suit and takes the bag from my hands. He passes me my food and then grabs his own. Looking down at the greasy goodness in my lap, I discover he brought me my all-time favorite burger. A chili cheeseburger from The Dew Drop Inn. I glance up and smile at Mason, who's watching me with interest.

It amazes me how easy food can change my mood these days. Before this pregnancy is over I'll be rolling everywhere just to get around. I remember my manners that have been branded into me by my mom and tell him thank you.

He just smiles and takes a bite of his hot dog. We eat in silence and it feels like yesterday didn't even happen. Mason's so easy to be around and can make anyone comfortable in his presence. I never feel judged, and even now, after everything coming to the surface, he acts like the same sweet Mason I met a few months ago.

When I'm full I start to feel better and my attitude dissipates. I exhale a deep breath and lie back on my bed to stare at the ceiling. "Man that hit the spot. Thanks again. I didn't realize I was so hungry." I hear the bag crinkle as he throws away the trash and then I feel the bed shift.

He lies beside me and looks at the ceiling too. "Now can we talk?"

I turn my head in his direction and watch his profile. He scrunches is brow while he thinks of what to say. With dread I sigh and agree because it has to be done. "Yeah."

"Good. I want you to hear me out before you say anything. I have to get this out and I know you." He smiles and turns his head to face me.

I can't help but smile back and nod while I wait for him say what he wants to say. He reaches for my hand and holds it in his. I feel the rough callus on the pad of his thumb as he rubs my palm, and I start to relax.

He turns his face away from me but continues to caress my hand. "Yesterday, when you announced you were pregnant, I panicked. Then I reacted before I knew what I was doing. However, I won't take it back. I know you feel like you can do this on your own, and I'm sure you can, but it's hard."

He stops and takes another deep breath. Event though I want to interrupt, I don't. I told him I'd be quiet and listen and I'm a woman of my word. "My mom raised us on her own and I see the load she carries and the effects of being a single mom. She wasn't always like that, though. When I was little she was happy, but then my dad was sent overseas and never came back. After that it was just the two of us and she was the sole provider for me. Luckily, the Army was good to us and we were left with a fair amount of life insurance, but Mom still worked and we eventually had to move to Mobile so we could live with her mother.

"When I was eight she met Grace's father. After they were married and my sister was born, the fucker emptied the bank account and filed for divorce. Shortly after, my grandmother died and she had no help." He finally looks at me again and tightens his hold on my hand as my heart squeezes for his family. We've never had such a deep conversation before, and I don't know what to think at the moment. For now I won't think. I'll wait until he leaves.

"I refuse to picture you like that, Jazz. Tired and resentful of the hand life dealt you. So like it or not, I'm going to help you. If you don't want me to know who the father is I'm cool with that. If you don't want others to know then I'm willing to be the name you give them instead. As far as I'm concerned, any asshole that leaves someone while she's pregnant is a complete waste. Especially someone amazing like you." He whispers the last part so low I'm not sure I heard him correctly. Then I see the pink rise in his cheeks and smile in his direction.

His story has left me speechless, so I just continue to look at him while I absorb his words. I'm dumbfounded that this guy is willing to sacrifice his life to help me out. Yeah, we've become friends, but I can't let him do this.

"I understand where you're coming from because of your mom, but I don't want you to give up your life. I'm not the only one who's gone through this, and I definitely won't be the last."

Releasing me, he sits up and places his elbows on his knees while he holds his head. I watch as his Henley stretches across his broad shoulders.

He's not overly built like some guys, but I'm sure he has muscle on his lean frame.

He continues to sit there for a minute before he concedes. "Fine, tell people what you want. But regardless, I will be here for you. It would just make it easier with you agreeing."

I sit up next to him and lay my head on his shoulder. He's my friend and I'd hate for him to be angry like everyone else. "Let me sleep on it. Okay? I'll let you know tomorrow." The offer is tempting, but I'm not sure if I can go through with it.

He rests his head on top of mine and puts his arms around me and squeezes. Then I feel that unwelcome rolling in my stomach that has occurred more often than I'd like. Morning sickness for me has become all damn day sickness.

I jump off the bed and feel the top of my head ram into Mason's chin. I don't care because I feel like my stomach is going to expel out of my mouth.

After I grip the toilet, my favorite food becomes my worst enemy. I really enjoyed that burger too. Dang pregnancy had to ruin my bad habit.

When I'm finally able to lift my head, I see Mason through blurry eyes and feel a cool rag on my forehead. I gulp for air and taste the bile that coats my throat. "Sorry."

He squats down and cleans my face for me gently. "See. Having me around might not be so bad after all." I can't say anything at the moment because my throat still burns, but he might be right.

Chapter Four

Mason

The last three days have been pretty good with Jazz. She's still not happy with my decision, but she finally stopped asking me to change my mind. To show her how helpful I can be, I bring her breakfast every morning and call later in the day to see if she needs anything. I don't hang out with her all day, though. I don't need her to feel smothered and start trying to convince me to change my decision.

It's the Monday after Thanksgiving and time to confront Jax. I know he just returned to Mobile yesterday and is moving Trudy into his new apartment, but this has to be done. He'll probably hit me again, but Jazz is worth it, even though it hurt like a motherfucker.

I drive around looking for his Jeep because he never told me which building he was moving in to, only the apartment complex. After another minute I spot it. Then I see David run down the steps and grab a box out of the back.

He stops mid stride when he spots my old Ford Ranger pulling in. His face forms that stupid grin that he thinks makes every girl "cream her panties" as he walks over to the window. I get out of the truck because my window doesn't roll down. Plus I have a feeling I'll need to go to Jax instead of the other way around.

"'Bout damn time." He slaps me on the shoulder, laughing like this is the funniest thing ever. "I wasn't sure you were going to show."

"Of course I showed up," I say in annoyance and look past him toward the stairs. I look back at David and wish he could be serious one fucking time. "Is he here?"

"Hell yes! He's been waiting on you to finally show your face. Now grab a damn box, fucker."

Finding that hard to believe, I just shrug like it's no big deal. I really don't want to fight again with Jax, and I won't throw a punch if he swings again. I would do the same if I were in his shoes. He's been a great friend since the day I met him and he's had to rescue my ass more than once. I might not be as tall or as built like David or Jax, but I can usually hold my own, unless it's two against one. When I first joined the frat I was targeted by a few of the other brothers. Maybe it's because I'm quiet and keep to myself. I don't really know, but in the beginning I was seriously thinking of quitting and moving into a dorm, but Mom wanted me to stay. Supposedly it looks good on future job applications. David and Jax had my back when one of the brothers decided to bring a girl to my room for a private party. He wouldn't take the hint, and he and his buddies acted like they made the rules and if they wanted to sleep with a girl in my bed they could. After a few sucker punches to the gut, they were thrown off me and Jax helped me off the floor. Needless to say I wasn't picked on after that and my bed was off limits to any more private parties.

Grabbing a box, I follow David up the stairs as he rambles on about some redhead he hooked up with over the weekend. Even though I couldn't care less, I nod my head while trying to analyze all of this visit's possible outcomes. Picturing Jazz in my mind eases my nerves some and makes this easier. I know she told me to confess to everyone the truth, and as tempting as that might be, I refuse to do it. My anger starts to escalate, and I feel my blood start rushing in my brain whenever I think of some piece of shit touching her then leaving her on her own.

"Calm the fuck down, dude. Don't go in there looking for trouble."

David's right. Even though my anger isn't directed toward Jax I can't say differently without giving away the truth. "Yeah, sorry."

We reach the door and David knocks loudly. I hear a movement on the other side before Tru opens up with a smile. It falls however when she sees me standing there and I feel like shit.

"Mason." Her voice is strained as she looks around awkwardly. "Come in." She turns to David and gives him an evil look, most likely because I've showed up unannounced.

David pushes his way in with the box he came downstairs for and places it on the bar. He sees me standing in the small entryway with my hands in my pockets not knowing what the hell to do now and decided to yell so the whole building can hear. "Hey, pussy. Grow a penis and get in here."

Taking a deep breath, I walk in his direction because he seems to be my only ally at the moment. He might be a dickhead at times, but he's a good friend when needed. And I definitely need him now. Before I get to him Jax comes out of the hallway and stops when he sees me."Mason? What the fuck are you doing here?" His eyes narrow as he stands there. I can practically see the image of him ripping my head off my neck reflecting in his glare.

"I need to speak to you." My voice is surprisingly steady and my eyes remain on him. When it comes to his sister I'm more than serious. I'm also determined. She seems to make me more without knowing it. Braver. Happier. Just more than I was before her. I guess love is the ultimate super power because I'd take on the world just to make her happy. And facing her brother and my friend feels like I'm facing the world.

His brow furrows while he eyes me up and down for a few seconds. Finally, he nods and turns back down the hall without a word.

I follow behind and pass Tru, who's sitting on the couch unpacking. She actually smiles softly before she continues what she's doing. Maybe that's a good sign that today will go well. Maybe I won't get a busted lip this round. I walk into the room and shut the door behind me, ready for whatever he wants to dish out. It's now or never. "I love her."

That's the first time I've admitted my feelings for Jazz out loud and it feels good … natural, like I'm meant to say it. I want to shout it to the world at times, but then I remember that she doesn't love me in return so I restrain myself. He still has his back toward me and I can tell he's tense. "I won't let her go through this alone, Jax. I only want what's best for her."

After a few seconds of silence, interrupted only by his breathing, he finally speaks. "You want what's best for her?" I'm about to say yes, regardless of his angered question, but he continues. "What's best for her is not to be pregnant at nineteen fucking years old or ever for that matter. What's best for her is to stay away from assholes like you who are unable to keep your pants up." He finally turns his eyes on me. Instead of the anger that matches his voice, I only see sorrow. "Do you realize what this means?"

I feel like I'm missing something, but since I'm not sure what it is exactly, I repeat my earlier statement. "I'll take care of her, Jax. I won't let any harm come to her and promise to make her happy."

He just stares at me for a second with confused eyes. Then he starts laughing, but it's not a joyful sound. "You have no fucking clue, do you? Do you even know my sister? How can you love her and not know a damn thing about her?"

"What the hell are you talking about, Jax? I know her and love everything about her."

"Then you're fucking stupid. Can't you see what this pregnancy means for her health? Her heart?"

Her heart? I feel bewildered by his rambling. Letting my brain drift back to the first time I met Jazz, a bad feeling settles in my gut. When the puzzle pieces fall into place I feel lightheaded and sick. Her heart. Her two open heart surgeries she had before her third birthday. I lean against the door behind me before I collapse from shock. Sticking my head between my knees, I try and remember to breathe. *Just breathe, Mason. It's going to be all right.*

"So that brain decided to wake the hell up I see." Glancing up, I watch him sit on the bed. The look of anger and sadness on his face must match my own.

Then my mind is on Jazz—her beautiful smiling face that looks so healthy; the mole resting on her left collarbone that I've pictured kissing every night for months; the sound of her husky voice that causes chills to surface all over my body; her contagious laughter. I love everything about her and knowing that child is a part of this woman causes me to love him or her just as much. Then I'm visualizing her pale skin after those couple of dances at Jay Jay's that first night, and the dark circles under her eyes. She has been tired and sleeping more than usual. Is the pregnancy already causing problems for her? If so, how do I make it better?

I finally take a breath after a minute and look toward Jax, who's resting his head in his hands. "What's going to happen to her?"

He looks up and shrugs. "I have no goddamn clue. Every case is different." He heaves a sigh while I just sit and lean my head against the door. "You really had no clue that pregnancy is bad for her heart, did you?"

"No. I never want anything bad to happen to Jazz. I don't know what my life would be if it did." I run my hand down my face and notice I'm sweating.

Jax is watching me with a defeated look. "Look, Mason, I know you care for my sister. It's obvious to everyone. I also know from the way you look right now, you had no clue what had us all upset Thursday. Don't get me wrong, I don't want her pregnant, regardless of her health. Then again, she's almost nineteen and not really a kid anymore, so her being sexually active is something I have to deal with. However, it has to do with her health more so than her being so young."

Feeling restless, I stand up quickly. Pacing in front of Jax is the only way to keep myself from walking out that door and running to her class. I run my hands in my hair trying to think of a way to fix this but nothing comes to mind. Desperation radiates from my every pore. I look at Jax and remember he's planning on becoming a cardiologist. He'll know what to do. "Shit, Jax. What do we do?"

He shrugs. "Nothing. It's her choice and I know my sister. She'll go through it no matter what. We just need to watch her. Make sure she doesn't get too stressed or exert too much energy." He comes and stands in front of me. "Mason, we're friends so I'm glad Jazz has you instead of some fucker who would use her. I hope you know what you're getting into, though. She was a handful before pregnancy so I can only imagine her hormonal." He gives a small laugh and tries to lighten the mood.

I force a smile, desperate to feel better, but I still feel as though I might pull my hair out if I don't see Jazz soon. I leave a few minutes later and head to her dorm even though she's not there yet. I'll wait until she's done with her classes. As much as I want to talk with her about her health, I won't. I know Jazz. She'll hate me constantly hovering so I'll just discreetly keep my eye on her.

Chapter Five

Jazz

I lie on my bed fighting another bout of nausea when there's a knock on my door. I feel like shit and hate moving my body, but I know it's probably Mason and he's been relentless lately. *Ugh! Why won't this kid keep the food down?*

When I hear the knock again I finally make myself get out of bed. "Hold on. Sweet Jesus, Mason, I just need to make you a stinkin' key." I grumble the whole way to the door while trying to get my heavy feet to cooperate. When I finally pull it open, my complaining stops because the last person I expected stands in front of me. "Tru?"

We haven't seen or talked in a week, and I've missed her so damn much. I want to cry and jump for joy at the same time, but I'm still too weak from throwing up a few minutes ago.

She gives me a small smile, and I automatically hate the awkwardness that has invaded our relationship. "Hey."

Oh screw being weak. I walk up to her as tears blur my vision and grab her into a hug and wail like my dog was just ran over. "Oh my God, Tru." I sniffle and blubber into her shoulder. I don't care because my sister is back. "I missed you so much and I'm sorry for making you mad. I'm sorry for your disappointment."

She pats my back and I notice she's crying too. "No, Jazz. I'm sorry. I'm sorry for being a selfish bitch instead of the friend you needed. I'm sorry for not checking on you or texting you back." She pulls me away and looks into my eyes that I'm sure match her red, leaky ones. "Most of all I'm sorry for being jealous instead of happy for you."

That catches me off guard. "What?" I wipe my eyes and snotty nose with the back of my hand. "What do you mean?" I look over Tru's shoulder and see a few girls watching from the hallway. "Excuse me, don't be so fucking nosy. If we wanted an audience, we would have sold goddamn tickets. Now move along." I shoo them away with my hand like they're rodents and ignore the eye rolls.

Tru starts laughing and grabs my arm to lead me into the room. "I see you haven't lost your people skills."

I sit on my bed and pat the space beside me. "Well, my God. Bitches are so nosy."

She sits down beside me Indian style while wiping her eyes. It reminds me of all those times we'd chat about stupid shit all night long. Well, I did the talking most of the time. "Our rooms are known for the drama. Of course they watch for it. Who needs reality TV if it's next door—live?"

After we compose ourselves enough to talk, we still remain silent. Where do we start? Tru must feel the same way, but instead of thinking about it, she actually starts the conversation.

"So, like I said, Jazz, I'm so sorry for not being here for you. Knowing I should have been, but not able to get past my own feelings is my only excuse. I was so taken aback at first because you are my friend and never mentioned anything. But the main reason was because I was jealous."

"Jealous? Why be jealous of becoming a walking vomit dispenser. I can't keep anything down and certain smells just ruin my day. My bladder is getting more action than I am and it ruins my sleep." I feel my tears start again and curse the hormones. "Geez, Tru! I can't stop fucking crying either. I'm either puking, peeing, or crying. So either way something's always being expelled from my body."

Tru reaches for my hand and squeezes. "Because, Jazz, I want another baby so bad sometimes."

"Another baby?" My voice rises a few decibels, and I'm sure the nosy bitches love it. I continue in a whisper. "What are you talking about?"

She wipes her eyes and nods. "I had a son last February. He didn't make it because he was too small. It hasn't been easy, and until I met Jax and your family, I thought I was going to drown in my grief. I miss him all the time and would love to hold him again. And even though it's better, it's still there. That emptiness."

Now I understand why she was jealous and my heart hurts for her. “I’m so sorry, Tru. I didn’t mean to get pregnant. I promise. I wasn’t trying to hurt you in any way. God, I’m so sorry you had to go through that.” I reach over and give her a hug. It’s all I can do for her and I hope it helps, even just a little bit. To be alone with no one to help? Wow! She is way stronger than most people. I would have crumbled into nothing. Now I feel selfish for complaining about something she’d love to be going through again. Why must I always be selfish?

“It’s okay. I know you didn’t purposely get pregnant, silly. I’m also happy for you. It was such a surprise and I just had to grieve for my loss. It’s something that hits every once in a while, but it’s getting easier.”

“Does Jax know?”

“Yes. He was the first person I told. I had to tell him everything before we started dating. He needed to know what a mess I was. And he was so patient and sweet when I told him. He didn’t look at me differently or judge me like I thought he would.” She smiles softly while wiping her eyes before she looks at me with a serious expression. “Please take care of yourself. I didn’t have the support or the money to do what should have been done. Brian was much smaller than usual and…” she stops and looks down with embarrassment “...sometimes I can’t help but blame myself. If I had only gone to the doctor more and bought the vitamins that were too expensive at the time...”

A need to change the subject sets in because I know her. She’s stubborn and no matter what I say, her feelings won’t change. She has to deal with her regrets her own way. “So since Jax was the first to know, am I the second?” She shakes her head and blows some hair out of her face. “Who was?”

"Benji," she says somberly, and I feel bad for bringing him up. He's only been gone for a month, but to me it feels longer. I knew they we're close, but I didn't know they we're that close.

We sit lost in our own thoughts for a few minutes before she speaks again. "Will you answer a question for me?" I can only nod my head because I'm dreading whatever it is. "Does Professor Wallace know you're pregnant?"

Shit. Panicking, I keep my outer appearance from showing it. I don't need her telling my brother about Ollie and me. I put on my familiar front and smile at her like she's lost her mind. "Why would Professor Wallace need to know about my pregnancy?"

"Isn't he the father?" She's watching me closely, and I hate keeping secrets, but I will keep this one.

"Nah. We've been over for a while." I smile like it doesn't hurt, but I still feel my heart twist when I think of his deceit and my own stupidity for believing him. I've been avoiding anything to do with that man and even dropped his class the first of November.

"Who is then? Mason?"

Seems like Mason's fucked up wish to play daddy is about to come true. "Yeah." I stare at my hands, unable to look her in the eye while I blatantly lie. "We hooked up one time. In fact, he was my rebound after Ollie and I ended it. It was no biggie."

"Are you two dating?"

I feel her eyes on me while I pick under my nails and think over the question. "Um, not dating romantically, but we still hang out. He was totally fine with the arrangement—no ties or regrets." I look up and smile. "He swears he's going to stick by me no matter what. Even though I told him not to."

"I believe it. He's a really good guy and he's wonderful with his sister." She looks at her watch before she stands. "Jax and I want to have you both over Sunday for dinner. Okay?"

After standing, I grab her into a hug and squeeze. "I've missed you so much, Tru. Thanks for coming by, and I'll get with Mason about Sunday." I watch her leave and sigh. I now officially have a baby daddy.

Racing through traffic, I look at the clock on the dash. We still have half an hour before Jax and Tru are expecting us, but since Mason's mom had to work an extra shift and use his truck, I'm picking him up from her apartment. I told him Grace could come but he says his neighbor will watch her. I'd rather her come because maybe it wouldn't feel so much like a date with her there.

I look at my reflection and check my appearance. I might have puked a few hours ago, but dammit, I will look good. Smiling real big, I see some pink lipstick on my front teeth and wipe it off just as my GPS tells me to take a right. Barely making my turn, I hear several honks from behind me and really don't give a crap.

After I pull into the apartment complex, I see several kids playing basketball in the middle of the parking lot and girls playing jump rope. They look happy and carefree, unlike me when I was that age. Hell, unlike me at this age!

My mind drifts to my childhood and how different it was compared to most children.

"But, Momma, I want to play with Lydia and be on her team," I cried with angry tears running down my cheeks as I watched my best friend and the other kids pick teams for the kickball game that was about to start. It looked like so much fun every time they had a game and I know I would have been be good at it.

Just once I wanted to play. I was never picked, though. Not because the kids didn't call my name, but because Momma wouldn't let me play. She said it wasn't good for me, but I felt fine. I just wanted to play!

"Honey, we've been through this." She knelt down to my level and looked at me with her pretty brown eyes that reminded me of Hershey's Kisses. "You can't get out of breath. It's not good for your heart."

I stomped my foot and crossed my arms in front of me. I was so angry and felt stupid for even thinking I'd be able to play. I didn't fit in with anyone, not even Lydia and she loves pink just like I did. When I heard the other kids laughing, I knew they already started the game without me. *Again.* Wiping my snotty nose, I stared at my mom. She needed to know how angry I was because she was being mean. "Well, I hate my heart then. I don't want it anymore." I took off to my room, not caring that Mom was yelling at me to slow down. I just wanted to be normal.

A knock on my window has me jumping out of my memory and out of my skin. Looking around, I see I'm parked. I guess I was so consumed by my memory I don't even remember doing it. I turn toward the knocking and see Mason standing there with a concerned look on his cute face. I step out the car and lock it but don't make a move to walk toward him because his attire catches me off guard.

Instead of his usual logo T-shirt and jeans, he's wearing a dark green polo and fitted khaki pants. He's even sporting some Sperrys on his feet. Now it feels like a date because we are both dressed up … but I always dress like this.

Well, not exactly like this. I mean I don't always wear something so tight, but I'll be fat in a few months and won't be able to fit into it anymore. It's a mid thigh sweater dress with a swoop neck that's the same shade of pink as my lipstick. I have a thin brown belt around my waist and matching five-inch high-heeled boots that reach my calves. I decided against the tights, though, because I seem to be having hot flashes lately.

We stand there for what feels like forever staring at one another. How did we go from comfortable conversation to uncomfortable silence? Before I can compliment him on his clothes I hear someone call his name. I look in the direction at the same time he does and see a girl about my age or older with dark, brown hair in a stylish pixie cut walking our way. She's staring me down with her creepy golden eyes like I'm a threat. *Oh hell no!* I straighten my shoulders and do what I do best—not take shit. I've never let anyone see my insecurities except for one person and that will be the last time. People like to play on your weaknesses and I refuse to be weak.

She finally looks toward Mason when she reaches us and smiles sweetly. "Here, idiot. You almost left your phone." She hands it to him and bumps his shoulder with hers playfully. I see some type of relationship here, but I'm not sure if it's a romantic one or not. In my opinion he can do way better than her, but I really don't care.

"Shit. Sorry about that." He turns toward me smiling and is completely unaware of the bitch stare this girl is still giving me. "Jazz, this is Chanda. Chanda, this is Jazz." Chanda? What kind of name is that? I internally slap myself for acting like I care … because I shouldn't … and don't.

"Jazz? Like a music genre? Maybe I should call you rap or rock. Hey, I know … techno."

Okay? Maybe I can hate her name after all. Plus only my friends call me Jazz, and I have a feeling Chanda will not be a friend any time soon, if ever. Instead of taking off my boots to throw down, I stick out my hand, gracing her with the manners my parents raised me with, as well as my Gucci white gold tennis bracelet with its chocolate diamonds. "Actually, I'm named after an exotic flower. Please call me Jasmine. Nice to meet you, Chanda."

Ignoring my polite introduction and protruded hand, she looks at Mason. "Remember, I need to be at work at midnight." Then she walks away.

"Well, she's lovely." I lower my hand and shake off the embarrassment before I get back in my car. Watching Mason walk around the car to get in, I fight down the urge to drive over Chanda while her back's turned. I have a feeling this won't be the last time the compulsion crosses my mind with that bitch.

Chapter Six

Mason

Walking around the apartment that Jazz is looking at to rent, I notice her excitement as she goes from room to room. I felt the same way when she told me about her talk with Trudy and how she said I was definitely the father. I knew everything would fall into place. I know she still needs to fall in love with me, but I'm a patient person. You have to be with Grace.

We haven't had an official date or anything yet, and I'm tempted to ask her, but I still can't get a read on her. Actually, I suck ass when it comes to reading girls period. My one and only girlfriend was my sophomore year and I thought she hung the moon. Little did I know she was screwing some older guy behind my back.

Following Jazz, I can't help but laugh at her animated face while she takes in the two-bedroom apartment that's in the same complex as Jax. When we went over last week Jax mentioned how a place was available and he had set this appointment up for Jazz to take a look. I'm very happy with this idea. Neither one of us likes the idea of her being alone at the dorm after the incident with Tru a few weeks ago, so I'm glad she'll be close to them, even though she'll be farther away from me.

I round the corner to the master bath and chuckle when I see Jazz lying back relaxing in the empty Jacuzzi tub. I shake off the vision of her naked flesh immersed in water that flashes in my mind and sit on the edge of the tub. "What are you doing?"

"I'm checking the size of the tub. Duh! I want to make sure it's deep enough."

She's so small I'm sure the sink is deep enough for her. "Jazz, the bottom will be like an abyss if you fill this thing all the way up. I might have to invest in a life jacket for you."

"Ha ha, rude ass." She swats my shoulder and starts to stand. "I'll have you know there are actually a few people smaller than me."

"Like who? Cohen doesn't count either." I dodge her fist and go into the master bedroom. I notice there is only one way to arrange your furniture with the way the outlets sit on the walls. It's nice, though. Way nicer than my mom's place. We walk around and I listen to all her plans for each room. She wants to make the second room the nursery, and while she tells me about how she'll place the furniture, I lean against the doorframe and watch her every move. The way she talks with her hands or how she'll occasionally run her fingers through her hair are things I've always loved. She's so full of life and spunk and can light up the darkest room when she walks in.

She turns toward me and bites the inside of her cheek. "So, I've been wanting to ask you something and I'm not sure what your reaction will be. Just know with this arrangement you're not obligated to do anything. Okay?"

Nodding my head, I walk to stand in front of her. "What?"

She looks up and bites her lip, and my eyes focus on her wet, pink tongue that sticks out for just a second. "Will you go with me to the doctor Tuesday? It's my second visit and I really hate going alone."

Smiling down at her, I feel relief course through me. The more time we're together, the more accepting she's become about us. This is a huge deal to me. "Of course I will."

After the lease is signed and down payment is paid, Jazz takes me back to my mom's. I have to watch Grace and finish studying for finals this week. I'm not too worried, though. I have A's in all my courses so I know I'll pass even if I flunk the finals, but I do need to keep my grades up for my scholarship.

It's the only reason I was able to attend college, and even though the University of South Alabama wasn't my first choice, but I knew I had to stay close to my mom and sister in Mobile. I'm lucky to have a well known university close by instead of just a community college. But even if I only had a two-year college available I would have went. I'm not one hundred percent sure of what I want to do yet, but I'm leaning toward biochemical engineering. I also love anything technical. To make extra cash I work on computers and hard drives for anyone who asks. I even do some formatting as well as fake IDs, but Mom doesn't know about that job. I guess you could call me a hacker, but I refuse to change people's grades in the system or hack into a bank like they do in those movies that give kids like me a bad name.

The whole way back Jazz is going on and on about her apartment and I'm happy for her. When we pull up, I hate saying goodbye—like always—so I decide to invite her up to meet my mom.

"Um, I don't know, Mason. Does she believe I'm pregnant with her grandchild?"

"Yeah. I didn't tell her until after you told Tru. I hope that's okay?" Mom definitely wasn't happy about the news, but she knows me. I take care of what's mine.

"Can we do it another night? When I'm more prepared. Plus, I'm sure your mom's getting ready for work and would like a heads up before company comes over."

Even though I'm disappointed, I agree. "Yeah. I'll check her schedule and we'll plan something." I open the door to the apartment building and turn in her direction. "I'll see you Tuesday."

I watch her pull away and walk up the concrete steps. When I get ready to unlock the door I hear the door across the breezeway squeak open. Turning, I see Chanda with her pack of Marlboro cigarettes. "Hey, Chanda."

"Hey, Mason. You watching Grace tonight?" She lights her cigarette and takes a deep drag while she watches me with her golden eyes.

Eyes that I used to think I loved when I was younger. We grew up together when I moved to Mobile with Mom all those years ago. She was into the same stuff as me and my friends: games, comics, and skating. Since she was my very first friend, we had a special bond. That bond broke after my heart did. When I found out through a friend that she was sleeping with his older brother, I lost all respect. I have never been the guy to get a girl, so when a girl like Chanda kisses you like she owns you, you fall hard. After she admitted to dating this other guy she ended up dropping out of school and left town with him and his band. She eventually came home after a while and *rock star* is nowhere to be found. Go figure. Now she lives with her dad and works at the local diner with my mom.

"Yeah. Mom's working the register tonight." My mom works two jobs to stay afloat: waitressing with Chanda and working the register at a truck stop gas station. I made her buy a gun last Christmas and take a few shooting lessons because she was robbed before. I hate that she works so hard and give her all I can. One day I'll let her quit and she can focus on herself for once. That's my plan anyway.

"I saw your girlfriend drop you off." She inhales another drag and I just watch as the smoke rises around her thin face.

"She's not my girlfriend," I state and immediately regret it.

"Then what are you two? Your mom told me she's pregnant with your kid."

"We're friends," I say, because it's true. "Things happened and now we're having a baby together." I shrug and turn around again toward the door, ready to end the conversation. "See you later." I don't look back and just walk inside to release a breath. I hope Chanda keeps her nosy self out of my business. She loves to gossip and spread lies. My mom thinks everything she says is true too, and I really don't need her spitting stories about Jazz.

I throw my truck keys on the scratched coffee table and walk down the hall. “Mom?” I reach Grace’s door and knock. No answer, so I crack it open. The light is off and it’s empty. Then I hear familiar laughter coming from Mom’s bedroom and head in that direction.

After I knock and get the okay, I walk in and see Grace sitting on Mom’s full size bed that sits against the worn, bare wall. She’s rocking back and forth looking at an antique hand held mirror that was our grandmother’s. “What’s so funny, baby girl?” I ask while kneeling down to get at her level.

She continues to giggle and then I see why. “Oh. You got into Mommy’s makeup again, huh?” I can’t help but laugh myself. Her happy, cherub face is covered in pink blush everywhere except her cheeks, and red lipstick is smeared around her lips.

Mom turns and gives me a tired but genuine smile while putting in an earring. “Sorry, Mason. She’s already had a bath so you just need to wash her face later.” She looks at her watch. “Shit, I need to get going.” She walks over and gives Grace and me a kiss goodbye.

“Keys are on the coffee table,” I yell as she rushes out the bedroom door. Her car is still in the shop so I let her borrow mine when she needs it. Chanda will take her if they work the same shift. “Love you, Mom.”

”Love you too.” I hear the door slam and turn toward Grace, who continues to look at her reflection in the mirror.

“Well, beautiful, it’s just you and me tonight. Want to walk down to the playground?” This of course gets her even more excited because she loves to swing. I can’t help the image that unfolds in my mind of Jazz and I walking hand in hand to the playground with our baby and Grace.

Chapter Seven

Jazz

Glancing around Dr. Parnell's office, I see women in all different stages of their pregnancy. Most of them are with their significant other, while I sit here and wait for Mason to show. He had a final in one of his classes and said he'd meet me here. I really wish he'd hurry. Whenever someone's eyes meet mine I feel like a sign is on my head that says "stupid girl who slept with teacher." I sit here alone trying to build my guard up again, but here in this top-of-the-line office with Mobile's debutantes and socialites, my situation pushes down on me. As I glance through the latest Cosmopolitan I feel scared and alone.

Then relief flows through me like a river when I hear his voice asking the receptionist if I've been called back. I look up and smile at him. "Over here."

He looks in my direction and returns my smile. As he comes my way, I get the same glimpse of the Mason I saw on Thanksgiving and feel my face become heated. Shaking it off, I return to my article and blame it on my nerves.

"Sorry I'm late. I went as fast as I could." He sits beside me on the black and white striped couch.

I look up and see him glancing at the gossip article that sits in my lap that I haven't been paying attention to. "It's okay. I told you the other day you didn't have to come. I would've been fine by myself." *But lonely.* I don't say those words out loud. In fact, I didn't mean to think them either.

Shrugging it off even though I do feel deeply grateful, I close my current magazine and point to another. "Will you pass me that one?" Before he passes me the magazine, I hear the nurse call my name. I stand up while Mason just sits there looking like his usual cute and awkward self. "You coming?"

"You sure you want me back there?" He stands and follows me to the back.

Laughing because he's so cute, I grab his hand as my answer. After I pee in a cup, I go to the exam room where Mason is waiting. Sitting on the exam table, I try to get comfortable but it's not going to happen. I hate the noisy tissue paper I'm sitting on because it feels so impersonal, or maybe it just reminds me of all my past doctors visits and why I wasn't "normal." I see the ultrasound machine in the corner and cringe. I hope I don't get that thing up my woo-hoo again.

"What's that face for?" Mason sits relaxed in the chair, watching me intently.

"Oh nothing." I shrug my shoulders. I really don't want to tell him about how embarrassing that was for me. However, he's relentless when he wants something and continues to ask me. "Fine." I walk over to the machine and pick up the wand. "Because at my first appointment they stuck this thing up my va-jayjay."

Of course Dr. Parnell walks in while I hold the culprit in my hand and point it in the air like Excalibur. I just smile and place it back in the holder before I go sit back down while Mason turns ten shades of red.

"Sorry, Doctor Parnell," I say meekly and smile. Glancing at Mason, I see the continued embarrassment as he reveals his cute dimples. I stick my tongue out at him like a two-year-old, but I don't care

"Jasmine. It's okay." She takes her seat and introduces herself to Mason. "I'm glad to meet you and congratulations on becoming a father." He nods, becoming shy again while she returns her attention to me. "So how are you feeling?"

"Good, besides the nausea and needing to carry a bag everywhere I go."

"That's pretty normal, but it should ease up soon since you're almost out of the first trimester." She lays me back and palpates my stomach. My dad taught me a few things growing up and palpate is one of them. "How's your breathing?"

I glance at Mason with wide eyes. We've never discussed my medical issues before. I like the fact that he doesn't look at me like I'll break. "F—fine. No problems."

"Good. Just keep a close eye on it. You know what the signs are I'm sure." She turns around and grabs a small square box with a microphone-looking thing on it.

"What's that for?" Mason stands and asks the question that I'm dreading. He grabs my hand and I feel better knowing he's there.

"Oh. This won't hurt at all. It's a doppler we use to hear the baby's heartbeat. Now unzip and pull down your pants." The excitement of hearing my peanut's heartbeat has me not thinking and I instantly do as she says, baring it all above my pubic bone. Then I hear a swift inhale and glance up to find a red faced Mason staring at my midriff and belly button ring. He licks his lips before bringing his focus to my face. I watch as he turns into sexy Mason again. *Wowzers!* His nostrils flare with each breath, and I feel dizzy and warm all at once. I want to breathe the air that he lets flow out of his mouth, and I want him to do the same to me.

Before I can act on my horny thoughts, I jump from a loud grating noise. As it gets louder it sounds more like a galloping horse or a stampede of rhinos coming our way.

"What's that? Oh wow! Is that the baby's heartbeat?" Smiling, I glance back up at Mason who's also smiling down at me.

"Yes it is. And it sounds really strong and healthy." After a few seconds of listening, she removes the microphone and wipes the gel off of my stomach. I don't even remember her putting in on.

“Now get dressed and take this ticket to the front. They’ll make your follow-up appointment.” She turns toward Mason and sticks out her hand. “Again, I am so glad to meet you.”

Mason politely shakes it. “You too.”

“Oh, and Jasmine …” She waits for me to turn in her direction after I’m done buttoning my jeans. “Don’t wear yourself out, okay? Take it easy and call if you need anything.”

I can only nod in agreement. I hope Mason doesn’t ask what she’s blabbering about because I have no clue what to tell him. After she exits the room, we head out and make a four week follow-up. I can still hear the galloping sound of my baby’s heart in my head and can’t help but feel excitement hum under my skin.

“Well that was pretty cool.” I turn in Mason’s direction when he speaks. “Want to go grab some food or something?” he asks with his hands stuffed in his jean pockets and a nervous look on his face. At least it’s not the same one that had me almost pulling his face down to mine so I could taste him. This is the Mason I’ve come to know and care for.

I look at my phone for the time and see it’s getting late, plus I really need to get my hormonal ass straight before I cross the line with him. I’ve sworn off relationships since Halloween and I really don’t want to ruin this thing between us. Whatever it is. “No. I really need to get back. I have my last final Thursday and a ton of laundry to do. Sorry.” I hate statistics just as much as folding clothes. I usually try and find a way out of both, but not this time. This time I need to stick to my plan. I really need to study for that stupid exam if I want to pass.

I see the disappointment and feel like total shit, if shit is an emotion. “Okay. I need to get to my mom’s anyway.” He turns to leave and walks to his truck parked a few spaces from mine. “See ya.”

OMG! I feel like such a bitch. He has been there for me when no one else has. The least I can do is get a bite to eat with him. Before he gets in his truck, I finally settle my internal argument and call his name. When he turns around I smile.

“Could you help me study while we eat pizza?” I watch his dimples appear while he nods his head. The sun catches his green eyes. *Oh sweet baby Jesus.* I have a feeling I’m in trouble.

After I go back to my dorm for my books, I head toward Mason’s mom’s apartment. Parking my car, I notice his truck is nowhere to be seen so I shoot him a quick text.

Mason: Still waiting on food. Gonna be few min. Go inside & wait 4 me.

Me: No. I’ll w8 here. I really don’t feel like meeting a stranger alone. Especially one that might want to kill me.

Mason: Go inside. Apartment B2. My mom wants 2 meet u & is expecting u.

***Me: Is she gonna kill me?* I can practically see his face smile from reading that.**

Mason: Def. not. Don't be a chickenshit. GO!

Me: Fine! I'm giving you the bird, asshole. And I totally am, while in my head I'm thinking about my game plan for survival.

He doesn't respond back, but I don't care. After I grab my bag, I slowly head up the front steps. The sound of children laughing reaches my ears. I hear someone across the way holler "hey, baby," but continue to ignore their lewd gestures as I ascend the stairs. Due to my freaky super spidey sense of smell, I feel my stomach start to turn when I'm assaulted by cigarette smoke and cheap perfume. I cover my mouth before I up-chuck all over the place and make a horrible first impression.

"These bother you?" I turn and see the girl from the other night standing there holding up her cancer stick with a smirk on her narrow face. She must be going to work because she's wearing a light blue button down blouse with white strips. It has the logo for The Waffle House on the sleeves and a name tag that reads *Chanda*. "Sorry," she says and takes another drag with absolutely no sincerity in her voice.

I feel too nauseous to argue so I turn and knock on Mason's door, trying to avoid breathing. "He's not home yet, you know. He usually comes by my place after school anyways to hang out. And I haven't seen him."

Breathing in deep when I feel a slight winter breeze, I look at her. "Well, I just left him and he's on his way here to meet me. We had a doctor's appointment." I reach down and caress my stomach. I don't know why I'm trying to piss this girl off. I shouldn't care if she likes Mason or if Mason likes her, but deep down I do. I tell myself it's because I don't like her and he can do way better. I watch her eyes squint in anger and brace myself for some more trash talk. Before she can say anything, the door opens and Mason's mom greets me. She's a few inches taller than me, which is no surprise. Her dark, curly hair is in a tight bun. She stares down at me with blue eyes like Grace's and a small beauty mark above her lip on the right side.

I smile my best smile even though I still feel sick from the breeze blowing the rancid smell of smoke my way. "Hello, Ms. Reed. I'm Jasmine."

"Hello, Jasmine. Come on in. And call me Brenda." She looks over my shoulder. "Chanda, I'll be ready to leave in five minutes. I promise."

We walk inside and I take in my surroundings. To the right is the living area with only a small TV on a cabinet and a worn brown couch that sits against the wall. The walls are a tan with an assortment of pictures of Mason and Grace posing at different ages. Mason was a gorgeous baby. I hope my child looks that cute. My eyes land on a quilt that is folded neatly across the top of the couch. Its bright colors hold my eyes hostage until I hear a scream.

I jump and turn toward the sound. Grace sits on the floor with her legs crossed, rocking back and forth while hitting herself with her small fist. I walk toward her, not really sure what to do, but Mason's mom just restarts a kid's video. Grace stops her tantrum immediately to watch.

"Sorry. That's pretty normal here." She walks to the kitchen table and pats a chair for me to come sit with her. "Now I hear that I'm going to be a Mimi. Believe me, I wasn't happy. Babies are expensive, but regardless I'll love him or her because they're a part of my precious boy." She gives me a small smile and gets up. "Are you thirsty? I have juice or sweet tea."

“No, ma’am. I am fine. But thank you.” I don’t see any weapons or body bags anywhere so I must be okay. Anyone who can raise someone like Mason has to be a special person.

She sits again. “I know you’re different from Mason on all levels. But I hope this baby doesn’t do anything to jeopardize his schooling.”

Confused, I ask, “Jeopardize how?”

“I’m not trying to come off as mean, but you come from money. I can tell. And there’s nothing wrong with that. But we have to work for every penny we have. And Mason has always worked hard in school and helping me out. So what I mean is I don’t want him to back off of his studies. He’s on a scholarship that has strict rules if he wants to keep it. And I’m afraid with him playing house he’ll get his priorities mixed up.” She glances at the clock while I sit there speechless. “Crap, I have to get going. Will you be okay to watch Grace until Mason gets here? I hate asking and I know she’s different but I’ve been late a few times already and the boss is getting aggravated.”

After a second I finally find my tongue. Out of nowhere I feel a need to gain her approval. “No, it’s fine. In fact my younger sister is in a wheelchair, so I’m sure I can manage.” My voice is small and shaky, and I notice my answer gains her attention. Instead of replying she says a quick goodbye and walks out the door. Once the door shuts I start to think of what I’m really getting into with Mason. Then guilt surfaces because of how this lie is not only affecting Mason and me, but everyone in our lives. I can’t help but ask myself if I’m really doing the right thing.

Chapter Eight

Mason

Today is a busy day because I'm helping move Jazz into her new apartment. Unfortunately I had to bring Grace with me because Mom is working extra hours for Christmas money. She does this every year, and since classes just let out for winter break, I'm staying at her place instead of the frat house. I just hope Jazz doesn't care that she's here.

When I pull up outside the dorm, I see David has already showed up with a few of the other frat brothers to help. Thank goodness because I'm sure Jazz has a shitload. I park and walk over to get Grace out before making our way toward everyone.

"'Bout damn time, pussy. Thought you bailed." David laughs with a few of the other guys, and I flip him off.

“Chill with the language. Grace is here.” I give him a stern look and point to my sister, who’s beside me.

“Oh shit. Sorry, dude.” He walks up the stairs and I follow behind shaking my head.

After we finally reach Jazz’s room, I see that she has two more guys I recognize from the house. They are packing and wrapping everything she points out, most of which are shoes. I keep my eye on them because I know these two guys bring girls home on a regular basis. She seems to be ignorant to their stares and continues to tell them what to take and what to leave with her beautiful smile constantly on her face.

I want to be the only one she smiles at, but I shake off these stupid caveman emotions and walk in, still holding Grace’s hand. I plaster a smile on before I speak. “Sorry I’m late but Mom had to work. I brought Grace too. I hope that’s okay.”

She smiles and walks up to Grace and me. “Of course it’s okay.” She bends down in front of my sister to get to her level, which isn’t very hard for her. “Hi, sweetness.” She smiles and glances up toward me with her sky blue eyes shining. “I got you something the other day. I figured you might like it.” She stands and walks to her desk. When she comes back she has a pink, children’s keyboard that lights up with the music. Grace quickly lets go of my hand to get her hands on it, and I watch as Jazz leads her to sit on the bare mattress. I literally feel my heart squeeze as I fall more in love with her.

David slaps my back and bends down to whisper in my ear, “Whipped.” He walks off to start carrying boxes downstairs. Turning around, I grab a box before following in his direction, desperate to not look so obvious.

Later that day when all the boxes are unloaded at her new apartment and the new furniture is placed where she wants it, we take a break and eat pizza. I hate that it's all we seem to eat, but she really enjoys it. Plus they have a soft pasta for Grace.

Glancing at my sister, I see she's asleep on the couch and I know I need to take her home. She's used to a set pattern in her day, so being around different people and different places can be very chaotic for her. She had a few tantrums but settled when it was time to eat, and she eventually went to sleep. I finish my food and look at Jazz, whose beautiful face hasn't stopped glowing today. "I think I need to get going and take Grace home."

"Aww really?" She stands up and throws her trash away. The guys left earlier so it's just us and it's really quiet. "She can lie on my bed. It will help break in the new mattress." She smiles, unaware of the images of us breaking in the new mattress running through my head. Shit. I need a hand job or a cold shower soon because being this close to my infatuation, unable to touch her, is giving me permanent blue balls.

I rub my hand over my face, debating. I really want to spend more time with her, but sometimes I get so worked up I think I'll literally explode. "Um. Sure." I go and lift Grace in my arms and carry her to Jazz's room. I place her on the bed and turn around slamming into Jazz. "Shit, Jazz. Are you okay?" I steady her and touch her face, shoulders, and waist making sure she's not injured.

She just smiles up at me. "Yeah. I'm good. Sorry."

In that moment, with her looking up at me and my hands resting on her waist, my mind conjures images of her slim body and the sexy ass diamond belly ring that rests on her soft skin. I can feel my dick swelling in my pants as my breathing starts to become shallow. Her smile falters and my fingers involuntarily squeeze her hips, which brings her flush against me. I've never wanted something so bad in my life than to kiss this girl—the girl who hooked me from just a photograph.

I watch her pupils dilate as her breasts brush against my stomach and her breath hitches. Having her react to my touch like that gives me the extra push I need to start bringing my face toward her soft features. When I'm about an inch away and I can taste her sweet breath against my tongue, there is a fucking banging at the door ruining the moment.

Her eyes go wide and she backs up. "I—I'm going to see who's here." She smiles awkwardly and runs toward the front door.

Fuck! I'm going to kill whoever that is.

Well I'm not in jail for murder. I figure I can't kill Tru because Jax will kill me and Jazz will be upset. Plus, I've heard about what she did to one of my frat brothers, so after she showed up I left with Grace and went home while they unpacked and did whatever girls do.

It's been a few days and I haven't heard from Jazz. I've been giving her time because she looked freaked out after the almost-kiss. I don't want to ruin it so I'll call tomorrow. Besides, I'm pretty busy with Grace and doing some software repairs for some of the professors to earn Christmas money. I have a great idea for Jazz's gift and hope it's not too much, too soon.

As I'm taking a break and making a sandwich, I hear a knock on the front door. I find myself hoping it's Jazz, but I know it's just wishful thinking. Chanda stands there all dressed up like she's going out, smiling showing all her teeth.

"Hey. You need something?" I ask.

"What? Now that you have a girlfriend I can't come over unless I need something? Oh I'm sorry. She's just your baby momma."

Even though we aren't as close as we used to be, we're still friends and she helps out with Grace. "Sorry. Come on in." I move to the side to let her by and feel her brush past me. After closing the door, I walk back to the kitchen and finish my sandwich at the table. "You want anything? I can make you a glass of tea or a sandwich." I hold mine up.

She moves and sits in the seat across from me. I notice her skirt rise as she crosses her pale, slender legs. I scoot my chair back to put some space between us. "Nope!" She pops the P and leans her elbow on the table "So where's Grace?"

"She's in her room. Jazz bought her a new keyboard and she hasn't stopped playing it." I can't help but smile when I think of how good Jazz is with Grace and the thoughtfulness of her gift.

"Well, with her money I'm sure she can buy whatever she wants. Where is Miss Royalty anyway?" She arches a brow and leans in closer, displaying her small cleavage.

These little mannerisms used to get me so hard we'd end up screwing anywhere and everywhere. Now it has no affect on me. Instead of wanting to see golden eyes lost in ecstasy, I want to see sky blue ones.

I lose my appetite and quickly stand to throw away my trash and to get away from Chanda. "Look, I don't know what's gotten into you but I'm not interested. I like Jazz. So please just back off."

She stands and walks to position herself in front of me while I lean on the kitchen counter. "So how come I've never heard about her before now? Neither has Brenda. Your own mother who knows everything about you." She taps her finger on her cheek while puckering her lips and thinking. "Something's going on and I intend to find out, Mason." She winks at me before she saunters away. She stops by the front door and holds the handle. "You know, we used to be best friends and would do everything together. I wouldn't mind that again."

She walks out and I exhale, rubbing my hands over my face. The girl from my past that I used to love just offered what I've always wanted … that is until a few months ago. I'm pining over someone who I'm not sure wants me at all. *Shit.* If I thought things were complicated with just the lie, now things are really fucked up.

Chapter Nine

Jazz

Is it wrong to not want to want to kiss your baby daddy who's not really your baby's daddy? If that confused you, then welcome to my world. I'm so frickin' confused that I decide to take a drive instead of sitting in my too quiet apartment. Even my reality television addiction isn't helping. I turn up *Tell Me how You Like it* by Florida and Georgia Line and sing at the top of my lungs even though I shouldn't. I need to release some of this frustration.

It's been a few days since I almost broke my own rule and I'm still worked up. Why do I keep seeing Mason differently lately? Why did I agree to this ridiculous plan? Why did I fall in love with my professor, who's a lying piece of shit scumbag who doesn't have the balls to tell me he's married?

I feel myself getting worked up and my chest starts to hurt as it tightens while my breathing accelerates. I start to take slow deep breaths in an attempt to calm down but it's not working, so I pull over on the side of the road. I reach in my glove box and grab a small paper bag to breathe into. I keep these just in case and haven't had to use one in a long time.

Once my breathing is back to normal my mind is still muddled so I decide to call Tru. She doesn't pick up. I shoot her a text asking if she wants to go with me for a retail therapy session. She says yes but she's finishing up the lunch shift at Jay Jay's so it will be a few minutes.

Making a quick but illegal U-turn, I head Tru's way and suddenly feel hungry. The nausea has eased up and I'm now able to keep more food down. I'm still not brave enough to try my favorite chili cheeseburger any time soon.

After grabbing a bite to eat and waiting for Tru to be done for the day, we go and hit the mall. While we walk around looking at all the faces pass us I get lost in my thoughts again. I can't seem to prevent myself from thinking about Mason here either. Maybe I'll ask Tru her opinion.

I turn around and see she's not by me any longer. "Tru."

"I'm over here." I follow her voice and see her looking in a window for Hot Topic.

"Why are you looking in there?" I eye the corset bodice that's showcased on a mannequin. It's black with hot pink ribbon laced on the sides and back with matching garters. "That is hawt!"

Tru just continues to eye it for a minute then walks in the store. I follow her in where she asks for one in her size. "Do you have fishnet tights?"

"What are you doing? I thought we were looking for a Christmas gift for Jax?" I've never been in here but I love the style. It's so dark and sexy. I need to come back after I have this baby. I see a short, plaid skirt and my mind wanders to Mason and what his reaction would be to me dressed as the slutty student. *Ugh!* There I go again. I am pregnant with my professor's child so I guess I am the slutty school girl after all.

"Yeah. But what do you get a guy who has everything?" she asks while paying the girl who's wearing heavy eye makeup and a lip ring.

"Um, I don't know … a gift card like I did?" The girl behind the register winks in my direction and so I wink back just for shits and giggles. Looping my arm around Tru's waist, I see her smile fall. I might flirt with her, but I've sworn off all romantic relationships. Male or female. I put my finger to my lips and say, "Shhh! What my brother doesn't know won't hurt him."

Tru gets my game and starts to play along with me. We're just in sync together and it's almost like some Yoda shit at times. "You ready, baby?" She smiles flirtatiously at me and pinches my butt hard.

We walk out together holding hands and laugh when we are finally out of the girl's vision. After a minute I finally get back to our conversation. "So why the sex kitten attire?"

"It's for your brother. I decided that a full show and strip tease with a lap dance to boot is what he's getting for Christmas. I also bought him some board wax and car cleaner so he'll have something under the tree."

I watch her eyes light up when she mentions the tree. It's her first one in a long time, and her apartment is Christmasland at the moment. Mom actually went through our attic and brought Tru tons of decorations that have accumulated over the years.

She shakes her head and looks at me. "What are you getting Mason?"

"Nothing. I mean, don't you think Christmas gifts are a little too personal for friends?"

"And having a baby together isn't personal?" She shakes her head and laughs. "What is going on with you two? I saw how flushed you looked when I came over the other day and how he rushed out of there."

I really want to talk to someone about this and that was my intention of this little outing Now that the time is upon me for my mouth to work I don't know how to start. I shrug my shoulders and look at my feet.

"I don't know. I mean we almost kissed the other day, but I'm not sure I want to cross the relationship line with him yet … or ever." I look up and see her intently watching me, so I stop and sit at a vacant bench. "He's great and I've always thought that, but lately he's been different."

"Different how? He's not mean under all the innocent cuteness is he? Because I will cut a bitch over you."

"Hold up, Rocky." I laugh because Tru usually doesn't voice her emotions and for her to get angry on my behalf is so touching but still funny. "No. He's still sweet, but he's showing a more intense side. You know, a manly side." She's still looking at me with confusion. "Geez. He's becoming like fuckably sexy to me. Okay? Every time we're alone I just want to … to. Shit, I don't know. Fuck him."

“Again,” Tru states, nodding her head and laughing.

“What?”

“You mean fuck him *again*. Right? Because you are pregnant.”

Shit! “Of course I mean again.” I laugh awkwardly and quickly stand to recover. Then I see a toy store and head that way. Grace would love something else noisy.

Tru follows behind me and we start to play with different toys and act like big kids. She walks over to some baby items and strokes them lovingly while emotion clouds her green eyes. When I stand by her she softly whispers, “I miss him so much.”

I remain quiet because I don’t know what to say. Losing a child in any way must be hard, but what she endured and the reason behind his death is so unfair. She takes a deep breath and wipes her eyes. “I’m thankful though. Thankful to have known him and thankful that when I do finally have another child I won’t take him or her for granted.”

She looks at me with a single tear running down her cheek. “Don’t take what you’ve been given for granted, Jazz. And if you feel a pull and attraction toward Mason, maybe you should try out an actual relationship with him.” She wipes away any other stray tears and smiles like she just didn’t knock me over with her words. “Now let’s go find some shoes I can wear with this outfit.”

The rest of the day I act like her words aren’t running around in my head and try to enjoy what’s left of it. After I drop Tru off at her car I have one destination in mind and can’t help but speed through traffic just to get there. My mind and body are at war over what I want with him. I don’t know which one I'll chose, but I hope the war will stop ripping me in two once a choice is made. But will it be the right one?

When I arrive I see his truck sitting in the driveway and start to panic. Deep down I was hoping he'd be gone and I wouldn't have to ruin this relationship, but he's here and this has to be done. I can do this. I can tell him this whole thing was a big mistake and walk away before our friendship is completely fucked. If he's determined to help me that's fine … but only after the baby is born, when my libido has calmed down. *I can do this.*

I get out and zip up my North Face jacket after I lock my car. The sun's down and the temperature has dropped so low my breath looks like smoke surrounding my face. Counting to ten, I try to calm my nerves. I see a few groups of people in one of the apartments across the way but they pay no attention to me. Thank goodness.

After I reach his door, I just stare at the 2B metal plaque for what seems like forever. Thoughts of our first meeting invade my brain. He looked so cute standing there with his hand out, holding my ID. I introduced myself and asked who he was but no words formed on his lips, only continuous gulping. I thought about calling security for either an ambulance or to haul his ass away, but finally he said "hi" and dropped the ID before turning and leaving me totally confused.

I shake my thoughts away and wipe the smile from my face. Finally, I knock and wait. No answer. I decide I'll knock once more but if I still get no answer I'm leaving.

"Coming!" I hear him yell on the other side of the door and my heart drops knowing what I'm about to do.

When he opens the door I'm speechless and feel my plan falling down the stairs. He's standing in front of me wearing only a pair of blue plaid pajama pants and looks fucking delicious. I see he has a toned body and a six pack that has my insides clenching together. Finally, I glance up at his face to see that his hair is in disarray from the towel in his hand. He must have just jumped out of the shower. *Oh my God!* Naked Mason is all I see now, and I have to bite my lip to keep from moaning out loud, but I'm purring on the inside.

He finely speaks and his voice caresses my skin because the sound is so low and deep. "Jazz. What are you doing here so late?"

I can't answer because the reason I'm here doesn't exist anymore. The only thing that exists is the power surge that runs between us. Taking a step in his direction, I unzip my jacket as I cross the threshold. My eyes remain glued to his, and I watch in amazement as his pupils dilate to overtake the dark shade of green. I throw my Jacket on the floor and press my chest to his stomach because I just have to be close to him. I need to touch him right now in a way we've never touched before.

His hand reaches over my shoulder and he leans into me to shut the door I left open. Then he places his hand on my shoulder and gingerly moves it up to my cheek where he leaves it and stares at me intensely. His touch is different than I expected. It's better. I push my face into his palm and smile at him because I feel calm and happy for the first time today.

His thumb rubs my cheek softly, and he returns my smile while wrapping his other hand around my waist. "What?" he whispers.

My smile widens because I see both Masons together in this moment: the cute, innocent one as well as the powerful sexy one. It's intoxicating and I feel myself getting lightheaded.

"Nothing." When he doesn't make a move, I have to ask because I need to be closer. "So are you going to kiss me or make me wait all night?"

I see dimples form in his cheeks so I place my hands hesitantly on his naked chest. It burns under my palms, but as they glide over his smooth skin I see him shiver.

I know it's from me and not the cold, but I ask anyway. "Are you cold?"

"No. I am so far from it, Jazz." The whisper and smile leaves his face and the innocent Mason dissolves and leaves only the one that speaks with a raw voice that matches his stare and causes my knees to buckle. "I'm so fucking turned on and hot right now. And it's all because of you."

Then he kisses me for the first time and I feel like an expensive chocolate being savored. I could get used to this.

Chapter Ten

Mason

I hear my alarm and curse at the damn thing. It always goes off while I'm having the best dreams. Last night's was more like a fucking fantasy—Jazz coming over and kissing me. I lick my lips trying to play it out a little longer. I don't want to get up but know I need to. Besides, the dream is gone and I can't get it back.

I go to move and feel something weighing me down. Slowly lifting my eyelids, I see golden hair all over my naked chest and my heart accelerates. *Holy hell! It was real and she's here. Asleep with me. In my bed.* Leaning my head back, I gingerly bring my hand to her golden mane and move some off her face. I smile when I see her button nose and puckered lips. She's even drooling on me, but I couldn't care less. Damn, she's beautiful.

As I watch her, last night plays out in my mind—Jazz coming over with red cheeks from the cold, advancing on me, and then finally kissing her. Man, I wish they made bubble gum that flavor. Well, maybe not. Because everyone would taste it and I feel selfish. No. I'll just kiss her and taste her that way instead. The taste of her drives me wild, but so does her softness. The pouty lips that pressed against mine, the softness of her skin when my hand rested on her waist.

I yawn and feel the soreness in my jaw, laughing. I can't remember kissing someone for so long it caused injury. I mean we kissed everywhere last night: the kitchen, on the couch, and finally ended up in here. But that's all we did. Well, I did feel her tit over her shirt but that's it.

"Mason? I'm home." Mom yells and taps my door.

Shit! "Hold on," I yell as she opens the door to show me her pale shocked face. Jazz jumps up looking around groggily before she stretches. My eyes watch hypnotically as she arches her back, and I notice she's still fully clothed. *Thank you, Jesus.* However, it is still causing me to get aroused. I lick my lips and my eyes flick back to my mother, who seems more pissed now than shocked.

"Mason Alexander, can I see you?" Mom asks sternly and shuts the door.

Taking a breath, I scrub my face with my hands. I feel the bed shift and see Jazz looking around the floor. "Hey, you don't have to go."

She looks up and uses her fingers to move the hair out of her face. It falls right back, though, and I smile. "Sorry, but yes I do. Your mom seems pretty upset. I don't want to be here when the shit goes down." She grabs her shoes and sits on the bed to put them on.

I sit up and slide my body behind her to whisper in her ear. "Stay. I'm a big boy. She'll get over it." I take her earlobe in my mouth and nibble before I start working my way down her neck. She tilts her head, and I feel the chills along her neck with my tongue.

"Mason? I really need to go," she says breathlessly. She stands quickly and shakes her head like she's attempting to clear her brain. "Look. We need to talk but not here. Why don't you come to my place tonight? I'll cook and we'll talk then. Okay?"

At least I know I'll see her again, but I still hate ending this … whatever it is. "I'll have Grace."

"Good. Bring her. She's really great." She walks to the door and grabs the handle. I think she's listening for my mom at first, but then she huffs out a breath and walks toward me. "Fuck it!" She grabs my face and gives me another taste for a few short seconds before she releases me and runs out the door.

After I pinch myself and go take a piss, I walk in the kitchen yawning. I see Mom has coffee brewed so I walk over and fix myself a cup. She hasn't looked at me or said anything, so I know she's pissed. She waits for me to sit down before she starts. "Mason, I know you're almost twenty-one and not a virgin, but I would appreciate if you'd keep that part of your life away from your sister and me."

"Mom, we didn't do anything besides kiss. I know better than to take that chance with Grace here." I lean back in my chair and take a long sip of my black coffee. Bitter and hot. Perfect.

"So her waking up in your bed was nothing? Do you really expect me to believe that?" I can hear the sarcasm in her voice, and I'm starting to get pissed. She never cared when Chanda and I were together, so why bust my balls about Jazz?

"Yes, Mom. I've never lied to you before. Why would I lie about something like sex?"

"Um, Mason, I don't know. Maybe because I just found out a few weeks ago out of nowhere that I'm going to be a grandmother. I didn't even know you were dating anyone. Besides that, I was sure you and Chanda were getting close again." I see her blue eyes start to build with unshed tears and my anger vanishes.

I never realized that my decision to put myself in Jazz's life would affect my mom like this. When I mentioned it, I knew she was shocked but I figured by now she would have adjusted to the idea. I get up and go embrace her frail and overworked body. I never wanted to add to her grief. I only wanted to prove myself worthy of Jazz.

"Mom, I'm sorry. I didn't know this was bothering you so much."

She sniffles and pulls away to pat my cheek. "Of course it affects me. My baby boy is going to have a baby. I'm only thirty-seven years old. Plus, I don't even know this girl who's going to have my grandchild. She's so different from us."

I exhale and smile. I'm glad her worries are easily fixed. "Well, that can be mended. Why don't we have her over for Christmas or maybe when you're off next? I'm sure Jazz wouldn't mind. We could go out and grab something or I could cook. I'm sure once you really get to know her you'll realize she's not so different."

She returns my smile and dries her eyes that have permanent dark circles under them. I wish she didn't have to work so hard. I can't wait to finish college and get a job to help her retire early, or at least quit one of her jobs.

"Okay," she whispers and stands up. "I've already spoke to Terri about my schedule for the week after Christmas. We can do something then." She comes and kisses my forehead. "I'm going to take a shower then go to bed for a few hours. Love you."

"Love you too, Mom." I watch her walk down the hall and finish my coffee. I reflect on every moment of last night and then of this morning. What did Mom mean about Chanda and me? She is so wrong about that, but I won't worry about it. I get up after my coffee is gone and head back to my room for a bit before Grace wakes up, desperate to smell the lingering scent of Jazz's perfume.

Excitement to see Jazz tonight makes the rest of my day pass by incredibly slow for some reason. I hold on to Grace with one hand and with the other I have a bag with some eggnog and some red poinsettias. Since Christmas is only a week away flowers are hard to find, and I know Jazz loves eggnog. Well, she did around Thanksgiving.

I take a deep breath and knock. After a minute she opens the door, and I smell something delicious and I know it's whatever she's cooking. She looks great, too, wearing a pair of worn jeans that have a tear in the knee and a pink off the shoulder sweater. Her hair is up in some kind of ponytail, but I can tell it took time to fix, It's not a quick hairdo like my mom usually wears. A few strands of white blonde hair frame her face and her bangs are clipped to the side. Man, she sure is pretty.

My ogling is interrupted when she quickly rushes back toward the kitchen and yells for me to come on in and get comfortable. I walk in and see Jazz running around everywhere in the kitchen. Pots and pans are piled in the sink and shredded cheese is scattered on the counter. To look so confident a moment ago, she sure looks like she's in complete chaos in the kitchen. I sit Grace on Jazz's new black suede sectional decked out in zebra throw pillows and a blanket lying on the chaise. Looking around I notice the sonogram picture in a black, beautiful picture frame hanging on the wall to match the other photos. She's also placed a huge, black, oval mirror above the fireplace. Black curtains trimmed in white surround the patio door. She's been a busy bee.

I place the bag on the black, round table that sits in the small dining area across from the kitchen. Looking around I see no flowers decorating her apartment and feel relieved. I definitely don't want to overload her with flowers, but I really wanted to get her something. Grace watches the large flat screen TV that already has Mickey Mouse playing. Jazz seems to know Grace already, and I smile widely while I turn my attention back to her in the kitchen. I don't know what to do now that she's in front of me. I've thought about it all day. Should I just go up and kiss her like I want to, or should I offer to help? Maybe she's like my mom and hates help in the kitchen. Shit! I can't just sit here. I stand up and take the eggnog and flowers out of the bag to place them in some water and pour a glass.

“Hey. Would you like some?” I hold up the eggnog and smile her way as she stirs something in the pot.

She glances and her eyes light up. “Heck yeah I do. The glasses are above the sink.” She concentrates again on what she’s cooking.

I clear my throat because I still feel out of place. “So what’s for dinner?” I ask while taking two clear glasses out of the cabinet.

“Well, pretty much the only thing I know how to cook that will actually taste good. Spagebbi.”

I take a sip of the thick cream and try not to choke from her answer but end up spitting eggnog out of my mouth. “Huh?” Starting to laugh, I see her reaction to the eggnog all over the floor and laugh harder. “Did you mean spaghetti?”

She starts to laugh as well and grabs a towel. “Nope. It’s spagebbi for me. Always has been, always will be. It will be this child’s favorite meal, just like it’s mine.” She bends over to wipe up the mess and lucky me gets a nice view of her ass.

I turn quickly when she glances at me and smiles. “Um. Sorry.” I can feel the heat crawling up my neck and face. “It will still taste the same right? I mean, I’m not going to find cheerios or anything else a toddler might mix in their food right?”

“Yeah, actually. I just added the gummy bears so we should be about set.” I turn and see her eyes smiling while she takes a sip of her eggnog. “I’m joking, dumbass. It’s just plane ol’ sauce with mushrooms and onions. But I do add a touch of bitters to it. It’s something my mom taught me. Adds a little tang, which I know for a fact you like.”

I feel myself relax again and smile. "Well, that I can handle. But what the hell is bitters?"

"It's a strong type of liquor." She must see my concern of her drinking. "Don't worry I only add two tiny drops and the alcohol is cooked out of it." Needless to say I relax.

After we eat and Grace is occupied with her keyboard in the living room, Jazz and I stay seated at the table. I know it's about to get serious. My hands get clammy while my nerves make their appearance. I'm positive my stutter will appear like it always does in tense situations. I'm terrified that last night was a onetime deal, and I seriously think I'll go fucking insane if that's the case. I mean, she's like my drug now and for her to just take it away after months of wanting will kill me. Taking a deep breath, I sit and wait for her to begin.

Chapter Eleven

Jazz

Sitting across from Mason I feel like a nervous wreck. When I left his apartment this morning I was a nervous wreck. When I went to the grocery store I was a nervous wreck. So basically I'm an apprehensive pregnant woman who is about to either ruin this relationship or take it to the next level. I've been thinking of what to do about the situation all day and it always leads me back to the thing I never thought I would do.

"So, Mason …" I lick my suddenly dry lips and nervously tap my food under the table. "About last night and this morning ... I hope you don't think I'm someone who does that all the time because I am so … so … so not." I pause to gain courage before continuing. "I wanted to ask you if you had any reservations of maybe doing it again and maybe we could actually do more.

You know what I'm saying? Maybe you don't because you haven't said anything since I started talking. Okay, well, what I'm trying to say is how about we become … I don't know … friends with benefits?" I take a much need breath because I was talking too fast while I examined the plum colored polish on my nails. When I finally bring my eyes up to stare into his wide green ones, I notice he's just staring at me with his mouth open. A mouth that definitely knows how to kiss and suck and … and … Shit! I feel myself start to blush from embarrassment. Maybe I read him wrong. I know he's different from other guys, but I thought every guy wanted to have a purely sexual relationship with no obligations.

He blinks and shuts his mouth. "Um. Wow!" He takes his hand and rubs it up and down his face, which causes his hair to turn into disarray. *So sexy*. "Did I just hear you right? Did you say that you want to be friends with benefits, or did I completely misinterpret your very fast speech?"

"Yes. That's exactly what I said. Since you are the *father...*" air quotes "...I figured why not? This way we can have our cake and eat it too. But if you're wanting it I have to tell you that there are rules." I sit up straighter and look into his dark green eyes as he stares intently at me. "We only sleep with each other. If for some reason you want a relationship with somebody else, can you please tell me beforehand?" I ask this and hope the small amount of jealousy that courses through me doesn't show. I don't know why it bothers me because I don't want a relationship with feelings and the crap that can cause pain. I smile and wait for him to agree.

What if he doesn't agree? What if I just made myself look like a slut or some nympho to a real good friend? I mean, I'm definitely not either one, but lately I've been so fucking horny it's scary. Some days I feel like humping my bedpost. Even masturbation isn't cutting it these days.

Finally he speaks while leaning back in his chair, crossing his arms. Dressed in one of his infamous black logo T-shirts and jeans, he looks yummy. "So you only want sex?"

Do I hear some disappointment in his voice?

"Yes. Plus it will play along well with the false gossip we are spreading around. So you in?"

He takes a deep breath and nods his head. "Yeah, I'm in." Standing up, he walks my way with that confidence I only see on occasion seeping through. When he reaches me he bends down and scoops me up effortlessly. He's stronger than what I imagined.

I wrap my arms around his neck and squeal. "What are you doing?" His smile displays his cute dimples and my heart goes pitter-pat. He sure is something to look at. Why the hell am I just now noticing when it's so obvious?

"Your room. I want to kiss you but Grace is playing in the living room, so I figured we could go in there."

"Mason, we can't have sex with your sister here. Geez." Excitement and nerves set in simultaneously and I can't decide which I want more. We did just agree to a FWB status and let's face it, people. My body has been craving his for a while now ... but not with Grace just down the hall. That makes it all seem wrong.

"No shit." He laughs and I feel the vibrations of his chest against mine. "I said I want to kiss you and I don't want my sister watching." Relaxing some, I let the anticipation overtake my nerves and can't wait to feel his lips against mine again. His smell is intoxicating and makes me dizzy. When he walks into my room, he gently lowers me to my feet and turns me around so we are facing one another. He brings his hands up, much like last night, and pushes an errant hair behind my ear before he tenderly brings his lips to mine.

I purr loudly when his tongue tickles my upper lip, and when I part my lips it invades my mouth. He does the unexpected and growls when I rub my tongue against his and suck it into my mouth. On their own accord, my hands run through his silky hair and pull him harder against me. I can feel the heat of his skin radiating against my body and it only adds to my own fevered skin. We continue this onslaught for a few minutes when I finally remember Grace down the hall.

"Mason," I say on a moan. "We need to slow down." I hate saying those words because I don't want to but now is not the time.

He kisses me one last time and then pulls away, exhaling and shaking his head. "Damn, I know it but I definitely don't want to."

I watch him blush like he can't believe what he just said, but it makes me feel desired. I stand on my tiptoes and kiss his nose before I turn and walk out my room smiling.

"So do you want to go out to get some food or something the next time I don't have Grace?" Mason asks while walking behind me.

I stop and turn to stare at him. Biting my lip, I think about his question for a few seconds. Would that be more along the lines of a date thing or *friends* thing? We usually only hang out with other people, so I guess that would be a date if we went solo.

I look in his eyes and smile to soften the blow. "I don't think that's a good idea, Mason. It would feel more like a date instead of the FWB arrangement we agreed upon." I see the disappointment in his eyes so I walk up and wrap my arms around his waist. "I'm sorry."

"No, you're right." Glancing up at him, I see his smiling face and cute dimples so he must be okay with it. "So when and how do you want to do this?"

The next few days fly by without Mason and I solidifying our newfound relationship. We haven't really seen one another because he's been working on some computer stuff and I've been busy with Christmas shopping and packing to head out to my parents' tomorrow. The other night Mason asked me if he cooked one night would I come over and get to know his mom. I wanted to say "hell to the no," but since he is my supposed sperm donor, I reluctantly agreed.

Today, however, is my dreaded appointment with my cardiologist. I haven't told anyone about this appointment because the last thing I need is for everyone to treat me any differently. I had enough of that shit growing up.

I walk up to the receptionist and sign in. "Hello, my name is Jasmine Coleman and I have a two o'clock appointment with Dr. Whitney."

I chose this particular doctor because he's good friends with my dad and he knows my history. He was practicing at Sacred Heart in Pensacola for years before he moved out to Mobile. I know he won't break any laws and tell my dad anything we discuss today either. *Thank you, HIPPA.*

After I take my seat in the dark blue chair, I grab a magazine to try and take my nerves off this visit. I've been really tired lately and I know it's a normal symptom with every pregnancy to an extent, but sometimes I don't even hear my alarm sound. Usually I'm a ball of energy.

After about another forty-five minutes and a few levels of Candy Crush completed, I'm finally called to the back. I sit at a nurse's desk while she takes my blood pressure and weight. "How are you today?"

"I'm good. Just getting ready for the big ol' fat man." She looks at me funny and quirks her brow in my direction. Obviously she doesn't get it. "Oh no! I mean Santa, not Dr. Whitney." I laugh because let's face it, it's funny … especially with the face she's giving me. I really needed that to help calm my nerves.

After that she leads me into an exam room. Its green floral wallpaper is outdated but the pictures and equipment look pretty new. Dad loved getting new heart models or charts when I was growing up. Every time one came in the mail he'd sit us down and explain how it works to push oxygen through our bodies. I loved his enthusiasm but definitely not the subject matter. It reminded me too much of what made me different. Jax on the other hand fell in love with the heart and chose cardiology as a career.

My eyes focus on the machine sitting in the corner and I know immediately I'm having another ultrasound. But this one is for my heart and not the baby's.

"Put on this gown and leave it open in the front. Make sure you remove your bra and shirt but leave your pants on." She hands me a hospital gown and walks out the door.

After I undress in the small changing nook, I look at myself in the mirror hanging on the wall and my eyes are immediately drawn to the scar that haunts me physically and emotionally. No matter how much I tan or apply those creams they advertise on TV it never changes or fades. Running my index finger down the center, I feel the thick tissue as it descends down and to the left. My first surgery was done swiftly and some mistakes were made, but only cosmetic damage was done. I remember the first time the look of it really affected my self-esteem.

Everyone was at the beach, including Brett. He was so cute and I couldn't wait to show off my new bathing suit. Maybe he'd finally notice me. I looked at my reflection in the mirror, admiring my first bikini—a milestone for any thirteen-year-old girl. I practically had to beg Mom for it, but it was so worth it. It was bright lime green with teal blue polka dots and I wanted to turn heads. I puckered my lips and posed in the mirror, trying to do it like the models on the magazine covers. Maybe if I looked like that he'd ask me to be his girlfriend. A huge smile formed with that thought.

Brett had never noticed me before at school. He was always into the athletic girls and not … not me darn it! I knew I wasn't allowed to date, but maybe … just maybe he'd take notice today and maybe even kiss me. I squealed and felt tingles in my belly from the thought.

"Wow, Jazz, that color looks so good on you. Especially with your tan and blond hair. Brett is going to flip." I glanced up from posing in the mirror to see Julie—or Jewels as I liked to call her because it sounded so cool—standing there in her purple bikini, smiling with her braces shining. She was visiting from Kansas and her parents rented the beach house next door. We had hit it off right away and it didn't hurt that her older sister had a crush on Jaxon so I was always invited over.

"Thanks," I said beaming and turned around. "You ready to walk down. I really want to get there before the snob squad shows up and takes the good spot. Don't want to miss watching the guys."

I grabbed my bag off my bedroom floor and noticed she still hadn't answered me. Looking in her direction, I observed her big, brown eyes staring at my chest and my stomach dropped. Suddenly, I felt filleted open. *Everyone will notice that I'm a freak.* Dropping my bag, I placed my hand in front of my newly developing chest, which forced her to look at my face.

She turned into a blurry purple blob as tears filled my eyes. I didn't want her to see me cry. I didn't want her to see my scar or anyone else to look at me like she just did. I was feeling normal a few minutes ago but it was ruined. I ran past her and went to the bathroom, wishing once again that I was normal.

The exam room door opens and brings me back, but I feel a wet tear running down my cheek. I quickly wipe it away and throw on the gown before I step out to see Doctor Whitney.

"Hello, Jasmine. How are you?" He shakes my hand and gives me a warm smile.

I sit on the exam table and try to get comfortable even though I know these things aren't made for comfort. "I'm good." Even though I'm not, it's just the generic answer.

"Okay, so rumor has it you're having a baby. Is that right?"

Instead of speaking, I reach into my handbag and pull out the first ultrasound picture of my jellybean. Licking my dry lips, I hand it over. He congratulates me and tells me that every case is different and most women have no complications. I just hope I'm a part of that majority. Unfortunately, my good mood is ruined during the echocardiogram when he sees a possible valve leak, but thankfully it looks minuscule. He further elaborates the disadvantages it could cause the farther along I get if the leak gets larger. I tell him I'm keeping the baby come hell or high water, and he finally ends his rant. He wants me to follow up every month to check my condition, but makes me promise if I feel any changes I'll come in sooner. After I agree I head home, depressed once again.

Chapter Twelve

Mason

Celebrating Christmas morning at home with Grace and Mom is great. Quiet is definitely not the word I'd use to describe it. With Grace's new toys everywhere while she continues to shred every piece of wrapping paper and Mom blasting Christmas music, I feel as though my brain might explode. However, all the noise can't drown out my thoughts of Jazz.

Yesterday I tried calling her so I could tell her Merry Christmas, but I only got her voicemail. Plus, I wanted to give her the gift I bought her. It's not much but I spotted it a couple of weeks ago—a pair of sterling silver hoop earrings with different charms you can attach. I purchased two charms to start it out. One is the letter J and the other is January's birthstone since her birthday is New Year's Day. I'm sure she has jewelry out the ass and any other thing a girl could want with her money, but it drew me in when I saw it behind the display glass. It cost a little more than what I'd usually spend, but I'm hoping her reaction will make it worth every penny.

Watching Grace destroy the house and laughing while I sit on the couch, I see Mom sit down beside me. Glancing at her wide smile and the crinkled edges of her blue eyes, I become aware that I haven't seen her this happy in a while. "Thanks for my earrings, Mason. You didn't have to get me anything, but I do love them."

"It's the least I could do for you. If I could do more, Mom, you know I would," I say, looking at the small cross earrings in her lobes. I can't wait to rid her of the worry she's always carrying on her shoulders.

She kisses my cheek before she starts to clean up the mess and begins to cook. I stand and text Jazz.

Me: Merry Christmas. Was Santa good to you? I wait a few minutes and start to think she might still be avoiding me but then my phone vibrates and lights up.

Jazz: Merry Christmas. Hope it's Gr8 for ur fam & u. Santa was okay. I think he's still pissed at me. What bout u?

Me: He'll get over it. He still luvs u. Mine is good. Grace is happy. I feel like sumthin is missing tho

Why did I just send that? It's too soon. Shit! Too late, though. I rub my face hoping my forwardness doesn't scare her away. Standing still, glancing at my phone for a few minutes, I hear a knock on the door. I realize she's not answering my text and fear maybe I did just fuck up. Shoving my phone in my pocket, I go and answer the door and see Chanda standing there in her pajamas. I notice she's colored her hair green and has a big smile on her face.

"Merry Christmas, Mason," she says with her hands behind her back.

"Merry Christmas." I'm still distracted by what Jazz might be doing this very second. Will she be staring at her phone thinking of that text and me? Will she be picturing the kiss we shared? I really just want to get in my truck and drive to see her for myself but I restrain myself.

"Mason? Don't just stand there. Invite her in," I hear Mom shout and my eyes focus once again on Chanda who's still smiling.

I move to the side and let her pass. I'm still not paying attention until I shut the door and she's directly in front of me. "What?" I know my tone is short but I'm really not in the mood.

She shrugs her shoulders and looks like she has a secret she's dying to tell me. "Nothing. I just wanted to give you your Christmas gift."

I notice she raises the hand that was behind her back above our heads. Glancing up, I see the mistletoe and get ready to back away. However, it's too late because I feel her lips on mine before her tongue invades my open mouth. I swiftly back away and wipe my face, ready to rip her a new one, but then another knock at the door sounds. I give her an annoyed look before going to open the door. I try not to feel bad for being a dick and acting like her kiss made me sick, but it did. She's not Jazz.

Seeing the delivery man standing there with a mechanical clipboard in his hands for me to sign, I shake off my guilt and take it from his hands. "Merry Christmas."

"Merry Christmas." Once I'm finished signing, he goes down the steps. When he comes back he has one large box wrapped in expensive silver and blue paper with an extravagant bow and two small, red envelopes.

"Um. I think you might have the wrong apartment. And when did delivery men work on Christmas morning?"

He smiles and arches a bushy eyebrow. "You Mason Reed?" I nod my head in affirmation. "Well, this is the right place. I am probably the only delivery guy working today, but you're my only stop. I get an extra Christmas bonus if this is delivered today." He hands me a card and walks away.

I glance at the package with the two cards before I focus on the card in my hand.

Merry Christmas. Hope it's wonderful and full of laughter. Since I won't see you before to give you and your family the gifts, I made arrangements. See you in a few days.

Jazz

I smile and stuff the card in my pocket before I take the gifts inside. Chanda and Mom are talking quietly as I place them on the table. Their eyes widen at the same time.

"What is that?" Mom comes over and rubs her fingers across the blue velvet ribbon.

I look up and see Chanda leaning against the counter with her arms crossed across her chest. I ignore her look and answer Mom's question. "Jazz arranged for Santa to make an extra stop."

Looking at the name tag in the pretty wrapped box, I feel something bump into me. I glance down to see Grace staring at the colorful paper and bows, smiling. “Hey, beautiful. Let’s go sit down and see what else Santa brought you.”

Taking her hand, I lead her into the living area again and place the largest box in front of her. I watch as she shreds the expensive looking paper, which is her favorite part. When she’s done I see a brown box so I take it from her while she continues playing with the wrapping. Opening it, I see another note.

I hope this works. I know how much she loves to swing and this way she can do it rain or shine.

I pull out the paper that shows what’s inside and see some sort of hammock swing with braces for the ceiling or a doorway.

“What is it?” Mom asks from behind. I hand her the paper because I’m speechless. I’m sure this wasn’t cheap and I’m stunned that Jazz would buy something like this for my sister. Grace would spend all day swinging if she could. She loves it and it helps calms her during her outbursts.

“Send it back.” I turn and look at my mom like she’s crazy while she hands me back the paper.

“Why?” I’m not understanding how she can’t see that this is perfect for Grace.

“Maybe because she doesn’t want her charity.” I look at Chanda standing beside Mom with a sneer on her face. Why she thinks she has a right to join the conversation, I don’t know.

I point my finger at her because I'm still pissed from the kiss. "You, butt out." Looking at my mom I ask again, "Why?"

"It's too much. I don't need handouts, neither does Grace. I don't need some rich girl trying to one up me on supplying for my child."

"Mom, listen to me. This will help Grace. It's perfect for her." I stand up and grab her shoulders so she'll look at me and hear my words. "You know how much she loves to swing. And if it's raining she gets really upset because she knows we can't walk to the playground. It helps her calm down when she's agitated and gets violent. It will keep her from hurting herself."

She huffs out a breath and I can feel a victory dance coming along, but I need to push a little harder. "Look. I'll pay her back, but I think we should keep it. Okay?"

After having a stare down with her, she finally gives in. "Okay," she whispers and gives me a hug. I watch over Mom's shoulder as Chanda rolls her eyes and leaves, slamming the door behind her. That is perfectly fine with me. I don't know why all of a sudden she's interested. She's been back home for months and never approached me about starting back where we left off. Honestly, I don't think I would've even if she did.

Christmas day goes on and little while later I finally convince Mom to open her card from Jazz. When she does she sees a spa day gift card at a fancy place downtown. I hope she uses it because she works too hard and deserves a day of pampering. I'm hesitant about opening mine, so I buy time by putting Grace's swing together. After an hour I finally get it up in her room and sit down to text Jazz again. I haven't heard from her since this morning and I miss her.

Me: Santa made an extra stop here. Thx. Grace <3's her swing.

I stare at the screen for about ten minutes before giving up. Wishing for her to text isn't going to help. Placing my phone on the coffee table, I walk back to the kitchen to grab another plate of food before Mom puts all of it away. She really outdid herself this Christmas and even brought home a pecan pie from the diner. Add a cup of coffee and my taste buds are in heaven. Taking a sip I hear my phone buzz and almost burn the shit out of myself from trying to run toward it. I really hope it's Jazz and not someone else. Thankfully, I didn't burn my tongue in vain. Seeing her name on my screen has me smiling like an idiot. Mom just shakes her head and continues to put the food away.

Jazz: Goodie. I hope ur not mad about yours. U R hard to shop 4.

Now that catches me off guard. Sitting there my eyes land on the red envelope on the table. I'm nervous and excited about what she bought me because I don't want to read too much into it. But why would I be mad? Standing, I walk over and pick it up. Opening the Christmas card, I see a gift card to Best Buy for a thousand dollars. What the fuck? I can't accept this. Reading the card I see her note.

Don't be mad. It's the least I could do after everything you're doing for me.

P.S. If you try to give it back I'm setting it on fire in front of you.

I text Jazz and tell her that she's in trouble and I might put her in an asylum, plus thank you. She doesn't text back of course, so I decide to call her cute stubborn ass tomorrow and every day after until I get in touch with her. I'm not sure when she plans on coming back to Mobile, so I'll ride by her place every day until I see her. It can't hurt.

With my mind made up, I enjoy my time with Grace and my mom. I can tell Mom is still uncomfortable about the gift Jazz gave her, but she's also excited about getting a spa day. Before I go to sleep, I text Jazz one more time to say goodnight. When my phone lights up, I feel the eagerness build until I see one of my childhood friends name across the screen.

"What's up, nutsack?" Besides Chanda, Ryan was one of my closest friends growing up. After high school he started working with his uncle at a local mechanic shop while I went to college, which has caused us to grow apart.

"Not much, dipshit. What you doin' tomorrow? I got a sick new board and want to take it for a spin. Wanna go hit the slab with me and a few others? You know, since you got that big ass nose out of them books maybe we can get you laid." There are always several girls that hang out at the skate park trying to either score some dope or some dick. Chanda was one of them.

He laughs and I just shake my head even though I know he can't see me. I'd hate to get him and David in the same room. They'll either become best friends or worst enemies.

After I agree and hang up, I lay my head down wondering what Jazz is up to. It feels like forever since my lips have touched hers and tasted her or heard that sweet moan that causes my hair to stand up and my dick to rise at attention. With her face the last thing I see behind my eyelids, I have a very vivid dream, which causes me to say fuck it the next morning and sleep in.

Chapter Thirteen

Jazz

The passing days have been just as grey as my mood since I left Dr. Whitney's office. I decide to keep everything he said to myself for now and just act normal. However, my mom sees through my façade and calls me out. I just blame it on being tired and leave it at that.

I decide to head home the day after Christmas to escape Mom's inquisitive stare and because Jax took Tru up to Atlanta for a surprise. He bought her son Brian's headstone, and it's already been placed with a beautiful flower arrangement to decorate the winter ground. I saw a picture and my heart just broke for Tru all over again when I gazed at the granite and bronze teddy bear swinging beside his name. He even had his footprints placed on it.

Tru believes they're headed to actually make the down payment and to visit, and I wish I could see her face when she finally sees it. She also took her new baby and other Christmas gifts with her. My brother, being the genius he is, decided to get her a puppy. And not just any puppy, but an African Rhodesian Ridgeback named Hero. He's so adorable with his big brown eyes and long, coffee colored fur, but I can tell he's going to be massive when he's full-grown. His paws are huge. Jax had said he wanted something to scare the shit out of anyone that might be a threat to Tru while he's in med school the following year. I'm happy for both of them, but jealous at same time too.

I pull into my apartment and decide to forgo getting my bags because honestly I couldn't give a fuck. If someone wants it that bad, then be my guest. Walking inside the first thing I notice is the poinsettias Mason brought me the night we made our agreement. Noticing they're dying, I freshen up the water and place them back on the table. The red vibrant colors are beautiful, and I find myself in a daze while I stare at them. *Mason*. His name runs through my mind, and I find myself wanting his company even though I've been avoiding him since our dinner. Am I really ready to compromise what we have for sex? Yes, he's a good kisser but after we cross that line what lies ahead? Will he look at me differently? Will he change his mind about claiming to be the baby's father? After everything with Oliver I'm just so unsure of myself, especially when it involves me getting naked. My confidence that was already dented is now cracked. No matter how well I dress, that scar feels visible to the world. I'm also scared of the hurt that could follow and ruin this relationship with Mason. He's become my best friend since Tru spends most of her time with Jax. With the new health issues hanging over my head, I don't want or need any heartbreak. Literally.

After a few more minutes of deep thinking, I decide to text him. Let's face it. I miss him and the way he makes me feel—desired and pretty. No, scratch that. He makes me feel beautiful … and like a normal person, not someone to coddle. That's something I have rarely felt growing up. I have always been the fragile one in the family and everyone constantly tried to coddle me. I've got news for them. Jasmine Coleman is not fragile and will not break easily.

Digging in my purse for my phone, I remember that I threw it in my luggage before I zipped it up. Geez, I have been out of it. Usually that friggin' thing is stuck to my ear for so long it's sweaty or my fingers get a cramp from constantly texting. Oh well. I guess my luggage is saved from the hands of a thief.

Slipping my black flats on, I grab my keys and head outside. The cold wind causes my blonde hair to block my vision as I walk toward my car. Grabbing the long strands and pulling it to the side, I see Mason's truck parked a few spaces down from mine. My breath catches and I feel the grey cloud that has been following me lift with just the thought of him being here. Fuck my phone. I have the real thing.

I see his dark head get out of the driver's side and even though I want to smile I don't, not until I see his reaction. Maybe he's pissed at me for avoiding him or for his gift. When he smiles and shows me those sexy ass dimples with his deep green eyes lighting up, it causes my body to hum. I launch my body into his lean strong arms and kiss the shit out of him. It's primal and rough because I can't help the feelings he triggers in me—the burning in my core that has me wanting to eat him alive and keep him with me every day. You know the euphoric feeling you get when you see the perfect shoes and it's the last pair that happens to be your exact size? It's way better than that.

I feel his fingers press into my back as he holds me up against him, and my lower half clenches with anticipation. I lick his lower lip and then kiss his cheek before I make my way to his earlobe. Damn it. He's tasty everywhere. Feeling naughty and unashamed, I say huskily, "Let's go inside."

"Yes, Mason. Let's go inside where you can introduce me to this sexy ass Betty. Dude … you've been holding out on me."

I hear the voice but it takes me a minute to decipher where it's coming from. Looking straight ahead over Mason's shoulder I see a guy I don't recognize. Even though he's wearing a beanie I can see his hair is bleach blond and reaches his ears. He's pale, but not sickly looking, and he has gauges in his ears. The rest of him is covered because of the truck parked between us. His blue eyes look at me over the roof of the truck, smiling, while he smokes a cigarette.

Mason places me on my feet but doesn't let me go as he smiles down at me. "Sorry, Jazz. This is Ryan. A friend of mine."

"Friend? Try best fucking friend ever. Taught him everything he knows." Ryan winks and walks over toward us. Now that I'm on my feet I can't see him over the truck.

When he comes into view I notice he's slender and has a similar build to Mason. Good looking but he has nothing on the guy to my right. I used to love checking out guys like him, but for some reason he has no effect on my libido. I won't dwell on it right now because I still have Mason's taste on my tongue. After that little appetizer, I'm ready for my entree. It looks like that's going to have to wait. Again.

I push my shoulders back and show my confident side. I love attention from guys, plus it makes me feel normal and not like a scarred, fragile girl. "Well hello, Ryan. I'm Jasmine AKA Jazz." I smile at him and feel Mason's strong arms tighten on me like a vice. The cold weather cannot penetrate the heat he's surrounding me with. "What made y'all stop by?" I glance up and Mason is watching me. *Love it! Just the effect I wanted.*

"Well, we're headed to beat up some pavement, but Mason said he had to drop something off and needed to catch you home. Or some shit like that. But I'm glad we stopped 'cuz I haven't seen Mason with a girl since Chanda. I was starting to worry."

Chanda's name causes me to pause while thoughts of her touching Mason play in my mind. I had no idea they used to date, and I feel jealousy simmer below the surface. I knew I didn't like that girl. Taking a deep breath, I pull away from Mason and start walking back to my apartment. "You two want to come in?" I don't wait for a reply and keep walking.

"Sure. If you don't mind. We have time." Mason's voice close behind me causes a secret smile to form on my face as I walk inside and hold the door open. I glance up and he winks as he walks by, taking off his jacket. I watch his ass shamelessly and wish I were the denim that encases it so snugly. My jealousy has evaporated with the heat that flows up to my cheeks.

Hearing a throat clear, I turn and see Ryan watching me with a smirk and nodding his head before strolling past me. I roll my eyes and he laughs loudly before he jumps over my couch and makes himself at home. *Geez! This guy reminds me of David.*

"What the hell, dude!" Mason hits Ryan's feet off my couch. I really don't care but I won't say anything. Angry Mason is so rare and hot!

Watching the curl of his lip and crease in his brow, followed by the intensity of his dark green eyes has me contemplating pissing him off more, but his playful and sensitive side causes me to feel warm all over. I'll just take both and enjoy them.

Mason sits beside Ryan while I head into the kitchen and grab a water. I need to cool off since attacking Mason is off limits due to company. "Drink?" I have to holler because Ryan has already turned on the TV. Is he deaf or some shit? He certainly knows how to blend in and make himself at home.

"Hell yeah!" Ryan sits up and rubs his palms eagerly together. "Bring me a brewski, woman."

Before I can answer, Mason throws his hands up in frustration before he turns toward Ryan. I laugh quietly because I think he's forgotten that I grew up with brothers and David. "Dude! Stop. She's not your fucking slave." Ryan seems to piss Mason off a lot. Maybe having this guy around will benefit me. I'll just have to throw him out soon because my libido is kicking into overdrive. "Besides, she doesn't have any beer here." Mason looks at me apologetically, and I smile and shrug while bringing them both waters.

"What? No beer? Why not? I mean it's cool if you don't drink and all, but living alone in this stylish pad I just figured you would have some beers left over from parties or somethin'." Mason's still glaring at Ryan, so he grabs his water and holds his hands up surrendering. "I was only playing. Calm the hell down."

Walking around the couch, I slip off my shoes and plop into Mason's lap. I'm rewarded with a grunt and strong arms wrapping around my middle.

Geez, he's fun to be around. Even this little bit of closeness is causing my earlier mood to be completely forgotten. "So, where were you two headed again? Pavement slapping or something?"

Ryan nods while taking a drink of his water. "Hell yeah, Betty! Going to slap it around and own that shit." He must see my perplexed look because he finally explains what I want to know. "Skateboarding, babe. Hitting that pavement hard with the stick. But only if Mason here promises to stay out of the ER. Pussy used to live there once a year."

Hearing that word has me hitting his leg. He just laughs but at least he apologizes. "Sorry. I forgot how chicks don't like my favorite word." He takes off his beanie and shakes out his platinum blond hair. I notice one half is shaved while the other half flips chaotically. He sees me looking and winks. I just roll my eyes because he's so like David it's weird and funny. I can't wait to get them together.

"Not as often as you asshole." I can feel Mason's warm breath across my neck and hear the smile in his voice. He's never been a big talker. When he does speak, his words and voice always have me listening. And when I talk about anything, and I mean anything, he always listens. His expressions are real and not some two-faced bullshit that guys like to use while trying to get in my pants. You know … the cocky smile and eyes that eat you alive, knowing the guy wouldn't hear a word coming out of your mouth even if you told him something important like "hey I think gonorrhea infested aliens just landed and demand all men cut off their penises." Yeah, Mason has always listened to me. Plus, he's always making me laugh and easing my worries. Even if he jokes about my size, which usually pisses me off. Size doesn't matter. It's how you work it, right? Well, that works for me and believe me, I work it. I want to be noticed and not looked over like I don't matter.

My family is so smart and they all seem to know what they want out of life. Not me. I have no friggin' clue. I've never been a brainiac like Jax or good with sports like Drew. Kenzie is an awesome writer and Cohen has the world under his fingertips. Me? Sports were off limits. I hated school and the only reason I'm in College is for the *experience* and because my parents forked out a shitload of money to give me the best in life. I'd most likely be dead without them. I can't write a grocery list down, much less a story. And I'll never be as awesomelicious as Co. So ever since I grew a set of boobs and an ass that looks great in jeans, I've relied on my looks for attention. Is it shallow? Hell yeah! Am I vain? Hell No! I know I'm not the prettiest thing out there, but I do have fashion sense and as long as my feet fit into some kickass stilettos, I can pretend I'm at model height.

Mason has always treated me like I'm special, but I've only realized it lately. I don't think he knows about my heart condition because he has never babied me. Honestly, he's been my ear—someone I can gossip and rant to without judgment. Always knowing when to speak or when to shut the hell up and let me vent. And I vent a lot. About everything. Well, maybe not everything. I've never told him about my past relationship. I'm good at keeping secrets and that is one I hope to take to the grave. I did tell him about my classes and that time I walked into the guy's bathroom the first day of school. That was hilarious and mortifying at the same time. I just said a few choice words and rushed out as fast as I could while laughter followed. I've even bitched about clothes and prices that seem re-donk-u-lous for a piece of clothing no bigger than a hand towel.

The point is he's always listened and only gave advice when I asked. He notices me. And not like a brother or family member would. Like I really matter. Why am I just now seeing how he's always made me feel significant? Is it because of the pregnancy and my sexually frustrated body? Maybe. This comfortable peace I feel right now while sitting in his lap is the first I've felt since our dinner. But do I want to ruin it with sex? Or do I want to try an actual relationship with him? I don't know.

"Hey. Where'd you go?" His lips caress the skin along my earlobe and I shift in his lap. The bulge in his pants is evidence enough that I affect him. Pregnant or not. I wonder if he notices my pooch and round belly that's developed. Goodness knows I have. I'm only a week from my fourth month mark and I know it's about to get real.

I shift in his lap slowly and turn, enjoying the way his breath hitches. My face is so close to his I can taste his minty breath on my tongue. "Nowhere. Just picturing you on a skateboard," I lie and shrug innocently. When his eyes focus on my mouth again I turn around to address my new friend while internally doing cartwheels. Being desired is so awesome. "So, Ryan, how come I've never met you before? I mean, I've known Mason for a while and not once has he mentioned you." I pointedly look at him and arch my brow.

I learn a lot about Mason during their visit and enjoy every aspect of this new knowledge. In fact, it has made my decision easier. I want to hear him play the harmonica and see him skateboard or slap pavement as Ryan calls it. I also learn that he dated Chanda his sophomore year. My jealous bitch peeks her head out, but I give her some chocolate and she returns to her hidey-hole and reality TV series. As Ryan continues to rant, he mentions he's in a band and I get excited because … well... because it's so amazeballs.

"You're in a band? That's so stinkin' cool! What instrument do you play?" Knowing my smile is probably as cheesy as Velveeta I still can't stop. I've always loved music. Country is my favorite of course, but any music that causes my imagination to surface I'm hooked. Listening to music alone in my room because all my friends were doing something I couldn't was my escape.

"Drums, baby." He winks and sits back, stretching his baggy jean clad legs out and crossing at the ankles. He places his hand behind his head before he continues, "I rock that fucking shit too. In fact we got a new gig and on New Year's. We're playing there for the first time. You two should come and please, please, bring friends. Jazz, not you, Mason. All your friends are dudes and ugly as fuck. Of course I'm the exception. I talked to Chanda already and she'll be there."

"Where?" Mason asks before I can. I'm still pissed about Chanda for absolutely no reason. I just don't like her.

"Jay Jay's down on Broad Street. Never been there myself, but the party usually comes to me, not the other way around."

The memories from two months ago hit me and I lose my smile. So this is the band that has taken over for Benji and Blaire. God, it still seems like yesterday that we were watching them play on that stage. But then I remember Benji's funeral and Blaire's rage before she left town and disappeared. I know it happened, but it still sucks. Kids aren't supposed to die, and Benji was still a kid. Of course he was fucked up, but aren't we all? I mean look at me. A girl with everything and I hate my scarred chest that has my left breast a little off kilter. Geez, I'm such a selfish person with my pity party. Benji and Blaire lost each other, Trudy lost her son, and here I am pissed at everyone because of a fucked up boob.

My breath hitches with these constant thoughts running in my head. Mason's grip tightens around my waist in an embrace, but right now it's not wanted. My overactive emotions take over and a tear slips down my cheek that I can't hold back. My throat burns with the yearning to mourn for my friends and even myself, even though I don't deserve it. This past Halloween night affected us all in some form; Tru losing two friends that were becoming like family, Jaxon watching Tru fall apart—which I know affected him more than he let on, me losing trust in the first guy I ever let see the real me, only for him to throw it back in my face. More tears start falling so I quickly jump up before the ever present water works start. I hate crying in front of people, especially when I know it's going to be an ugly one. *Ugh! My looks are still on my brain.*

Slamming the bathroom door, I collapse on the floor while grief takes over and shakes my body. Not caring if I'm loud, I let go. Everything is hitting me now for some stupid reason that I can't explain, other than being pregnant. My body feels tense and ready to explode, so I bang my head on the door just to try to alleviate the hurt and rage. I hear knocking and talking in the background but my mind replays everything from Halloween night to the following week after. I hid from almost everyone in that time because I was grieving selfishly for my loss. But nobody I loved or really cared for died. They are all still around. So why can't I get over my loss?

I'm not sure how much time has passed when the tears stop. I feel tired, so I stand and look at myself in the mirror, hoping beyond everything I won't see the girl I've been staring at for the past two months—the one who I'm disgusted to be. The one who's stupid enough to fall for a married man. The one who's still selfish and thinking of all these stupid things instead of worrying about anyone else for once.

I splash water on my face to wash away the salty tears that have mixed in with my mascara. Red angry blotches are everywhere, especially my nose. I look like hell. After I'm done cleaning my face, I listen for any sign that

I'm not alone. Not hearing anyone in the other room and feeling embarrassed for my female showcase of emotions, I debate on hiding for the remainder of the day or seeing if Mason and Ryan are still around. If they left I can't blame them. I want to run from myself. The latter is the winner so I crack open the door and walk into the living room where I left them. Instead of two people I only see Mason pacing back and forth. His back is turned my way as he runs his hands through his hair and talks to himself. I can't help but smile. He's so quirky. I don't know what I'd do without him. That last thought makes our arrangement come to mind and I can't help worry about ruining us.

Before I dwell on it too long, he turns and sees me standing there. I'm sure I still look like total shit, and I feel like the word homewrecker is tattooed on my forehead. Feeling vulnerable without makeup, I look at my bare feet. "Hi"

"Hi." After a few seconds with neither of us speaking he comes close enough I can see his feet come into view. "Are you okay?"

Keeping my eyes downcast, I concentrate on his Adidas. "Yeah. Sorry about that." I shrug my shoulders and change the subject. "Where's Ryan?"

"Um … I told him to leave."

My head comes up and my eyes widen with surprise, realizing we are alone. And there's a bed. "Why?"

"Well, after you ran out I explained about Benji and he felt like shit. So I gave him my keys so he could leave. I hope that's okay. I couldn't leave you like that. But I can get him to pick me up." He places his hands in his front pockets and rocks back and forth on his feet nervously.

Something melts in me with his words. He stayed behind while I cried just so I wouldn't be alone, even when he could go hang with his friends. How many guys would do that? None. Feeling warm, I walk and lay my head on his chest while wrapping my arms around his waist and squeeze him against me. The tears start back up because of his consideration for my well-being and it just can't be helped. *Crap!*

Chapter Fourteen

Mason

Seeing her disheartened face with tear streaks running down her delicate cheeks breaks me. I want to make it better but I know I can't. I hold her instead and hope that's enough. Seeing her so broken and upset is so different than the Jazz I'm used to but no less beautiful, probably more beautiful. No make up to hide those beautiful lashes. No lipstick to cover those heart-shaped lips that cause me to lose myself when she smiles. The warmth from her tears seeps through my sweater. I hold her tighter wanting to absorb her pain. Watching my mom all these years and hearing her tears through our thin walls makes me aware that sometimes crying is needed to feel better. The pressure of life becomes so much at times that you need to relieve it. So I'll be her shoulder. I'll be her warmth. And I hope one day I can be her hero.

I eventually leave later that night and head home. I need to get Grace because Mom is working. I hate it though. I've had Jazz all to myself today and she even fell asleep on my chest. It was the best fucking feeling—the feel of her white blonde hair sliding between my fingers and the sound of her steady breathing as she inhaled and exhaled. I hope she dreamed of me. Maybe my closeness allowed her to have good dreams and finally relax. I tried to listen to her heart a few times but it wasn't loud enough. The urge to fix the thing that can give her to me or take her away forever is overwhelming, but I'm lost and helpless without a solution. She had curled into me, the steady rhythm of her breathing against my side, and I knew how precious this moment was. Then I felt a different vibration and realized it was my phone. Ryan was outside waiting for me. I placed a small kiss on her cheek and laid a blanket across her small body before I walked out the door. Now I lie in bed thinking about everything that has taken place the past few weeks and wonder if Jazz feels the same way about me that I do for her. And if she does, will she and I have time to explore it.

Happy New Year

Walking into Jay Jay's I feel a change in the air. Maybe it's because I haven't been here since before Benji's funeral, or maybe because it's New Year's Eve and it's packed. Jazz's nineteenth birthday is tomorrow but Jax and Tru are surprising her with a cake tonight. Her parents called and invited me to a party tomorrow afternoon for her, but I'm still trying to figure out if she wants me there. We've texted back and forth but that's about it. Our last kiss was the day she came home from her parents and I feel like maybe she's changed her mind. Maybe "us" is something one-sided and she doesn't want it. The birthday gift I bought her is still in my truck, wrapped in pink—her favorite color.

Following David and trying not to get shoved, I start to worry about Jazz in this rowdy crowd. I wish they would celebrate somewhere else instead, but Trudy had to work since she's been out of town.

I finally see Jazz through the crowd, and I stop and stare like a fucking moron while people shove me. It happens in slow motion like in the movies, and I know I will never forget this moment. It will go into my "Jasmine file" that's filling up pretty fast.

I feel sweat drip down my back as my blood heats from the look of her. Long blonde hair falls down her back. Her makeup is flawless as usual and she's wearing her Christmas gift I got her, but tonight she looks like she's happy and glowing. Maybe it's from being pregnant. Maybe it's from the lights flashing around the room. Whatever it's from, I'm grateful because she deserves to always be happy. She smiles when she sees me and I smile back. Straightening my spine, I make my way to the table and the girl of my dreams. Trudy is our waitress and she brings over a pitcher of beer and several chilled glasses. Jax keeps his eyes on her until she disappears and then he turns in my direction.

"Hey, man." He reaches his hand out and I accept it. He introduces me to a few of his teammates that showed up. I feel the overwhelming need to kiss Jazz in front of them, which is new to me. They seem nice but I still don't like the thought of them being so close to Jazz. We're not official and I really don't need the added competition.

After a few minutes of yelling my name over the music during introductions, I feel a body slide against mine and look to see Jazz looking up at me.

"What took you so long?"

Bending down to answer, I slide my arm around her waist. This might not be a kiss, but hopefully it has the same effect. "David's primping. He took forever to get ready." Smiling, my eyes wander to her pink lips. "I missed you." Why the hell did I say that? But it's too late to worry about what she thinks of my confession. It's the truth. I always miss her when she's not around me.

Her eyes widen for a millisecond but her smile remains. "I missed you too."

Hell yeah! Inside I feel like dancing but I know that won't earn me any points with her, so I squeeze her tighter. My palm spreads around her stomach and I notice her bump. Even though I didn't help conceive the baby growing inside her, I will always love the both of them. I kiss the top of her head before I hear Ryan in the crowd surrounding the table.

"'S'up, mothafuckas!" He runs round smacking people's hands and some girls' asses until he sees the death glare Jax gives him. Putting his hands up in surrender, he backs away from David and Jax and then comes toward Jazz and me. "Well hello there, Betty."

I roll my eyes at his nickname for Jazz. "Hey to you too. You almost got your ass kicked." The thought has me laughing. Sometimes he needs his ass kicked.

Running his hands through his hair, he shakes it off. "Whatever. They don't want any of this." He flexes his arms and kisses his muscles like an idiot. "Besides, I'm about to go on stage and blow all them assholes away."

Jazz laughs beside me. "Those assholes are my brothers. Or a least one is."

"Please tell me you're joking, Betty. I don't want to be related to those guys." He puts a hand over his chest like he's been shot, and this has Jazz bursting out more giggles.

"Sorry. It's the total truth."

"Why would you be related to her anyways?" I ask.

Grabbing Jazz out of my arms, he picks her up bridal style. Thank God she's wearing pants. "'Cause after I show her my moves she'll be begging to marry me, and I can't deny her anything."

He stalks away headed for the dance floor and I can't be upset. I trust him and he knows about how I feel. Besides, Jazz is laughing and blows me a kiss that I feel in every pore on my body.

Sitting at the table I can't help but continually glance at Jazz as she dances with Ryan. It's obvious to me she's pregnant now that I watch her from the side. The white lace material clings to her bump as she moves. Then the crowd swallows her up and even in her white, knee high boots, she's still too short to see. The thought of her pregnancy has me thinking of her heart. I turn toward Jax, who's kissing Tru as she drops off another round. "Is all this okay for her?" I encompass our surroundings with my arms.

"Yes and No." He takes a gulp of his beer. "There's no smoking in here so that's good. But she might get tired easily so just keep your eyes on her."

I nod my head, feeling better, and look for her in the crowd.

"So who's the dick she's dancing with?" Jax asks me. I follow his stare and see Trudy walking out toward the dance floor to bring Jazz a water.

"He's a good friend and the drummer to the new band Janet hired." He just nods his head, still staring daggers Ryan's way. "Don't worry. He's a good guy and has been involved in MMA stuff most of his life. He'll protect them."

Right about that time I see a tall guy with a black faux hawk and tats covering his arms walk up to the girls. He grabs Trudy from behind and starts to dance. Before I can get my feet going, Jax is there and shoving him off of her. The guy has at least an inch on him, but he doesn't back down. The music dies and the crowd makes room for a fight. I'm standing beside Jax and soon David is too.

"What the fuck, dude? You got a death wish?" Jax is in his face ready to kill, but the guy just laughs coldly. I see a lip ring catch the light and a tattoo of a black, demonic claw on his neck. It looks so real like it's tearing up his flesh, just as evil as this guy who's obviously jonesing for a fight.

"Whoa, whoa!" Ryan pushes his way between the two and turns toward the guy. "Lyric. Not. Tonight. We need you to play. Not fuck up this gig." The big guy looks like he could eat Ryan for breakfast, but he actually seems to take his words into consideration.

"Besides that, I can't have you knocking the shit out of my future brother-in-law." Ryan looks toward Jazz. "Ain't that right, Betty? You gonna marry me now, right?"

Jazz laughs and you can feel the tension leave the room with the sound. When she gains her composure she addresses the question. "First, buddy, you need to buy me some food 'cause I'm friggin' starving. Then we'll discuss marriage." She winks and I walk over to her. Jealousy is a bitch and I've learned I don't like it. I hold her close and turn back to the commotion.

After a stare down with Jax, Lyric shakes his head and sticks his hand out around Ryan. "Sorry, man. I had no idea she was taken."

Jax visibly relaxes and accepts his hand and shakes it. "Well she is." He looks at Ryan and smiles. "And apparently so is my sister."

Janet comes and breaks up the party and tells Ryan and Lyric they have ten minutes until show time.

I grab Jazz and take her back to the table and away from the crowd. "You okay?"

"Yeah, I'm good. But I'm not the one that was grabbed. Trudy was. But I know she was ready to kick the guy's ass."

She's probably right, but I know for a fact that Lyric is nothing like Craig. From what Ryan told me the other day, he's the lead singer and founder of their band Lyrical Obsessions, as well as a badass MMA fighter. Supposedly he did a lot of underground matches in his hometown of New Orleans, but he only trains here. I'm sure his cold stare alone could probably bring down most people in the ring. I'll just keep that to myself for now. Ruining her birthday is not part of my plans for tonight.

An unwanted face is sitting on David's lap when we return to the table. Chanda sneers her bright red lips in our direction until she sees me watching her. Then she smiles like the friend I've always known. "Well did you two decide to actually date or are you just going for seconds, Mason?"

"Excuse me?" Jazz and I say in unison. David turns and looks at Chanda and something happens that I never saw before. He stands up and deposits her loudly onto the floor.

"What? Did you fuck her too?" Chanda hollers at David's back as he walks away.

He turns back around and looks at her like she's worthless. "No, Babe. That's you. Just a Fuck. She's my sister." He continues on his way until he reaches a group of Trudy's friends and wraps his hand around one girl's waist. And it's not just any girl, but Elle from Trudy's dance team. Then he kisses her and she doesn't argue. It's about damn time. He's been pining for her almost as long as I have been pining for Jazz.

Chanda's face is red with embarrassment when I face her again. She has to realize she can't come into our circle of friends and attack one. But that's always been her problem. She doesn't think before she speaks or does something. A side of me sees my friend from years back and feels the urge to help her, but after what she just said about Jazz I won't. The girl on the floor isn't the one I used to know and has never been the same since she returned home.

After she stomps off, I sit down and Jazz lands in my lap. I've never been good at reading girls, but I hope this is flirting. Soon the innocent flirting vanishes as the band starts to play and she's dancing against me. I groan from the friction of her ass against my erection. She has to notice what she's doing to me. After another song starts up, her hips begin to twist. I grab her by the waist, desperate to stop this torture. I put my head on the back of her shoulder trying to control my thoughts before I bust a load in my pants. "You have to stop that," I breathe into her ear.

"Stop what?" Her voice sounds so innocent and maybe even breathless. I can't help but imagine her yelling out my name as I sink into her. Beating off to her vision is getting old, but if it's what I gotta do, I'll do it. "This?" She swivels her ass on my dick again, so I grip her hips tighter. I haven't paid one bit of attention to the band and what they sound like because I'm getting my very first lap dance. Even if it's an unofficial one. It still counts in my book.

"Mmm hmm." I look around but everyone is absorbed in the music. Thank God! My hips thrust up on their own and I feel her breath hitch. *Hell yeah*! She's affected by me too. "You like that?" I don't know anything about talking dirty, but I feel like I have to or I'll bite my own tongue off.

Lifting my head, I place a kiss on the side of her neck and taste her *peaches 'n cream* skin. I want to eat her up. My hips thrust again as she pushes down on me. My hand reaches the hem of her shirt and I feel a war inside my body raging on. Should I touch her skin or wait for her permission? Luckily she answers my unspoken question before I just do it and feel like shit when the lust-filled haze fades. She takes my hand and slides it under her shirt. The feel of her warm skin above her black tights is amazing. I've dreamed of feeling her skin for so long, but it's softer and smoother than I imagined. I kiss her neck and feel her hips shift again. "If we don't stop, baby, I am going to ruin my jeans." I continue to thrust my dick against her ass. My hand inches up and I can feel the swell of her breast right above it begging me to touch and squeeze it. To claim it and her. However, the applause breaks through my brain and I know the band is done as well as our little session.

I'm breathing hard and fucking stiff as a board. "I need to go to the restroom." I watch her hair move with every breath I exhale as I remove my hand. She stands and straightens her shirt while I adjust myself. Everyone is talking about the music as they find their seats, so I discreetly make my way to the restroom. After splashing cold water on my face, I stare at the black pupils in the mirror. What the hell just happened? I hope this isn't just part of our agreement. I mean we had a chance the other day and nothing happened. I feel like we're more than friends and definitely more than friends with benefits. If that is all she wants, then I can't do this. No matter how much I want her … I love her more than that.

Chapter Fifteen

Jazz

My mind is so fogged up with Mason that the whole evening is a blur, even the cake and birthday song sang by the Adonis called Lyric. I usually eat up the attention, but not tonight. My panties are so wet from Mason that I can't help but wait for the night to end. He doesn't know it yet, but he's staying with me so I can get what I've been wanting for weeks. I even used my birthday wish on it—a heated night of sex with the Mason that's been showing up since Thanksgiving Day. Geez! If anyone knew the thoughts that were running through my sexed up head and how I continuously have to cross my legs to alleviate the ache, they'd think I'm a nympho.

Sneaking a peek at him as I blow out my candles, because I can't help it, I see he's looking at me with more heat than what's coming off the wick. I'm so affected I have to brace my hands on the table and lock my knees, determined not to fall. The cheers going around act as temporary distraction. Key word: temporary. I can't get the feel of him against my ass out of my brain or the calluses on his fingertips against my bare stomach. Who knew a few months ago I'd be lusting after my friend? I sure the hell didn't. But then again, I was so absorbed in another relationship I never noticed how Mason has always been around when I needed him.

After I blow out the candles and get a few hugs, I hear a voice I haven't heard since last semester. "Happy Birthday, Barbie."

I turn at the feminine squeal and see my friend Cory from my English class and the only reason I actually passed. She was always helping me when she saw how frustrated I'd get. I never had to ask her and I'm grateful. Like I said before, I suck at school.

She's one badass girl and so different from Tru and me, but she fits into our duo. They've only met a few times at lunch but they seem to have hit it off, especially when she learned about Trudy busting Ashton's beak. Ashton is my brother's ex and the biggest cunt around South Alabama. She likes to judge anyone that's different from her. And Cory is definitely different in every way possible. If she were anything like Ashton we definitely would not be friends. Luckily for me that's not the case.

She's so pretty and her style enhances her features and her brash personality. She's from New York and I love her accent and constantly get her to repeat words like coffee. It's so funny. Of course she's taller than me, but who isn't? She loves black and her hair is silky and so black it almost looks blue. It reaches her shoulders and her bangs kiss her forehead tenderly but allows her green eyes to pop, especially with her black eyeliner. She loves to wear black netting up her arms and shows off her small midriff and tiny waist. I swear she can't be bigger than a size one. Tonight she's rocking the black and nets as usual, but she has on a black, Star Wars sleeveless shirt that says "JEDI. So back the fuck off" on the front in white letters. It's ripped right under her breast and falls above her belly button. Her black pants are rocking a huge Yoda belt buckle with shiny bling and her favorite black knee high boots that have buckles down the side. She calls them her "don't fuck with me" boots. You would think she rides a Harley and is part of *Sons of Anarchy*, but she's a geek through and through. And I can't help but love it. The chick has an addiction to anything Sci-Fi. Her whole dorm room is dedicated to Hans Solo and his posse. Considering my pink addiction, nobody would ever see us as being friends but we are and it rocks.

I give her a happy squeeze. "Thanks, girlie. I didn't know you were still in town. Figured you'd be celebrating at Time Square instead of here with us southern folk."

"Well, I decided to stay warm this New Year's instead of freezing my tits off like other idiots. And I mean my family." She gives a fake shiver and grabs her boobs. "Besides, I only have so much to spare and it's not a whole lot."

We laugh and soon Tru joins in and gets the same New York Cory welcome. "Oh my God, Cory! You totally missed it. I thought Jax was about to lay out some guy that had his paws all over Tru"

"Aww, man! I always miss the testosterone filled fun." She fake pouts before she grabs a drink from a passing tray. The girl gives her a look, but then see's Tru and changes her mind. Tru is now in charge of all waitstaff, and the girl knows who to push and who to step away from. "So who was the guy wanting his ass kicked?? Cory looks around and I join in trying to find the tatted up adonis with a bad attitude.

Tru spots him first. “There. By Mason and the band’s drummer.” I look their way, Mason winks at me and my face turns ten shades of red. Totally unusual for me. I never get embarrassed unless I’m naked, and I’ve rarely been naked in front of anyone.

“Jazz? Are you blushing like a virgin? Oh my God! You are.” Cory laughs and nudges my shoulder. “How fucking sweets is that? My girl is in love.”

I glance up quickly and eye my friend. Trudy just smiles at me. “I am so so so so not in love. And I wasn’t blushing either. I just got hot.”

“Sure you did. And by hot you mean nipples hard and horny. Then I’ll believe you.” She leans in and whispers before I can argue. “He’s uber lick-o-licious and I think he loves you too.” She backs away while her words just play over in my head like a damn merry-go-round. “Now, bitches, I need to dance.”

Before I know it my thoughts are distracted by my friends lining me up on the dance floor. I keep my hands on my stomach as we make our way through the active crowd. Then I hear the song and squeal. The Wobble has every single girl on the floor shaking their ass. I can’t help but laugh happily and enjoy my birthday. Plus the start to a new year with new friendships. Maybe now I can leave my mistakes behind and enjoy my future family and myself.

After one more song has kicked my ass, I make my way to our table. Before I reach it, however, Lyric gets back on stage and announces we have one minute until midnight. As everyone gets ready for his or her kiss, I look around for Mason. This will be my first New Year’s kiss and I want it to be with the one guy who makes me feel special. The one guy who believes I’m more than a pretty face. The one guy who might just love me. But I don't see him. Maybe he went to the restroom.

Shrugging my shoulders, I decide to wait before I bust up in the men's room. Standing by the table, I let my eyes roam over every male, but I still can't see him in the crowd. Being short sucks sometimes and this is definitely one of those times. I decide to stand in one of the chairs. Probably not the smartest idea with these boots, but desperate times call for desperate measures, right? And this kiss is an emergency dammit! Slowly, I pull myself on the chair and stand to my full height and the added two-inch heels don't hurt either. Our table is unfortunately in the middle of the bar, so I have to turn in a circle to scan the whole place. I hear the countdown starting and feel like a complete loser with no one to kiss me while everyone is paired up. Even Cory is sitting on the bar beside Chris, ready to kiss into the New Year. Mason is going to get an ass chewing when I find him. Making one more turn, I lose my footing and start to fall. Nobody hears me due to the crowd screaming along with the countdown.

"Five."

"Four."

"Three." My heart drops and I hold my baby bump, bracing myself for impact.

"Two."

It doesn't come though. Instead I feel strong arms.

"One."

Keeping my eyes squeezed shut, I hold my breath as everyone yells "Happy New Year." Then I feel soft, warm lips crush against mine. Dumbfounded, I open my eyes and see familiar deep green ones looking into mine. Mason.

Wrapping my arms around his neck, I practically jump into his mouth, rubbing my tongue against his and feeling the moist warmth and smelling his intoxicating scent. Best fucking feeling ever! He loses his balance from my attack and sits in the chair I just fell from. Wanting to crawl under his skin, I straddle his lean body and start to grind against his hard length.

"It's time to go. I want my birthday wish." He doesn't argue and we leave before anyone can stop us or ask questions that I'm not ready to answer. Honestly, I don't know how to answer them. Leaving his truck at the bar, we take my BMW and haul ass to my apartment. Luckily the drive isn't awkward like one might think. I keep myself occupied. I'm so hot and ready explode I do something I've never done before. Well, actually two things: one is giving a blow job and two is doing it to someone while they drive. When I reach for his crotch, I feel nervous excitement mix with my pheromones. What if I don't do it right? What if he thinks I really suck at sucking dick? *Only one way to find out.*

Mason grabs my hand as I reach for his zipper. "What the hell, Jazz?" His voice is breathy and deep. The sound is nothing like the porno movies I watched as a curious teenager. It's more real and actually sexy. Instead of laughing from the fake acting, I find myself rubbing my face into the crook of his neck and inhaling. Damn! Why does he smell so good?

Licking under his ear, I love the chills I elicit along his skin. "I need to touch you. Please, Mason!" When his hand lets go of mine, I slowly get to work. He actually helps with the button of his jeans before I dig in like it's

Christmas morning. When the smooth, soft skin over hard muscle is resting in my palm, heat builds deep in my belly and my moan is surprising to both of us. "Let me know if I'm doing something wrong," I whisper before kissing his pulse and then dive in, eager to get my prize.

"Holy damn, b—baby!"

His hips thrust up with the first contact of my tongue on the tip. The salty taste mixed with his obvious enjoyment is friggin' amazing and I want more. Wrapping my lips fully around him, I feel his fingers thread through my hair. When I suck in, his grip tightens as he says words that would make a sailor blush. I work my way from base to tip several times, getting him moist, and let my hand grip the base, following my mouth's lead for more friction. I don't know how long I've been at it or if we're even at my apartment, but I plan on keeping it up until he comes. I don't have to wait long after that last thought. Mesmerized by the feel of him actually getting harder and longer, I scrap my teeth lightly on the underside of his dick. Then he explodes and holds me against him as he pumps his hips.

"Fuck, Jasmine! Fuck … fuck … fuck!"

With his last thrust I swallow every last drop before sitting up. Looking into his features shadowed from the streetlights, I see his nostrils flaring with his labored breaths. I smile and try to comb my hair that has gone everywhere while he fixes himself and wonder what's next. Should I kiss him or ask how I did? I hope he liked it. Maybe he faked it like I have in the past. But I taste come in my mouth, so maybe not. I try not to let these thoughts dampen my newly discovered sex goddess but what if I did suck? What if he decides that he got what he wanted and now wants to leave? Like Ollie. And why the hell am I comparing the two?

“Come here.” I look up just as he grabs my face with both hands along my cheeks before he brings his mouth to mine. This kiss is different. This kiss is gentle, slower, and deeper, not desperate like before. This kiss answers my unspoken questions and confirms Cory’s statement from earlier. Mason Reed loves me. But will he still after he sees the real me? If he learns my secrets? Soon these thoughts vanish with the feel of his mouth on mine while his skilled fingers comb my hair. Now it’s my turn to be breathless, and he does a damn fine job too.

After he’s done giving me a kiss that causes my toes to curl, he continues to hold my cheeks while his eyes take in my whole face almost reverently. His eyebrows arch under his dark shaggy hair like he’s trying to figure me out. I hope he doesn’t see the mistakes I’ve made and my selfishness. I only want him to see how he makes me feel: happy, healthy, and—

“Beautiful,” he whispers, and my whole body feels warm just from that one word that passes his lips.

Wanting to lighten the mood and ease up on some of this seriousness, that I’m definitely not ready for, I wink in his direction. “You’re not so bad yourself.” I know it’s corny and totally not the time, but it does cause him to smile. I kiss his nose because he’s just so dang cute. Then I make myself pull away. “Wanna crash here tonight?”

“Definitely.” He gets out of the car and walks my way to grab my hand. “Is this okay?”

Looking at him I see his worried look. It can’t hurt to hold his hand. Right? I mean it’s not like he just proposed or anything. Besides, I just had his extra appendage in my mouth so holding hands is totally fine. I think. "Um … Sure."

We're silent on the way up and while I unlock the door to my messy apartment. "Excuse the mess, but I couldn't find something that really fit." I pat my bump and it reminds me of my upcoming doctor's appointment. "Mason? Would you mind going with me next week to the doctor? I know classes start back up, but I'm supposed to find out the sex of the baby and Trudy will be busy."

Actually, I never asked Trudy. Mason is my first choice, but if he can't go I'll ask her. Or Cory. We sit beside each other on the couch and it feels normal, not weird like I thought. The fire I felt earlier is still simmering, but definitely not overwhelming like before.

"Yeah. I'd love to go but let me make sure I can get a sitter if Mom needs to work." He puts one arm around me and pulls me close. "Happy Birthday, Jazz." His lips land on my temple.

I can't help but smile. Tingles run through my body and a sigh escapes me. "Thank you." Feeling tired all the sudden, I start to doze off as my body relaxes. All the dancing really did a number on me, topping it off with my first blow job followed by ultimate make out session. Yeah! I'm pooped. Before I know it my brain is swarmed with sweet dreams of Mason.

Chapter Sixteen

Mason

My dick is straining for release as I pound into Jazz, but no matter how hard I thrust or how deep I go, this fucking hard-on won't go away. I watch as her perfect breasts bounce with each thrust and I'm scared I might hurt her. But she only smiles at me with the same look she always gives me. Not turned on or hot like I've seen lately. Just sweet and friendly like before our first kiss. Maybe I'm doing something wrong. Maybe I'm not enough to please her. What if she is just doing it and really didn't want to? I probably need to stop, but she feels like heaven under me and I'm not sure I can.

"Jazz. Please, baby." I don't know what I'm asking. All I know is she needs to give me something. Anything. Tell me to stop or try a different position. Just give me some reaction dammit! Grunting, I thrust deeper and stay there.

"Mason." Finally she says my name but her lips don't move. Maybe I just missed it. "Mason?" Again, her lips remain smiling.

Leaning into her warm body, I'm determined to taste her sweet swollen breasts but I can't seem to reach them. What the hell? After the third try I finally make contact. But it's not the warm skin I was expecting. It taste like cloth and invades my entire mouth while absorbing all the saliva and causing it to become dry. Suddenly, I can't breathe and start to cough. Jazz screams my name right before I feel a sharp-ass sting on my shoulder blade and let out a yell while sitting up. "Shit!"

Looking around in a daze I see a very dressed Jazz in bed beside me under the blankets looking scared to death with wild hair. Glancing down at myself I realize I'm on top of the blankets and also very dressed. And very turned on. My face turns red with embarrassment because she just witnessed me having a wet dream about her and humping her bed. Rubbing my face to gain a few extra moments, I can only hope it wasn't obvious. Then I hear her muffled giggles and know she definitely heard me. Shit!

With the urge to hide, I get up and go the bathroom, avoiding her smiling expression. Once inside, I splash cold water on my face and just stare at my reflection in the mirror. I take in my flushed skin and glazed dark eyes and wonder if she could ever fall in love with me. Someone who loves to play video games and loves anything technical. If I had a chance of looking confident and cool in her book, I'm positive it's scratched out and has the word weirdo written in red in its place. I close my eyes and try to disappear. Rushing water hitting the porcelain sink drowns out all the noise in the room. However, I can still hear my heart pounding against my rib cage as the dream replays in my head with my newfound embarrassment closely following its tail. What am I supposed to do now? She knows I was just dreaming of us having sex, but of course the dream was justified. She gave me the best BJ I've ever had tonight. So I shouldn't be embarrassed. It's not like I jizzed on her sheets or called out her mom's name.

Feeling slightly better, I turn off the water and dry my face on her pink bathrobe that hangs on the back of the door. Inhaling her scent that lingers on the fabric puts me at ease and I start to feel myself calm down. I see Jazz as soon as I open the door. She's standing in front of me and she's no longer smiling. Instead she wringing her hands nervously and refuses to make eye contact. Why is she acting nervous when I'm the one who just dry humped her mattress? Maybe I did freak her out. "Jazz? I am so, so sorry. I guess the events from tonight, which happens to be the best night ever, mixed in with my dreams and became the best damn dreams I've ever had." She's still rubbing her hands, but at least her eyes are making contact now. I can't read her thoughts tonight and I really wish I could. I take a step toward her, desperate to make this awkwardness fade. "Do you want me to leave? Are you uncomfortable? Shit! Of course you are. I just raped your mattress." Looking around, I spot my phone on her dresser. "I'll just call a cab and leave."

"Don't. Please don't go."

I turn and face her again. She walks in my direction this time but stops a foot away. "Okay. I'll stay, but I'll sleep on the couch."

She still looks scared but I see resolve in her sky blue eyes. "Can I trust you?" After my nod she steps closer and takes my hand. The softness of her touch helps ease my concern. "Good. I want to show you something. It's the one thing that I have always tried to hide from people. Something that has haunted me all my life." She takes a breath so I remain silent as she leads me back to the bed. "Sit."

After I do as she says she backs away. Before I know what's happening, she's shimmying out of her black pants. "What are you doing?" I don't know if I should panic or smile. I'm leaning toward panic, though, because I don't want her to feel obligated in any way to do something she doesn't want.

"I'll ask the questions. So I just need you to sit there and listen." After she kicks her pants to the side, I allow my eyes to travel up from her pretty, arched feet to her tanned, muscled calves and soft thighs. Her white lace shirt obscures her upper half so I hurriedly bring my eyes to hers and see her searching stare. "Do you like what you see, Mason?" My heart hammers in my chest as she waits for my answer. Can't she tell after all these months that I love everything I see? Every freckle, curve, and imperfection. But my tongue vanishes with my nerve and no words form. "Was that your first wet dream about me, Mason? And please be honest. I need honesty right now."

Honesty might make me sound like a pervert. But she only wants a yes or a no, not the details of my late night showers and a washcloth. "No."

She gives me a small smile. "Good. When you see me in these dreams, what do I look like?"

"Like you." I don't know what I'm supposed to say but I decide to stick with honesty. Tonight is about laying it all on the table with her. "Beautiful." Nothing could have prepared me for this. I had no clue that the change I felt when I stepped into Jay Jay's would come to this.

"Beautiful for me is only an illusion. I know every makeup and beauty trick there is to enhance my features. It's something I've been doing since I was a teenager. I'm not good at a lot of things like others, but fashion and flirting are the two subjects I've excelled in." She gives me a forced laugh, and I swallow hard. I want her to see what I see, but I know she needs to get this off her chest—whatever it is. "But I want to show you the real me. I trust you and you've become a very important person in my life." She stops and just stares at me. If she thinks I'm going to run from her she's wrong. "Do you know how I became adopted by the Colemans?"

"Yes."

Her eyes widen and she seems surprised but continues. "Well, the first surgery was an emergency. And there was a mistake made. But to doctors the cosmetic part isn't important." She places her shaking hands on the hem of her shirt. After a few stalled seconds I see her lift it slowly over her head. I pinch my arm. This has to be another dream because my fantasy for the past four months is standing in front of me in her white panties that have bright green bows on the sides and matching bra with a bow dead center, nestled between her perfect cleavage. My dick has been reawakened and is now ready for round two. Or three if you count the dream. I can tell she likes my reaction because she gives me a heated look. "You like? Well give me a second and you will see that this too is an illusion. Thank goodness for Victoria Secret." She turns her back toward me and I see the dip in the small of her back before it curves create her pretty ass in a fucking thong.

My loud swallow and heated blood can probably be heard by the family next door. I can't help it and my inner male dominance is starting to take over. A vision of putting her against the wall so they hear her scream my name and know who can please her is overwhelming, but I know she still has more to say so I wait.

"I was pretty much dead when they brought me into the OR, or so I was told since I don't remember. But I still see it everyday."

She reaches around and unclasps her bra, and I watch as it falls to the floor in slow motion. My breathing speeds up when she turns toward me again in that damn thongs and a breast cupped by each hand. She has a baby bump that sticks out, but it just adds to her sex appeal.

"You see, I should be thankful for the doctors saving my life, but I'm not because I'm a selfish person. Sometimes I get so angry I just breakdown, especially when it involves guys or clothes."

She takes a step and stands right in front of me. I'm eye level with her hands that hold her tits, but I gain control and look at her sad face and notice moisture in her eyes. "Now, you can leave if you want to after this and I'll even let you out of our agreement. But the past week has me wanting to show you the real me."

Then she lets go and reveals herself to me. And I see the real her. And it's not perfect like my fantasies. It more beautiful because it's why she's here, right now, with me.

The scar rests between her breasts. It starts out faint and narrow but gets jagged as it moves toward her left breast. It's thick and has caused her left one to look like it's missing a piece where it indents, but it's no less sexy to me. Looking up, I see her face is looking away and her white-gold hair obscures her profile. I hate that this has given her a complex but love the fact she doesn't show people freely.

Hesitantly, I reach up and slowly trace my finger over the top of the scar down to her left breast. I hear her breathing shudder, and when I look up her eyes are wide and on mine. I take my other hand and grab her waist to pull her closer to me. My breath is fanning her chest and her nipples tighten.

"Beautiful," I whisper before I slowly put my lips on her scar and kiss it. Pulling away, I watch her reaction. She's squeezing her eyes shut tightly and a tear runs down her left cheek. I stand up slowly and hold her face in my palms.

"Look at me, Jazz." She shakes her head as another tear falls. "Please look at me." I wipe the wetness with my thumbs and wait. Finally she opens her eyes and stares up at me. She needs to know she is the most beautiful creature to ever enter my life. She lights up my every day and has made me want something for myself for the first time since I was little. "You are so beautiful. This only adds to it."

"No, Mason. You're wrong." Her voice is thick with sadness as she tries to shake her head again.

"Can't you see? These scars make you who you are. They allowed you to live so you could be there for Trudy when she needed you. Allowed you to touch so many lives that would be bored without you. And mine. I was so lonely before I met you. But I didn't realize how much I needed you. You allowed me to feel young again instead of like an old man." I place my hand over her heart feeling the steady beat. "Because of this scar the most beautiful noise is the beating of your heart. I love this part of you most of all, Jazz. This heart that loves so many people and will stand up for the weak. The scar is beautiful to me. And I love it." I take a deep breath before I continue. "And I love you."

I stop breathing and wait for something to happen. Anything. And when I'm sure nothing is going to occur, it does. She reaches up and grabs me around my neck before pulling my mouth down to hers. And I lose myself in her wet kiss. The warmth from her mouth is intoxicating and hungry. It's angry and determined, just like my girl.

Reaching around her small waist, I pick her up and turn toward the bed before laying her back down. This causes her to giggle but I swallow it in my mouth, desperate to continue my exploration.

"God you feel so good under me."

I make my way down her neck and love on her freckle that I've been obsessed with since I met her. The taste of her skin on my tongue is driving me crazy. I want to eat her up, but I don't want this to end too quickly either. When I get to her scar I give it small kisses until I get to her left breast. Looking up at her face I ask, "Is this okay?"

She gives me a small smile and I can't help but smile back. "Yeah."

Keeping eye contact, I lick down her scar to the indention of missing tissue and swirl it with my tongue lovingly. "Mmmm … You taste amazing." When I get to her nipple I do the same but pull it into my mouth and suck deep. She moans and arches her back. "Damn that's hot."

"Don't stop." Her voice is begging me for more, so I reach up and play with her other breast as my mouth continues to devour the left one. She likes it when I scrape my teeth over her tight nipples and so does my dick. Her breathing is fast and shallow and mixed with her moans I might just come in my pants.

Standing up swiftly, I pull my shirt over my head and quickly discard my jeans. Before I take my boxers off I look at her. "Are you sure? I mean, really sure?" Because this will change everything to me. Our relationship, the arrangement, everything. But I don't say those words.

She sits on her elbows in only her panties and flushed skin, and the tent in my pants becomes the Big Top Circus. "Yes. I'm positive. Now hurry up and get back over here. Because I'm cold."

"That's my girl. Still bossy and sexy as usual." Pulling down my boxers, I quickly pick my wallet off the dresser looking for the condom that's been there forever. God I hope they don't expire.

"Mason, what are you looking for?"

"Condom." Which has in fact has expired. Shit! I run my hands through my hair in frustration. "It's expired."

"It's okay. In case you've forgotten I'm already pregnant. Plus I just had full check up and I'm clean."

My frustration dissolves and I'm standing by the bed again, fully erect. "Thank God. If I don't get you tonight I know I'll die of blue balls."

She laughs as I climb on top of her again. I kiss her heatedly on the mouth before working my way down her neck again. Once I make it to her scar, I feel her shiver while I lick it, letting my fingers caress down her body. Feeling her cute pregnant stomach, I stop and look at her.

"Jazz?" When her eyes meet mine I continue to tell her how I feel. "I want you to know that I. Love. You. Every part of you. And this baby is a part of you. Therefore I'll love him or her just as much and promise to be there. No matter what."

She smiles and nods. I see a shimmer of tears in her eyes, and since I don't want to make her cry again, I lighten the mood by letting my hand reach her underwear. "Now where were we?" Tracing the hem, I watch her pupils dilate with desire and her chest move when her breathing hitches. Bringing myself up on my knees, I help her out of them. When I see her exposed flesh it's my turn to breathe roughly. "I'm one lucky bastard." She starts to giggle. "Oh really. And here I thought I was the lucky one." Glancing in her direction I can't help the surprised expression on my face from her words. She can have anyone.

"Mason?" She reaches up and touches my cheek gently. I feel dazed and frenzied. I thought having her naked under me was all that could set me on fire, but having her look at me with emotion in her sky blue eyes dissolves me into nothing. "Do you know how amazing you are? All the nights you've helped me get through so much since I've met you. The relationship you have with Grace is so beautiful and I know she loves you. Having you, one of my best friends, care about me the way you do. And not to mention how you willingly jumped in to father a child that's not yours. You are the best person I've ever met. You're wiser than your age and I care for you so damn much that I can't think straight. I want to be like you one day and hope you can teach my child how to be like you as well."

It's not a declaration of love, but I'll take it. Grabbing her hand from my cheek, I kiss her palm tenderly before I bend down and gently kiss her swollen belly. I need to please her, so I kiss and lick my way down to her mound.

"Can I taste you?" I've only done this once and it's been a while but I need to do this with her. I need to taste every inch of her and leave an impression that she'll never forget. I need to ruin her for anyone else.

"Yes. But I'm scared. No one has ever been so close to me before."

Excitement has me smiling like a victor over her words. "Don't worry, baby. You'll like it."

I hope she more than likes it. I want her to fucking love it. Standing once more, my knees hit the end of the bed before I grip her sweet rounded hips and drag her to the edge.

"Spread your legs and put them over my shoulders." My voice sounds strained. A growl erupts when she does what I say and her pink, moist flesh is in front of my face. I can't help but rub my nose against her and inhale. "Fuck, you smell so damn good."

Then I get to work, sucking and licking every crevice while watching her body jump and hearing her breathy moans. Before I know it she's gripping my hair and grinding her hips against my mouth faster and faster. Then she hollers my name and I taste the best fucking thing in my life.

Chapter Seventeen

Jazz

Holy hell! Fuck a duck and shit on a goldfish cracker! My fingers grip the blanket beside my naked body as Mason and his gloriously talented tongue continues to attack my wet pussy. Yes! I just said the word I hate, but right now at this very moment that is what it is. A pussy! Even though I had one orgasm already, he is working on number two. Thank you men everywhere who love to do this for a woman. What have I been missing? Why didn't I ever let myself do this before with Ollie? Oh fuck him. He has nothing on this sexy guy between my thighs.

I feel the same tension in my body that I did a few moments ago start to build. The lapping of his tongue as he tells me how beautiful and sexy I am is addicting. If death is going to knock on my door, then please let me die after this next orgasm. Biting my lip, my hips thrust up on their own because I have lost all control of my body tonight. My moans even sound sexy to me, like I'm made to do this in life. Maybe I can be a voice over in a porno one day.

"Ahhh!" His finger slowly enters me as he sucks my clit and I lose my shit. My body thrashes against his mouth and I might have possibly ripped some of his hair out. But I can't care at the moment because I'm once again in sex Heaven as I yell his name until I feel relaxed and like a marshmallow.

"Say it again." His voice is close and the shift of the mattress causes me to open my eyes.

"Say what?" He's above me again and the feel of his bare chest against my sweat covered one is glorious. Returning his smile, I run my finger over his full lips and watch as he sucks it into his mouth.

"My name. Say my name again."

He's so easy to please. "Mason," I whisper. "Mason. Please make love to me."

I feel his shiver or maybe it's mine. I meant to say fuck me, but I realize that Mason is better than just a fuck. He's a guy who will devote his whole heart into anything he does and sex is one of them. He's very thorough and ready to conquer whatever quest he's on.

Before I know it he's nestled between my thighs and I feel his mouth on my neck and the head of his dick against my opening. Instead of just diving in, he kisses his way down to my breast before returning to my mouth. Squirming under his weight, I wrap my legs around him, desperate for him to enter me. Torture is the only term I can come up with. He just continues to assault my mouth and breasts affectionately.

"Damn it, Mason. You're killing me." My words come out in quick pants because the feel of his teeth scraping across my sensitive nipple is achingly wonderful.

He comes up and smiles again before he kisses me heatedly, doing all the things he just performed between my thighs to my mouth. Then he plunges into me and I moan from the feel of him. Oh wow! I'm so sensitive and I don't know why. But I like it. A lot. Maybe it's from the pregnancy or his earlier ministrations, but damn I could definitely do this all day.

"Damn it, Jazz. You're tight."

He thrusts deep and I feel his balls slap my ass. Soon our bodies make music as they slap and slide against one another. Our moans and grunts sing a song that matches it perfectly. Too soon the heat and tightening is back and I feel the euphoria building.

"I'm going to come." And I do. My hips move against him and grind as I ride out my orgasm.

He becomes a beast then by lifting himself on his knees while holding my legs around him and fucking me hard. It hurts so damn good and keeps my orgasm going and going. Soon he lets himself go and follows me over the edge. His strangled cry probably wakes my neighbors, but they can go to Hell. I always hear the two of them going at it.

Sweat dripping skin, heaving chests, and our warm bodies lie there for minutes with no words. They're not needed. I know without a doubt that everything between us is different now. Everything has changed since last night. I knew it as I got dressed for the evening; I just didn't think the change would make me this happy.

Holding hands as we sit and wait to be called back to the exam room, I can't help the smile that has remained on my face since New Year's night. Mason and I have been spending every moment possible together. And I guess you could call us a couple and not just FWBs. I mean we haven't actually been out on a date or anything because he always has Grace, but he's usually at my house if I'm not at his. I even went to see him skateboard with Ryan yesterday. I'll just say that the ride home was almost as hot as watching him ride his board. Who knew skateboarding was so sexy? Even when we're apart during classes, I find myself watching the clock until I can see him again. Weird I know, but totally true.

New Year's morning I woke up to French toast and a pink wrapped gift on my night stand. It turned out to be a gorgeous silver charm bracelet with three beautiful charms already attached: a pink heart, the letter J, and one that says "Best Mommy." I haven't taken it off since Mason put it on me and don't plan to either. After being fed a yummy breakfast, we picked up Grace and headed to my family party at the beach. Mom and Dad were so happy that Mason and I are actually a couple that they just talked and talked about future events that we could go to together. Jaxon and Trudy even seemed in good spirits, but ever since Christmas Tru has done more smiling.

And that makes me happy. We are actually planning a girls' spa day soon, and Cory, Trudy, and I are going to get our hair done then have a much needed slumber party. No penises allowed, and that makes me sad now that I have Mason's.

Glancing in his direction I watch him as he reads an article. He's is so cute reading through the parenting articles I could stare all day. Wrinkles form in between his eyes as he reads with so much concentration, and when his face pales while his eyes widen unexpectedly I burst out laughing. When I take the magazine out his hand, I look over the page that caused him to almost faint and see a woman nursing her baby on a nipple cream ad. I have to admit I get a little pale myself thinking about it, however I won't admit it. To be so sensitive about breasts you'd never believe that he loves to motorboat me any chance he gets. I guess today he's bashful Mason and last night he was lustful Mason. My man and his dual personalities. Got to love it.

"Jasmine Coleman."

When my name's called I am jumping up and forgetting my purse because I'm eager to find out the sex, but luckily Mason grabs it and follows me. After the normal exam of temperature, blood pressure, and peeing in a cup, I'm lying on the exam table with him holding my hand, standing beside me. Our eyes are glued to the sonogram machine that Doctor Parnell is turning on.

"Alright, Jasmine. Do we want to find out if we have indoor or outdoor plumbing? Or will it be a surprise in a few months?"

"Are you crazy? I need to start planning names and nursery themes. So of course I need to know."

She nods her head and starts to probe my belly. She takes several measurements and pictures before she finally moves on to the main event. The waiting is killing me, but seeing my baby on that screen makes it all worth it. The sickness and nausea as well as the emotional roller coaster ride I've been on for the past several months seems like it never happened while I watch that screen.

"Well today is a good day. It seems your little girl is quite the model. She's showing off."

It takes me a few seconds to understand what she just said, but when it registers I squeal with exhilaration. I'm having a girl. I watch my little girl on the screen sucking her thumb and I fall in love all over again. My eyes are watering from happiness and I feel Mason kiss my cheek. I look his way and see a handsome smile. "It's a girl."

"I know. She's going to be just as beautiful as her momma too."

Reaching up, I run my free hand through his brown shaggy hair before I pull him down to touch his lips with mine. It's gentle and soft but still full of emotions.

"Thank you," I whisper against his lips.

"No. Thank you."

After wiping the lubricant off my middle, we check out and make our way to my car. "I'm starving. Want to go get some lunch?"

"Sure. What are you in the mood for?" He opens my door and I get in while deciding what sounds the most appealing. But even though I'm hungry I am not sure I can eat with the news we just learned. I'm having a girl.

"Why don't we get your mom and Grace to meet us somewhere? And maybe Tru and Jax. Then we can tell them all the news. And how we're having a little girl."

He stops the car and puts it in park again before we can even pull out of the parking lot. I look in his direction and see him looking at me in a strange way, like he can't figure me out. My heart rate picks up in fear of my happiness coming to an end.

"Mason? What's wrong?" I ask cautiously.

"We're. You said *we're* having a little girl." He smiles and grabs my face before he kisses me. "I've been waiting for you to say that. To accept me as a part of you two." Kiss. "Thank you for this." He kisses me again and moves one hand to my stomach. I'm speechless and so happy. All I can do is kiss him in return and hope I'm not rushing this.

After making arrangements to meet everyone to eat, we head over to the restaurant and see Trudy holding hands with my brother. They look so good together. Thoughts of them giving my little girl a cousin invade my brain. That would be so awesome, but I know Jax really wants to get through med school first before he has babies, or at least that was the plan before Tru walked into his life.

Mason comes around and opens my door. After helping me out, he kisses my cheek. "I love you."

Hearing those words seem to cast a spell on my body. One that causes me to become speechless and warm. I can't say it back because … because … hell, I'm scared. I care for him so much, but I'm just now discovering my feelings. Jumping into love again even though it feels that way ... No way Jose! So I smile and kiss his sweet lips as response before wrapping my grey shimmery scarf tightly around my neck. It's January and the wind is killer here in Mobile.

We meet Tru and Jax outside the restaurant. It's a nice local deli with some amazing soups. I can't wait to feel my toes again. Even in my cowgirl boots with warm socks my tootsies are cold. After we sit by the window I start to worry about Mason's mom Debra. She should be here by now. "Where's your mom?"

"I don't know. I'm going to call her." He pulls out his phone and excuses himself.

I can't help but think she doesn't like me. Even after the few conversations we had she seems kind of cold. I just figured it's because I'm new, but now I'm not so sure. Feeling a warm hand encase mine, I glance up and see concern on my brother's face.

"You okay?"

I shrug not sure how to answer. "I really don't know. His mom hasn't really been welcoming to me. But I thought we were making progress." Seeing Mason make his way back to the table I tell them not to say anything to him. Stubborn as ever, Jax is hard to convince but after a quick kick in the shin he agrees. Smiling at Mason while he sits down, I see his expression is gloom. "She okay?"

"Yeah, but she got called into work. Chanda has Grace at the house. I need to get her soon though. She has a date or something later."

On one hand I'm aggravated with the thought of Chanda having Grace, but then I feel relief that she has a date and maybe she'll stop being a bitch toward me. I wouldn't care if I could bust her in the mouth, but with me being pregnant that is a definite no-no. Smiling with the thought of a daughter, I rub my tummy and my bad mood disappears.

"Well then let's call Mom and Dad on speaker so we can share the news with everyone."

After our food is delivered and Mom and Dad are called, Mason and I announce we're having a girl. I instantly reach across the table and latch hands with Tru. Relief is visible in her eyes and I'm sure if I were having a boy this would be torture for her. Jax and Mason do a bro-hug before he envelops me in a mean bear hug like he's always done growing up.

"Congrats, Jazzy girl." His familiar smell surrounds me, and I can't help but feel my eyes water. We're no longer the kids that would constantly fight or laugh together. We've grown up and it's bittersweet. I dry my tears before anyone sees. Today is about happiness.

Mom and Dad are thrilled and can't wait to see the sonogram video. I promise to come up real soon to show them. After being interrogated by Dad about my health, we finally say our goodbyes and finish lunch. Walking out to our cars I grab my friend in a hug.

"We still on for our girls' day, right? Cory has already stocked my cabinets with all kinds of junk for our movie binge."

"Wouldn't miss it." She squeezes me before my brother steals her away.

Once we reach Mason's mom's apartment we go up hand in hand. Going in the door we see Chanda on the floor playing with Grace and watching Disney on the TV. When she's not giving me a "go to Hell" look, Chanda is very pretty. I can see why guys like her.

Mason walks over and kisses Grace on the head. "Hey, sweet girl." He puts his attention on Chanda. "Thanks for coming over."

Standing up, she walks over and grabs her jacket that is lying on the couch. "No problem. Like I said, I love Grace and anytime I can watch her I'll take it. I'm going to go." She turns to me and catches me off guard with her smile. "Look, Jasmine, I'm sorry for the other night. I guess I'm used to being the third woman in Mason's life. I got kind of jealous." She sticks out her hand that's decorated in intricate tattoos and rings. "We good?"

Being raised in the Coleman household has always taught me to forgive and forget. So why not?

"Yeah. We're good."

While shaking her hand I get a feeling I shouldn't forget when it comes to her.

Chapter Eighteen

Mason

Tonight Ryan and I are headed to Jax's apartment for a guys' night. Actually it's an excuse to be close to the girls, but nobody wants to call it that. A few games are on ESPN and beer is what it's all about. David swears Jax and I are turning into pussies. But hey, at least we're happy!

David's having his own girl issues. I don't know what happened between Elle and him after their kiss on New Year's, but every time I bring it up David changes the subject. Either he was shot down again and didn't get any, or he actually likes the girl. I really think it's the latter.

Ryan invited himself to the party and called Lyric to show up later. He actually has a fight this weekend he wants me to go to but it depends on Jazz and my mom's schedule. It would be awesome to see the guy in action though. Ryan says he's a sadistic beast in the ring. That's why they gave him the name "Devereux the Demon." The name fits because New Year's night he looked possessed while smiling at Jax.

"So, Betty coming by tonight with my bay-bay?" Ryan asks while drumming on his leg as we pull into the apartment complex.

"My baby, asshole. And no. She has plans with some friends. They're having a slumber party or something." I shrug, not really sure what girls do.

"Hell yeah! Girls half-naked in pajamas." He rubs his palms together. "I'm in."

"Not happening, dude. I don't want to interrupt them or have Jazz think I don't trust her." I park my truck in front of Jax's building and get out. I head up the stairs while fighting the temptation to check on my girl.

Ryan quickly catches up and slaps my back. "Come on, man. I won't mess with her. I want to check out some of the others."

"Only Jax's girl and her friend Cory are there. It's not like they are running around naked. I'm not even sure they will be drinking. Tru rarely does and Jazz is pregnant."

After I knock, David opens the door with a beer in hand. "Hey, dipshit. I see you brought another pussy."

Ryan gets flustered but I place my hand on his chest to hold him back. "Not tonight, David."

Ryan smiles and I can tell he's about to be a smartass. "You know what they say. You are what you eat. So I guess that's why you're a dick."

Jax and I bust out laughing while David looks Ryan up and down ready to kick his ass. After bumping chest with him he finally joins in and they shake hands. "Hey Mason. I think I like this motherfucker. Even if he is ugly."

Ryan shrugs and takes the beer I hand him. After I sit down Jax's new dog Hero runs over and jumps in my lap. He's only four or five months old but heavy as hell. These dogs are bred to attack lions in Africa, so I can only imagine the damage he'll do to an intruder. The police have been worried about some drug dealer in Atlanta coming after Tru since her attack a few months back. So far nothing has turned up and sometimes no news is not good news.

We turn on the TV and watch some SEC football bowl game that's on. I really don't care for sports, but I'm enjoying the guys bantering back and forth. We order pizza a bit later, and soon Jax walks to the back with his phone in hand. Bet he's calling Tru. Does that mean I can call Jazz? What the hell! I'm going to do it anyway. Making my way to the bathroom I notice I'm feeling loose and I have a buzz. I guess it's justified since I drank a six-pack on my own and I hardly ever drink. Pulling out my phone, I see blurry numbers so I squint to see them better. After a few minutes of trying to dial my girl's number I get it by just pushing talk twice. When she picks up I hear laughter and music in the background.

"Hey, you. Having fun with the guys?" She sounds breathless and it reminds me of our post-sex state.

"It'd be better if you were here." At least I think that's what I say. I'm not buzzed, I'm drunk. Geez! I am a pussy. *Ha! I said pussy.*

“Yes, you did say pussy. Are you drunk, Mason Reed?” She laughs. I’m surprised because she hates that word. However, I’m also horny from hearing it leave her mouth. The background noise fades and the sound of her breathing is all I can hear on the phone. Maybe she walked away from the noise and wants to be alone while talking to me. My dick starts to strain against my jeans with each exhale. “Mason!” she says, and my name sounds so damn erotic.

I swallow before I can answer. “Yes. But not too drunk. Because now I have a hard-on.” I rub my palm over it and notice how sensitive it feels, like every nerve has surfaced and are causing shock waves to shoot up my spine and down my legs. I sit on the commode before I fall over.

“Really?” Her breathing becomes deeper and her voice becomes sultry. “How hard are you?”

A growl bubbles up from my chest. The thought of her on her knees before me clouds my vision. “Very. So fucking hard.” I rub my palm over myself again and again. My hips start to thrust up from the sensation.

“Good. Can you feel my hand as I touch you? Can you feel me stroke you? Do it, Mason. Touch yourself and think of me doing it.”

What the Fuck? I think we’re going to have phone sex. A total first for me. And as hot as it would be, it’s just not good enough. I need more. And she’s close by. Only a building over in fact. Making a quick decision that I know will mostly piss her off, I take a deep breath push end on my phone. Hanging up on her was the only way to walk over and surprise her. At least that’s what I think in my drunken state. Walking through the living room I see the guys are into another game. Ryan catches my eye and sees something in my stare. Maybe it's my need for Jazz or my hard-on tenting my jeans, but he knows where I'm headed without me saying a word.

He jumps off the couch and runs my way. "Whoo hoo! Titty time, boys!" He runs past me out the door but comes back in and grabs his beer. "Can't forget my friend, can I?"

I'm unaware of Jax and David following behind until I get to Jazz's door. Looking at Jax, I see he's carrying Hero like a baby. For someone so strong and mean looking it's weird seeing him holding a puppy, regardless of whether it's a gigantic one.

My phone has been vibrating since I hung up, but I plan on making it up to her. Knocking on the door I brace myself for her wrath, but when it opens I'm caught off guard. Her hair in pigtails with pink tipped bangs falling to the side of her face. The background noise of Ryan yelling some shit disappears, and I can only hear the blood rushing in my brain as I stare at my girl, who happens to be standing there in tank top and pink superman pajama pants with her hand on her hip, giving me a death glare. Without words, I wrap my arms around her waist and bring her flush to my body while never breaking eye contact. She smiles and wraps her arms around my neck. I know instantly I'm forgiven.

"Surprise."

She laughs. "Hi." I love it when she says that one sweet word. It reminds me of New Year's.

"Hi to you, too."

Noticing how cold it is, I move her inside and shut the door. Before I can do anything else she places her cold hands at the base of my skull and pulls me down so I can taste her lips. She tastes of all the things I love: fall weather, Christmas time, and hot chocolate. Mine! The word whispers in my brain and I deepen the kiss. Then Ryan interrupts. Asshole.

"Hey, ass wipe. Stop kissing my bay-bay's momma."

Jazz pulls away due to her giggles and I join in. Hers are contagious, especially when she snorts. "Let's go get him before he destroys your place and humps your friends."

"I don't think Cory will let him near her unless he wants to get shanked. That girl is lethal and can wave a lightsaber in a pair of six-inch heels like no one's business."

We sit on the couch beside Cory, who is sporting a princess Leia hairdo and giving Ryan a "what the hell" look as he tells everyone how he and Jazz are getting married, but she wants to wait until after Ryan junior is born.

Cory quickly cuts him off. "Hey, it's a girl, you weirdo. Besides, it's my baby not yours." She winks at Jazz.

"Whatever! Like anyone will believe that. You couldn't get her knocked up because you don't got the goods. And, baby, I got plenty of the goods." He takes a swig of his beer and fist pumps David. Those two are going to cause some major trouble.

"Please! I'm sure I have more of the goods than you two combined." She points to Ryan and David, who quickly lose their smiles. "Besides that, I got mad skills. Don't I, ladies?"

Tru and Jazz loudly agree. “Sisters before misters.” All three bust into giggles. Jax and I join them while Ryan and David continue with the comebacks. Well, Ryan anyway. David seems to be quieter than usual. Maybe it’s only compared to Ryan.

After about thirty minutes or so my phone rings and I see it’s Chanda. I know she’s off tonight and so is Mom, so I don’t know why she’d be calling me.

“Who is it?” Jazz asks with concern. She’s probably worried Mom was called in and I’ll need to leave.

“Chanda.” I kiss her cheek when she turns her attention away from me and back to the group. “I’ll be right back.” Walking outside to face the winter chill, I answer. “Hello.”

“Mason?” Her voice sounds strained and people are in the background laughing loudly and making it difficult to hear her.

“Yeah, Chanda?”

“Can you come get me? Please?” She sniffles and I hate when any girl cries. “My ride left me.”

“Well, I’m kind of at Jazz’s with a bunch of friends … and I’ve been drinking.”

“Oh.” She starts to really cry and talking becomes difficult, but I can still make out some of what she says. “I’d call a cab but he left with my purse.”

Well shit! I exhale and rub my hands through my hair. “Okay, tell me where you’re at and Jazz and I will come pick you up.”

She tells me and I hate the idea already. This part of town is rough and why she's down there, I'll never know. Actually, it's probably because of some lowlife guy, but who she dates is none of my concern. She's not the girl I knew back in middle school and high school anymore. She's been different since she came back almost a year ago. Even though she's always been wild and free it's more intense now. I guess you could say she's more reckless and selfish, always lying to her dad, asking for money or stealing it, and flirting with older men in suits trying to find her ticket out.

Well that's what she said when I confronted her one night.

I was taking our trash out this past summer and watched a car pull in that really didn't belong in my apartment complex. It wasn't the worst place to live, but BMWs, Audis, and Mercedes usually didn't come around. Suspicious, I watched and saw Chanda get out of an all black Mercedes with chrome detailing. When the guy drove off I saw someone that looked to be in his late sixties or so and dressed for business in an expensive looking suit. I hated that someone I consider a friend, or used to anyway, would sell herself for money. I had to say something.

Shaking my head, I go back inside and to Jazz's warmth. It's fucking cold out and I hate getting her out this late at night. Maybe Jax can come with me and drive. I think he's only had one beer, unlike the rest of us.

Jazz scoots over and I notice how she stays there instead of cuddling next to me like usual. Nudging her with my elbow, I get her attention. Her eyes look tired with dark circles under them. I'm immediately worried.

"You okay?"

"Yes."

Okay! She's obviously upset. Short answers are her way of simmering under her pretty skin. I need to make this better.

"Sorry about that. Her ride left her and took her purse." I wait for her to look at me before I continue. "I need to go get her."

She pales before her cheeks turn red. Her eyes narrow and I know she's pissed. It's scary and cute at the same time. Should I hold her or run for cover? Instead, I'll sit here and watch. "So you're leaving? To go get her? But you're drunk."

Her shout grabs everyone's attention and I feel eyes on me but ignore them the best I can. "I wasn't going to drive. I was going to get someone to drive me. And yes, I was going to go get her but planned on coming back after I dropped her off. I can't leave her stranded. She's off Decatur Street and you know that's not the safest part of Mobile." She stands and places her hands on her hips.

Jax cuts in before she can argue. "He's right, Jazz. That part of town is definitely not safe for anyone." He looks at me and stands. "I'll drive you, but I need to go grab my keys." He pulls Tru up from her seat and gives her a kiss. I watch as Hero stands on alert and can already see his protectiveness of her.

Standing up, I grab Jazz. I kiss her nose and hold her tight against my chest. When her arms return the embrace I feel my heart slow down. I'm not afraid to admit that I was scared to death of losing her over something so stupid like Chanda. The last thing I need is for her to think something might happen between us. Tipping her chin up with my finger, I kiss her lips once, twice, and then a third time before I tell her I love her and pull away. She never says it back and that's okay with me. For now.

Chapter Nineteen

Jazz

I have a "come to Jesus" meeting with myself after they leave to go pick up Chanda. My anger over the situation disappears and a new anger forms. I feel angry with myself for being the same selfish person that I usually am. Just because I wanted to keep Mason close and because it's another girl, I let jealousy overtake me. After he leaves I lock myself in my room and think of Mason and how he's not like Oliver. He's not with someone else and cheating. He's a good guy helping a friend out in their time of need. Just because she has a va-jayjay doesn't mean he shouldn't still be a friend and help her out, even if she was a bitch in the beginning.

I eventually cry myself into a fitful sleep but wake up a few hours later. My jelly belly thinks my bladder is either a trampoline or tumbling mat.

I notice a heavy weight on me when I try to move, so I turn and see a sleeping Mason with parted lips a tousled hair. He's so sexy and cute all at the same time—practically perfect. Scooting out from under him, I hurry in the bathroom, desperate to get back to his warmth. I strip down first and enjoy waking him up without words, only actions.

The next morning we wake and I'm all smiles, but when I think of my behavior the night before it falls. "I'm sorry." I kiss his slightly stubbled cheek and repeat myself. "I'm so sorry for being selfish last night and wanting you all to myself. But honestly, I think Chanda still has a thing for you and the thought of you and her together had me jealous and paranoid."

He leans to his side and props up on his elbow while watching my every move. I love how his dark hair falls against his forehead and over one eyebrow. When he smirks I feel my insides quiver again. "I like you jealous. It means you like me."

Lying back down on my back I turn my head and face him. "Of course I like you." I touch his nose. "You make me laugh and you look good on my pink duvet." He kisses my finger once it reaches his lips.

"What else do you like about me?" He's playful this morning and I love it. All is forgiven.

I tap my finger to my chin and stare at the ceiling. "Hmmm. Well you do make killer French toast."

He climbs on top of me and straddles my naked body. Nuzzling my neck, he whispers, "Anything else?" Shivers race from my neck down to my toes as a laugh erupts from me because it tickles.

"Nope. Nothing. I think that's it."

He sits up smiling and looks at my body while holding my arms above my head. Man, I'm glad I shaved. "Nothing, huh?"

My laughter dies as his green eyes start to smolder. To know that he gets turned on and heated from my scarred chest is something I never thought I'd experience with anyone. Beautiful is what this sweet man makes me feel. I love how he caresses my body during sex or when we're just sitting on the couch. I love how he devotes his life to those he cares about and is willing to give a few dollars to the homeless. I love him.

"I love you, Mason." The words slip out without trying. My soul needs him to know how he makes me feel, how much he means to me. Us.

His stare reaches my eyes and he smiles with so much love that it's a moment I will remember for the rest of my days. I know I'll never love someone as much as him and hope one day I'm worthy of him. He bends down and catches me in a sweet kiss before his mouth travels to my baby bump. He repeats his words of love, and I feel a river of happiness flow through me that has me glowing from deep within.

It's so stinking hot for March. I'm sweating every second. A pool sounds wonderful but the apartment still has theirs locked up. I had asked them if I could use it but the guy in the office said it was still too cold. Douche bags. Don't they know I'm hot? Can't they see my sweaty face and damp clothes? So instead of swimming to cool down, I settle for summer clothing to keep my temperature down from these damn hormonal changes.

When I walked into the dentist office last week in shorts everyone looked at me like I lost my mind. Who cares if everyone else in Mobile is still wearing sweaters and jackets? Not me, that's for damn sure! After I slide on my blue and white flip-flops that match my Maxi dress perfectly, I head out the door. I have another appointment and Mason is meeting me there after his class.

Classes for me are light and only on Tuesday, Wednesday, and Friday mornings. I plan on taking the summer off, and honestly I doubt I'll come back. College isn't really my thing and as far as the experience goes, I think I've had enough. Sleeping with one's professor is experience enough in my book.

Dropping out has been on my mind since I felt the baby kick for the first time. That caused the reality of the situation to really sink in, and I kind of had a mini freak out about having a person inside me. If you really think about it, it's pretty weird.

It was the week after the Chanda rescue and I was with Mason and Grace at Tru's. We just finished dinner and were watching American Idol when this chick comes on and screeches like a fudged up bird. It was so loud my child jumps inside of me for the first time. At least that's what I say caused it. While big bird was screaming on TV, I started screaming for real which caused everyone to start screaming. Poor Grace. I didn't mean to freak her out, but shit, I was freaked out myself. So much so, I couldn't calm down to tell anyone what was happening. So I finally just grabbed Mason's hand and held it against me to show him. Mister cool and confident just smiled and kissed me. This calmed me down because he obviously doesn't think I'm about to be ripped open like in the movie Alien. Unlike me, he didn't have a lunatic moment that caused a hilarious riot for my whole family. Even Ryan found it funny and he's picked on me every time I see him. I warned him the next time I'd kick him in the balls. He finally got the hint after I actually did it. Since then almost everyone wants to feel, everyone but Tru that is. I asked her after it happened, and she just said it was too soon, but I found out shortly after, that Brian's birthday was a few weeks away. I could tell she was happy for me but sad for herself and wanted to be alone. So we left and I called Jax letting him know what had happened. He immediately left practice and headed home.

After I pull into the Doctor's office, I look around for Mason. I don't see his truck so I head in and do the usual sign-in and waiting game. After I take my seat, I place my hand on my stomach and feel the flutters that my princess causes against my palm. It still kind of freaks me out.

"How far along are you?"

Looking up I see a woman in her early thirties, maybe mid thirties. She's dressed in nothing but a designer soft green pant suit with black trim. Her hair and eyes are brown, and she's wearing square framed black glasses. She's pretty, but she could be a knock out with my help and some contacts. "Six and half months."

"Wow, you're tiny for being so far along. When I was that far with my last two I was double in size." She laughs. "Do you know the sex yet or are you going to be surprised?"

"Oh no! This girl here has to know what the nursery will be decorated in. And it's all pink." The things Mason has done to the nursery are beautiful. He and Ryan painted it with pink and white vertical stripes on all walls but one. It will eventually be painted with some mural of princesses and castles. Mason won't allow me to do it or even help so I'm getting Cory. I warned her there better not be a green, wrinkled Yoda face or I'm going to coochie punch her. She just laughed like I wasn't serious, but I am totally serious.

"How lovely!" She smiles big and I can tell she's a genuine person. Some of my parents' acquaintances are so fake it makes me gag when they come around. "I have two girls already and honestly, I want another." She pats her small tummy. "However, my soon to be ex-husband wants a boy. Since he's a cheating bastard, he doesn't really get a vote." She looks up surprised by her outburst, and I can't help but laugh. "I am so sorry. I really shouldn't have said that. Anyway, back to the subject. I don't think I can handle a boy though. I'm like you when it comes to pink."

We continue to talk and she tells me that she's only fourteen weeks pregnant and her daughters are nine and six in age. Complete opposites from each other too. The younger of the two is a huge tomboy while the older is a prima donna. We don't mention the ex again and I'm glad. I feel as though it's still a fresh wound. Soon, I feel the couch dip beside me and look to see a smiling Mason beside me.

"It's about time." I lean in and kiss his cheek.

That's not good enough however. He gives my new friend and the whole doctor's office a show with a heated kiss that has me wishing we were alone. My toes curl and my body shifts in his direction desperate to get closer. He pulls away before I can climb in his lap and a whine erupts from me. Of course he only laughs at me.

"How are my girls today?" One hand is around my shoulders while the other goes to my belly and she kicks immediately. It's like she knows him as her daddy even though he's not by blood.

“Well, she’s great and her mommy is wonderful now.” Remembering my manners, I turn ready to introduce Mason to my new friend who I’ve just met and have yet to learn her name. Before my eyes meet hers my world stops and my blood turns to ice. I feel sick and disgusting all at once and desperately want to wash myself clean. Sitting beside her is her soon to be ex-husband and my ex-lover.

Ollie.

I’m frozen as he stares at me while the cold blood rushes in my head and my breathing stops. I thought that seeing him was enough to have me freaked out, but when Mason stands up and shakes his hand while smiling like my world didn’t just turn into a huge clusterfuck, I start to see spots in my eyes. Everyone’s voices are drowned out by the pounding and rushing in my brain.

I feel my daughter kick several times, so I take a much needed breath. Hurting her is not in the cards for me, so I try to smooth my features and produce a pleasant smile. I look at Mason and the wife. I refuse to make eye contact with that piece of shit for fear of him seeing the truth. However, fate has a different plan.

“Jasmine. How are you? I noticed you dropped my class last semester right before midterms. You were so good I really wish you wouldn’t have left.” He sticks his hand out for me to shake and like an idiot I do. I’ll do anything to keep the truth from Mason and have him look at me with disappointment. I feel his finger rub across my palm and my stomach rolls.

I quickly pull away before I vomit. “I learned it wasn’t for me. Life happened and I have other things to worry about.”

My name is called so I say goodbye to his wife. She stares at me with a look of comprehension in her brown eyes and I have a feeling she knows. I hate it. This woman did nothing to me and I ruined her marriage. I tore her home apart because I fell for her husband's lies. And now her family is suffering the consequences.

Needless to say the appointment is short and quiet, full of yes and no answers with awkward moments. Mason has been nothing but quiet, and I feel as though a red A is displayed on my body somewhere. He only kisses my cheek before he leaves and I want to cry but know it will do no good. He shouldn't want to be with me and won't once he's discovered what I've done to that poor family. Just because I love him doesn't mean I'm worthy of him. I'm tying him down and holding him back from a real family. I'm being selfish. Again. I leave the doctor's office and head home with torment running through my mind. Even my usual remedy of Blake Shelton and a candy bar doesn't brighten my mood or take away my worry. Mason said he had to go meet Chanda to get Grace. Lucky for her I feel like being alone so the thought of him around Chanda doesn't bother me as much as usual. The girl might be civil around me, but we are far from friends.

Today's bizarre encounter has given me a headache. Instead of studying like I need to for this semester's midterms, I crash on my couch. Or at least try too. Before I know it a loud banging breaks through the silence. It continues and I realize it's coming from my door. Bastards!

Opening it before looking in the peephole, I'm surprised when I'm shoved aside and Ollie walks in. "What the fuck are you doing?"

"Oh don't be so damn dramatic, Jasmine. You know why I'm here." He takes off his sport coat and lays it across my couch like he's home from work and does this every day. The nerve of this asshat.

My mind is still groggy from my almost nap so I'm trying to take it all in, but when I look at him standing in my apartment, I know it's real. I see the lust cloud his eyes as he takes in my cleavage that has developed with pregnancy. The memories of us that surface are unwanted and feel wrong. He needs to leave. I straighten my shoulders and roll my eyes.

"Sorry, bud, but I have absolutely no idea, and besides, you're definitely not welcome here or anywhere else around me."

I'm filled with Bravado and anger, but we both know I'm too small and pregnant to make him leave with force. Jax isn't, but he's at baseball practice. Tru might be but she has enough drama in her past and I'm not willing add to it. Besides, the asshole in front of me won't lay a finger on me. Or at least I hope not.

"I'll leave after I get some damn answers." He walks in the kitchen and looks in my fridge. What the hell! "The beer in the fridge better not be yours." He sits at the bar and takes a sip of his water. "So tell me. When is my son or daughter due? And why the fuck didn't you call me?"

My breath falters and heartbeat picks up. I refuse to say anything. There is absolutely no way he could know the truth. Mason acted like the devoted father and boyfriend the whole time we were in front of them. "I have no idea. Ask your wife. I think she's three months or so along."

"Jasmine … Jasmine … Jasmine." He sighs while shaking his head and looking at me like I'm a child, like he always did. "Do really think I'm a fool? I know for a fact that child is mine." He finishes his water before he stands up and walks toward me. "You're lying. It's written all over you and your behavior." I'm backed into the door and his body becomes flush with mine—no more tingles or heat like before, only cold fear and disgust. He reaches up to touch my lips but I quickly turn my face away so his hand makes contact with my cheek instead. "You were so into me all those months ago that there is absolutely no fucking way you spread those warm thighs for anyone else." Clicking his tongue, he backs away and grabs his jacket off the couch. I exhale with relief and open the door, ready for him to leave.

"Leave. Now." My voice croaks as anger clogs my throat.

Passing me, he stops and turns my way. "You know the beer and liquor in the fridge is not suitable for a child. Especially mine. Keep that in mind, Jasmine. I know people and I usually get what I want, and having a lot a children is something I've always wanted." He winks and smirks like a true asshole. "I'll see you around, baby." He struts out with his coat thrown over his shoulder, leaving me shaking with his warning.

I watch him leave and when he's gone I go inside, desperate for all that to be a dream and I'm actually still asleep on the couch but I know it's not when I hit my toe on the chair leg. *Shit that hurts!* And that means it really did just happen and I need to make sure it doesn't happen again. Plus it's time to tell Mason the truth. If he lets me go, then I can't blame him. If he stays I'll be the happiest girl in the South. There is only one way to find out though.

Locking my door, I walk to the window and watch Oliver get in his black Escalade. My focus is solely on him and I never see the other person watching from their car or expect things to go from bad to worse.

Chapter Twenty

Mason

I know today is going to be messed up. Last night I should have just stayed at Mom's instead of coming back to the frat house when she got home early this morning. Instead, I fell back to sleep and missed my alarm, along with my first class. I've had a bad feeling all day and trying to push it out of my head is useless. Things just have just gone from bad to worse.

Watching Jazz's face pale after I shake Professor Wallace's hand was a kick in the gut. For months now I've been wondering who the guy is, but I never expected this. I've always respected him and kind of looked up to him. He even suggested I join my fraternity and wrote my letter of recommendation to the school's engineering program. He's actually really smart, plus he helps with the biochemical program and that in itself can be difficult. He's even called me a few times to fix the class projector and his personal computer. I never would have imagined this. The whole situation is fucked up and if I'm feeling this way I can only imagine how Jazz feels.

Driving in silence, I let everything sink in until I pull into Mom's. When I'm inside Chanda is feeding Grace dinner and gives me a run down while I just stand there. I'm sure my face shows my lack of interest in what she's telling me. Everything is a blur and I feel like shit. Feeling a tap on my arm, I see her standing in front of me.

"Hey. Earth to Mason." She waves her hand in my face. "Everything okay?"

"Yeah. Just had a long day." Sitting beside Grace, I watch Chanda and notice she still has a limp. When Jax and I picked her up that night I noticed her knee was skinned pretty bad and bleeding. She says the guy she was with pushed her down when she tried to stop him. I don't know how she finds these assholes, but for some reason she's attracted to them.

"Are you sure? You look like shit." She comes over again and feels my forehead. "You're not sick. Do I need to kick your baby mama's ass?"

My eyes narrow as my temper is alerted. "Don't touch her, Chanda. I mean it."

Hands up in surrender she backs up. "Alright, ass wipe. Chill!" She looks at the clock before grabbing her coat and heads for the door. "I'll see you later."

Half an hour later I'm cleaning the table off when the phone rings. It sounds eerie and a bad feeling sets in my gut. "Hello." I hear crying and it sounds like a woman. Instant panic sets in. "Hello? Jazz, is that you, baby?"

It's a woman but not Jazz. "No … no, sweetie. My name is Ginger." She takes a deep breath. "I'm sorry. But you sound just like him."

Okay? "Can I help you?" I don't want to be rude but this is weird.

She clears her throat. "Is this Mason?"

"Um … yes."

A relief filled exhale comes through the line. "I've been calling every Reed in Mobile today trying to find you. Is your mom home?"

"No, ma'am. But can I ask who this is, because I'm really confused."

"I'm sorry. I'm obviously not myself today. This is your grandma Ginger. And I called to tell you something terrible happened to your dad last night. Your father had a massive heart attack last night and passed away."

She continues talking between tears, but I'm not hearing anything. Her words regarding my dad have stopped my ability to think. I feel my stomach drop as disbelief and confusion war. I quickly shake the feeling of confusion aside and think her words through. It's crazy and this woman is crazy, because my dad died overseas. Years ago. "I'm sorry for your loss. Truly, I am, but you have the wrong person. My dad died when I was little."

There's silence for a few long seconds. "No, sweetie. You're mistaken." She pauses for a moment. Your dad … was his name Gregory Reed? From Indiana?"

What the hell? Now instead of confusion I feel anger. I sit down before my legs give out. Hearing my dad's name spoken from this stranger's mouth has me floored. Try as I might, I can't think of how she might have that information other than she's telling the truth. And the truth hurts.

I'm sitting on the couch when Mom gets home at midnight. Other than feeding Grace and putting her to bed, I haven't done shit. I turned off my phone earlier and ignored the knocking. My fury and hurt of the situation about my dad has me ready to go off on somebody, and I know the next person to piss me off will get it. This feeling is so foreign to me. I hardly ever get upset and I've never felt something like this. Rage, pure and not so simple rage. The lady who's actually my grandmother told me she and my dad have been trying for years to see me, but Mom refused. I just don't understand why she'd do that. The idea and vision of my dad I've had all these years was a lie. My entire past was basically tainted by a lie that stole years from him and me. He wasn't a hero who died overseas. He wasn't even in the service. He was an electrician. Someone who hated confrontations and loved the Beatles. This whole situation is fucked up. I'm pissed off and I don't want to take it out on just anybody. There's only one person that deserves it and she just got home.

"Hey, honey." She puts her keys on the table and takes off the sweater she's had for years. It has stains and a few holes, but she keeps it around. It used to give me comfort because it was a constant. Now I feel pissed off while looking at it. Why not get help from someone or the family who wants to help? Why struggle so damn hard to make it when you don't have to?

I take a deep breath so I won't go off the deep end. Words are hard to form but I need answers. "How did Dad die again?"

She looks at me warily and I see the moment when she decides to lie again. "I told you ... he died during Desert Storm." She doesn't continue, only grabs a drink from the fridge and comes in the living area.

"But how did he die?" Resting my elbows on my knees, I wait for her answer and keep my eyes trained on her.

"I really don't like talking about the details, baby. You know how upset I get." She sits on the opposite end of the couch and faces me. "Now, how was Grace this evening?"

I'm not dropping the subject. Not this time. Whenever I asked as child she'd say the same thing then switch the topic. How did I not see the lie? Standing, I walk over and pull out the picture of the man I missed out on. He looked like a normal guy but his eyes and smile are the same as mine. I see a piece of him everyday in the mirror and I had no clue. Thank God for the Internet and Facebook. After Ginger told me about Dad, she mentioned a sister I never knew about as well. Her name is Symone and she's seventeen. "Who's this then?" I stick the picture in her line of vision and watch as her features turn from confusion to sadness, then to anger and confusion again.

Snatching the picture from my hands, she stares at me like I betrayed her. "Where did you get this?" Her anger causes it to come out as a hiss.

It doesn't affect me though, not like it usually does. I'm not trying to make her smile and cheer her up tonight. I want some damn answers. "The internet. In fact, it's off my sister's Facebook. A sister I knew nothing about until a few hours ago. She lived with that guy..." I tap the picture that's still clutched in her fingers "...who happens to be my father. Who was well and alive until last night." My voice is loud, but pissing neighbors off and waking people up is the last thing on my mind.

“How … who?” She wipes her tears and takes a breath. “What do you mean? Until last night?”

I turn my back and rub my hands down my face. “Oh! Now you give a shit about him or me for that matter? Well, Mom, I received a call from a lady named Ginger, who claims to be my grandmother. She says he had a massive heart attack and died last night.” When I turn around again I see her face is covered behind her hands and her shoulders are shaking. “You know what else she told me? She said that they’ve been begging you for years to see me. To let me visit, but you refused. You even told them I didn’t want anything to do with them.”

She continues to cry while I wonder what to believe anymore. “I don’t understand how a person can deny a child a family. Do you know I haven’t been a kid since I was eight? I have always felt like I had to be the man of the house. Giving up every social aspect of my life to help you out. And all you’ve done is lie to me. All these years you have done nothing but lie.” I wipe the tears that run down my cheek. “What about the medals mom? The medals I took to school to show everyone my dad was a hero. Where did you get those?”

She finally looks up and it kills me to make her cry, but dammit I deserve the truth! “Where did you get them, Mom?”

“Some were my dad’s but most were from novelty shops.” She watches me for a minute while I hunch over to catch my breath. “Mason, you don’t know the whole story. Let me explain please. I did what was best for us. He had an affair. He got her pregnant and he decided to leave us. Not just me. He walked out on me and you.”

"If he didn't want me, then why try to see me all those years? Why didn't you let me make the choice about having him in my life?" I stop and gain composure. The sound of her tears and horns honking outside are the only noise throughout the apartment. "I'm leaving and going to Indiana to pay respects to a man that was stolen from me. To meet a family that wants me to know them."

I go to my room and turn my phone on. I see several texts from Jazz and Chanda. Ignoring them, I call a cab and start packing. I hate leaving Jazz but I need to do this. I go to text her but open Chanda's message instead. And my legs give out on me so I sit on my bed. There on my screen is a picture of Professor Wallace leaving Jazz's apartment with a cocky smirk on his face. Jazz is behind him and even though I can't see her face I know it's her. She's wearing the same dress from earlier. My Jazz with the guy who really got her pregnant. Throwing my phone across the room, I hear the crack before it hits the floor in pieces.

After grabbing my bag, I kiss Grace on the head and go wait outside for the cab. Sitting on the steps I can't help but picture Jazz and Professor Wallace. Their bodies wrapped together and sweaty, planning their family while I'm at home watching Grace. Then I think of Professor Wallace's wife. The sweet lady I met today and how he and Jazz are sneaking around not only my back but hers as well. Fucking home wreckers. That's what happened to my parents and that's what's happening to Mrs. Wallace's family.

Hearing delicate footsteps pattering on the cement sidewalk, I see a shadow approaching and recognize it immediately. *Jazz*. She stops when she sees my face. Maybe it's the anger or the tears in my eyes, but I'm grateful. I don't want her anywhere around me.

"Mason?" Are you okay? I've been calling and I need to talk to you about today. I need—"

"What, Jazz?" I explode and she jumps from my unexpected outburst. "You need to tell me how you fucked a professor? You need to tell me how you're pregnant by a man who's old enough to be your own dad? Guess what? I already know. And I also know how you ruined a happy family. How you continue to ruin them with your games and lies. How can you even stand to look in a mirror, knowing what you're doing to people's lives? God you make me sick."

I refuse to look at her as the words continue to spew from my mouth, refuse to watch as I hurt her, even though I want to cause her pain like she's caused me. So my eyes are trained on the parking lot. I see my cab pull up just as Chanda gets close to the steps. Standing, I walk past Jazz and keep my eyes trained on Chanda who watches me. I see the smile that lifts the corner of her mouth. "Well, Jazz. Two can play at that game."

I wrap my arms around Chanda and kiss her like I'm fucking her, kiss her like an asshole who doesn't give a shit while the girl I love and thought loved me watches. When I'm done I unintentionally look over at where Jazz had been and see she's gone. Pushing away from Chanda, I grab my bag and hop in the cab. Hopefully to a place that will help me forget the lies everyone has been telling me all my life.

Chapter Twenty-One

Jazz

I'm numb, so numb that I don't feel the sun's warmth or the breeze as it lifts my hair from my face. It hasn't been brushed and I haven't worn makeup since my heart was stomped on. It's been two weeks and I'm positive I look horrible, but honestly, I just don't give a shit. All the reasons to smile and laugh or think of myself are the last thing on my brain. All I want to do is get the last time I saw him out of my mind, get the kiss he gave someone else to leave my thoughts and nightmares. But it stays there no matter what I do. My tears finally left me a few days ago after I arrived at my parents' house. Tru thought me spending time with my family at the beach would help, but I know nothing will help. Nothing will take away the broken heart that I carry in my chest or wash away the shame I feel throughout my entire being. I ruined a family and the one person who I love left when he found out how disgusting I am. He's right. How can I continue to look at myself in the mirror?

"Honey?" The sound of my mom's voice snatches me from my thoughts. I turn and see her standing behind me and notice her worried expression. I should care that I'm doing this to her, but like I said earlier, I'm numb. "You really need to eat. You're seven months pregnant."

Turning around, I look out toward the water, ignoring her words because I have no appetite. College students are everywhere and cover the white sand with their suntanned bodies. Spring break is supposed to be a happy time for someone my age, but instead of enjoying it I'm trying to block everything out. I spot Jax, Tru, McKenzie, and Cohen playing and laughing. Thanks to Mom telling him to leave me alone, he decided to take everyone to the beach. He's been on a rampage since I showed up at their door that night, ready to fight the world to make me stop crying and feel better. He doesn't realize I did this to myself and deserve everything I'm feeling, but I couldn't tell him that. I couldn't stop sobbing from the pain that scorched my body long enough to breathe or speak more than Mason's name. Supposedly they drove to his mom's, but she also had no idea when he'll be back. I don't remember most of the first week or the drive that night. All I remember is Mason and Chanda together. Kissing. Touching. Even fucking while I watch. It's been in my mind so much that I don't know what's real or imagined. All I know is that he hates me. And he left.

Mom sits beside me and wraps her arms around my shoulders. "Jasmine, baby, please tell me what happened. You seemed so happy last time y'all were here. How can I make this better?"

Should I tell her the truth? Should I risk her hating me too? Nothing hurts anymore so why not tell them. Keeping my eyes trained on McKenzie laughing while Jax holds her in the water I open up. “It was a lie. It was all a lie.” My voice is strained and scratchy to my ears. I guess when you cry for a week straight with no words that’s normal. “Mason isn’t the father.”

“What? Then who is?”

I sit there and count to ten before I let the words I’ve kept to myself for so long slip through. “My biology professor.”

With her intake of breath at my confession my numbness disappears and I feel disgusted again. Shivering, I wrap my arms around my middle and feel my daughter kick. A daughter who will be fatherless because of lies. “He’s married and already has children.” I want to look at her but I can’t. My tears build up again while my throat starts to clog and burn. “I didn’t know, Momma. I promise I didn’t know.”

Her arms encircle me and I lose the battle, allowing the tears to return. She doesn’t push me away like I thought. Instead she holds me closer and whispers in my ear how much she loves me and how we’ll get through it. As a family.

After it’s all out in the open I actually feel relief. My heart is still broken, but I’m not a leper to the family like I thought. Tears are shed and hugs are given while some sort of peace is settled in my soul. I will get through this with or without Mason.

When I return home I decide to drop out of college. Mom and Dad were fine with my decision. They said that it was just added stress and agreed that I should wait to see if I wanted to go back. They even offered to keep the baby if I wanted to move back home and attend Pensacola Junior College. I don't see it happening, but you never know.

Cory is staying with me for now and I'm grateful. The quiet always gets me thinking about Mason, so with her loud mouth here for distraction the days pass quicker. In fact, I invited her to my appointment with the heart specialist to keep my thoughts on lock down.

"So, I need to tell you something and I hope you're okay with it."

I look up and see her biting her nails while she sits across from me. I shift on the exam table and feel my nerves. "Okay ... shoot."

"Um … well … I'm kind of seeing someone. Or just his appendage anyway." I just stare, praying it's not Mason. I don't think she'd do that, but I can't help the feeling of jealousy that settles in my belly. "It's Ryan."

Relief has my breath rushing out. "Thank God. I thought you were going to say Mason."

Now she looks offended. "Oh hell no! There's only one thing I want to do with his appendage. And that's stomp it a few times with my spiked heels. And how can you think that? You're my girl."

"I know but my mind and emotions have been recently screwed over. Sorry."

"It's cool. I know you've had a ton of shit handed to you lately." She comes over and gives me a tight hug. "Are you okay with me fucking Ryan?

I mean I know he's friends with that shitdick. And he's an annoying ass, but he knows how to lay it on me to make me scream out and purr like Chewbacca. That's for damn sure." She winks at me and I can't help but laugh as she thrusts her hips repeatedly and lets out exaggerated moans, especially when the doctor walks in at the exact same time. Luckily he keeps his professional face on and shakes our hands like he didn't just catch her dry humping the air.

After a few questions we do another echo and learn that I will need a procedure done shortly after delivery. It's not open heart—thank goodness—but involves them routing a new valve through one of my main arteries and directing it to my heart. This should fix the issues of breathlessness and dizzy spells. I just wish it could fix the sadness that still has me crying at night.

Later that night we order pizza a watch a movie with Tru and Hero. Cory loves anything sci-fi but also has a soft spot for zombies. I notice her constantly looking at me throughout the movie and it's starting to piss me off.

Throwing my zebra pillow at her when I catch her again, I ask what her problem is. "Do I have something on my face? I have been bathing lately you know."

She rubs her nose where the pillow hit. "Ow, bitch. That's my sniffer."

"Then stop staring. You're giving me a bigger complex than I normally have. Now tell me what's going on."

"She's staring because your boobs are as big as mine and the cleavage you're sporting is amazing." Tru laughs while shoving popcorn in her mouth. Her confidence has made her cocky. I wink at her because I love her and she's just so dang cute.

"Now. You..." I point at Cory "...what is going on?"

"Well Ryan just texted me." She bites her lip and a bad feeling settles in my chest. "Mason is home."

My recovered good mood disappears and my gut feels like someone just kicked me. I feel the burn in my throat and I swallow, continuously fighting the tears. *No more crying, Jazz. You are over this, remember?*

Cory and Tru both come over and hold me. My head lays on Tru's shoulder as she tries to reassure me. "Don't do this. You didn't deserve the things he said to you. You didn't know about professor douche bag's family. No one did."

They continuously tell me how it's not my fault. How he should have told me he was married instead of lying. My dad has a lawyer as well as a private detective looking into it. If he did it with me, Dad is positive he will do it with other students. Hopefully that'll provide enough proof against him. If not, then after the baby is born he wants a paternity test to use as proof. I don't want that bastard in my life or in my daughter's life. I even told them about the subtle threat he made of taking away my child the day he showed up at my apartment. Dad's positive he's bluffing. If anyone on South Alabama's board was to find out he slept with a student, then he'd be fired. Why risk it?

Once a few minutes have passed I'm more pissed than sad and decide to try and let it go. "I'm good. Just a surprise, that's all." Shoving pizza in my mouth, I smile and show my cheesy grin. Literally. This causes them to laugh and the subject seems forgotten. For them anyway.

When the girls leave the next day for class I decide to go to the gym. I know it's weird for a pregnant woman to work out, but I feel my ass jiggle whenever I move. That's my cue to do some toning in my derriere. Instead of getting a membership to another gym, I go to the one on campus—no fees because I still have my student ID. I talk to the girl behind the reception desk and she shows me what's safe and what's not. My heart condition is no one's business, so I just nod and do as she says. After a good forty minutes my muscles are burning and I'm sweating like a pig. That is definitely enough.

After I grab my towel I feel someone staring in my direction. Trying to be discrete, I look in the mirror in front of me and see a guy I recognize from Jax and David's frat house. He's really good looking with blond hair and brown eyes. He smiles and starts walking over and suddenly I feel out of my element. Where did my flirtatious side go? She must still be buried under a rock because I'm feeling scared and shy instead of sexy and confident. Should I leave or stay? He's standing behind me before I can make a decision.

"Hey. Jazz, right?"

Turning around to face him, I trip on my bag that sits at my feet and my face smacks right into in sweaty, muscled chest. "Oh Shiznit!" *Sweet lawd baby Jesus! He smells yummy.*

He laughs as I pull away but keeps his arms around my waist. My child kicks me hard and I'm positive he felt it because he moves away.

"Little kicker in there, huh?" He shakes his hand like it actually hurt. Unintentionally, I watch his muscles and veins roll up his arm like waves. His forearm gracefully flexes and my eyes follow the movement to his bulging bicep.

Slapping myself for being weird, I bring my attention back to his chiseled face. "Yeah, she's like me I guess. Small and feisty." I stand there like a dumbass, not sure what else to say. "Um … I don't remember your name, but aren't you with the same frat as David and Jax?"

He finally backs away and takes a towel out of his back pocket to wipe his face. He's very good looking, but I feel nothing: no need or urge to flirt; no need to fantasize about driving him wild. What the hell is wrong with me? Am I ruined for all other men?

"Yeah. I even helped you move into your apartment." He sticks out his hand. "My name is Bo-Bo, but they call me Bo."

Shaking it, I laugh. "Bo-Bo? What kind of name is that?" If my laughter offends him I really don't care. Besides, he's laughing with me so it must be okay.

"Yeah. I know. My name on my birth certificate is top secret. So I just stick with Bo-Bo?"

After the laughter stops the awkwardness surrounds me again. I grab my bag ready to go home where I'm comfortable. "Well, Bo, I really need to get going, but it was nice seeing you again."

I hurry past him and rush out the door. Before I get to my car I hear my name being yelled very loudly. I know exactly who it is and smile. Turning I see Cory. When my eyes land on Ryan it falls though. Instead of walking my way with her he goes the opposite direction toward an old black car. She hugs me when she reaches my side.

"Hey, chick."

"Hey." I look toward Ryan's direction again, but he's gone.

"So who's the hottie with a body eye fuckin' you, lil' mama?"

I shake my head with confusion and look where her eyes are directed. When they land on Bo and he waves. I just ignore it and turn back to her. Might be a bitch move, but I'm pregnant and recently heartbroken, so frankly I couldn't care less

"Nobody important."

We start walking and she talks about how her classes suck ass without me since I dropped out. I don't get another word in but I'm fine with it. I'd most likely bring up her relationship with Ryan hoping Mason is mentioned. She seems to have more energy than me lately and keeps the conversation going. I really miss my old self. Maybe she wouldn't be a glutton for punishment.

After I arrive back home I feel lost in the quiet, so I walk to the nursery and look around. The white crib I ordered finally came in last week. It looks beautiful with its curved, ornate wood and hearts carved in the head and footboard. It took a while to get David and Jax to put the damn thing together, but after I told them I'd do it myself, they finally showed up. Right now it's sitting in the middle of the room because Cory is still working on the mural. It looks beautiful with a pale yellow castle on a grassy hill and whimsical trees surrounding the valley below. Fairies and sweet creatures are placed in different locations within the kingdom. I sit in the white glider with its pink cushion and rock back and forth while playing with my belly. Smiling and laughing genuinely for the first time in weeks, my stomach rolls with her active movements and I feel a peaceful warmth settle over me. I know deep down it will all be okay. Maybe not today. Maybe not tomorrow. But one day.

Chapter Twenty-Two

Mason

On my flight back home I think of my family. Not just mom and Grace, but Grandma Ginger—AKA Gigi—Grandpa Frank, Symone, and even the woman who stole my dad away from us all those years ago. Her name is Candice and she is someone you can't stay mad at. Believe me, I tried. She has bright red hair and a fiery personality to match, but she can also make you laugh if you need it.

When I first arrived in Indiana I was surprised to be greeted with so much warmth and hugs. A feeling of being wanted settled inside my gut, as well as some guilt. Was I betraying my mom from being here? Instead of dwelling on the question, I pushed that thought to the back of my mind and embraced them as much as I could. These people were interested in my life and even wanted to meet Grace when I told them all about her. Symone was awesome and the total opposite of me. In fact she reminded me a lot of Jazz with her outgoing personality and never ending energy. She had her mom's hair but our dad's eyes, just like me, and that one little trait meant the world to me. Somehow the man I didn't really remember left us something to remember him by. Where I was tanned like my mom, she was pale like hers and had a lot of freckles. She liked to date but has avoided anything serious because she's determined to travel or attend a University far away from home. I used to have the same dream, but I knew deep down I couldn't leave Grace. So instead of Virginia Tech I stayed in Mobile.

The day of the funeral was surreal. I stood there listening to all the stories of a man I will never meet or never know how his voice sounded saying my name. He was successful and owned a small electrical company here in town. Candice is really not sure what she plans on doing with it yet. They have money from his business and I'm proud of them and angry with Mom at the same time. If she wouldn't have run and let him in, she wouldn't have had to work herself so hard all these years. She could have done more for herself and us. But she didn't and I may never understand why.

When Symone sang a song called *Daddy's Hands* at the service, I listened with envy. The relationship she had with him was something I'd never experience and it pissed me off at times, but I couldn't change that no matter what I did, so I just tried to enjoy the time I had left with everyone else. I refused to look at the lifeless body in the casket. When everyone asked why, I told them that was not how I wanted to meet my father for the first and last time. I'd rather have the videos and pictures.

Through all the commotion and chaos during the visit my mind always had one constant: Jazz. The thought of her and the baby on their own; the baby girl with no dad; Jazz without me. Most importantly, me without them. Man it hurts in the worst way when I think about it because for all these months together they were mine, or that's what I thought anyway. And now that they aren't anymore I feel like something vital is missing. My heart.

No matter how pissed I was and still am, she is always there. Her smile and laugh invade my thoughts and I've even had a few detailed dreams of the two of us together. The night of our first time constantly replays in my mind. No matter how many thoughts I have, I can't get over the picture Chanda sent me. And the more the image inhabits my thoughts, the more I feel like I made a huge ass mistake. Did I just jump to some stupid assumption? Should I have looked at the photo better and really studied the details? Yes. I always study details and take time to make a reasonable theory that is probable. Not that night, though. I just jumped to conclusions. I mean, I don't remember seeing any intimacy between the two of them and her face was blocked. Who's to say she wasn't giving him the finger or holding up her pointiest stiletto to use as a weapon? Nobody. And since my phone is smashed, I can't check. So instead I battle the feeling of complete dread as I decide what to do.

After getting my luggage, I head to a waiting cab and head to the frat house. I missed midterms and need to get with my professors about the death in my family. Gigi gave me a copy of Dad's obituary as proof in case there are any issues. Seeing as I've never missed any previous tests and my grades are high, I can afford to make a zero on the test. I'm not too concerned.

I head to my room ready to crash for a little bit, but before I get there I see David coming down the hall. His eyes narrow and he looks like he's going to rip my head off. I brace myself.

He walks over and gets right in my face. "You have some serious balls, fucker. I really, really want to kick your ass back to wherever you just came from, but I'm going to leave it for Jax. He'll be happy to learn you're back. I will say this though … Leave. Jazz. Alone." He shoves past me so hard I drop my bag.

After going to my room, I lock the door and look around. The first thing I see is the picture of Jazz in a frame by my bed. It's the one Jax gave me all those months ago to make her fake I.D. The one that caused me to fall in love. I stare at it for a few minutes before I shove it in the drawer. After the encounter with David, my need for sleep is gone and now I just want answers. Going downstairs, I use the house phone to call Ryan and let him know I'm back and need a ride. He says to give him a bit so I grab something to eat. A few guys are in the kitchen discussing only God knows what, but I know they are staring at me. Who knows what rumors are going around this place? Maybe I shouldn't stay here, but I'm not going to run or put up with this shit. They can just kiss my ass and get over it. None of them have any clue what happened that day. Then a thought occurs to me. Maybe I don't either.

Later that day Ryan takes me to get a new phone since I ruined my old one. He knows some of what happened because I called him while I was in Indiana so he could check on Mom and Grace from time to time. I mentioned the photo but not who the guy actually is or that he's married, only that he's the real father and how we've been lying to everyone all these months. He really didn't understand why I jumped in the middle of her drama to begin with, and he probably never will. Being in love is something I doubt Ryan's ever experienced. After we get a bite to eat, we head to his uncle's car restoration shop. Pulling in, I see Lyric talking with Jim, Ryan's uncle, beside a fine Pontiac GTO. I really don't know a lot about cars, but this one is old and a classic. It's nothing but shiny black and chrome with silver flames on the hood. I help them wire some stereos and tell him about my sister Symone and how she's coming down the week after next for her spring break. She wants to meet Grace and see the campus at South Alabama. Mom probably won't be thrilled, but I honestly couldn't care less. I'm still pissed about the whole lie. But I miss her too. Forgiving is easy, but forgetting her lies will be a different story.

"So, dude, is your sister hot?" Ryan's driving me back to my mom's place so I can tell her everything. I give him a look that tells him to back off. He laughs and shrugs his shoulders while looking back toward the road. "No worries. I already have a regular booty call."

"Oh really? You found someone who can actually put up with your dumbass for more than a few seconds?" Looking out the window as he parks his car, I see my truck in the parking lot. I can't wait to see Grace and Mom.

"All I need are those few seconds to have her screaming my name. Besides, you know her. It's that chick Cory. The mouthy brunette. And she likes to purr and make some weird ass noises, but dammit, boy, she is like an animal."

Cory's name immediately brings Jazz to mind. My heart feels hollow with how things turned out. I ask what I want and need to know. "How's she doing? With the pregnancy and all?"

He shuts the car off and looks at me like I've lost my fucking mind. Maybe I have because since that night I haven't felt the same. I haven't felt right.

"Why ask? It's only going to make things worse? So don't worry about it. Personally, I don't give a shit about that two timing bitch."

My head turns in his direction as anger and rage cause my heart rate to spike. I'm ready to knock his teeth in. "Shut your fucking mouth. You don't talk about her like that. Got it?" My voice is full of venom. She might have screwed up some things in life, but who hasn't? Nobody will talk about her like that.

"Whatever, dude."

I get out and slam the door before grabbing my bag and making my way up to my mom's apartment. Not looking back, I knock on the door. With the way we left things I don't feel right about just walking in, so I wait until Mom opens it.

Hearing the lock turn from the opposite side, I feel my body tense. I'm not ready for another round with her, and I hope it doesn't come to that. When her face appears I watch her blue eyes get watery and her body crumple before she throws her tiny frame against me.

"I'm so sorry, Mason. So, so sorry." Her body shakes against mine so I squeeze her harder and tell her I love her. She's my mom and I'll always love her.

Her reason for keeping my dad from me is one I will never understand. Hurt and heartbroken, she wanted to make him suffer the way she suffered, so she decided on a whim the only way to do that was to keep me from him and lying to him about how I didn't want to see him or his mistress. When she was scared that he'd get a lawyer and claim his rights, she gave him everything in the divorce. The house, the business, and car. She threatened to take it all since he was in the wrong and had an affair.

After an emotional discussion and reunion, I tell her about the family and Symone. She seems hesitant about meeting her at first but soon realizes how I need that family as much as I need her and Grace. After the uncertainty disappears, I watch some excitement build as she talks about everything we can do while she visits. Hell, I'm even excited and have an urge to call Jazz to tell her all about it. Reality slaps me in the face with a hard ass glove and I remember she's no longer a part of my everyday life. Dammit! I really need to see that photo again because the feeling from earlier is still hanging over me like a black cloud—the feeling of knowing I totally fucked up.

After dinner I walk to Chanda's apartment on a mission to find out the truth. I hope she's home because now that everything is falling in place, the last piece is still missing. And like they say, save the best for last. Jazz is truly the best for me, but I still need proof she didn't cheat on me. The longer I'm away from her, the more I just want to take her back regardless of what she did or didn't do.

I knock on Chanda's door and hear the grumble from her dad on the other side. When he answers the door a strong aroma of alcohol and stale cigarettes invades my sense of smell and takes my breath away. He must be drinking again.

"Excuse me, Mr. Stewart, is Chanda home?"

He squints with red, dazed eyes and rubs his long, greasy beard. "Chanda? She hasn't been home for three fucking days. Do me a favor will ya, Mason? If you see her tell her she owes me some goddamn rent money or she can take her bony ass and move somewhere else. Got it?" He mumbles something else and slams the door in my face. Feeling defeated I walk back to my mom's for another restless night of dreams that leave me wanting more. So much more.

After Symone arrives in Mobile, I take her to meet Grace and my mom. The apartment is completely spotless and feels warmer than it has in a while. Mom has even taken the next few days off to enjoy some time with us. She's even pulled out a recipe book to prepare some home cooked meals—totally out of the ordinary. Pulling into my regular spot, I look around for Chanda's car and still don't see it in sight. Frustrated doesn't even cover what I'm feeling. I don't know if she ran away again or if she's actually missing, but every time I ask her dad, I get the same response as the first time. I could just go and ask Jazz, but seeing her will only have me begging her to forgive me. And if she's with Professor Wallace it will only make the situation worse. She's just way too beautiful for me to resist. And cheating is something I'm totally against. Especially with all the shit that has happened in my family recently.

"Wow, Mase. Mobile is so much bigger than my town. Morgantown is just full of cornfields and tractors, nothing like this." She's animated with her facial expression when she talks and her dimples show when she smiles.

Even though I hate the nickname, I let her continue to use it. She's my long lost sister and I want to make her happy. She's totally right about Indiana. Cornfields are on every corner. "It's pretty cool. Kind of easy access to anywhere you might want to go. You can go two hours west and be in New Orleans or go east and arrive in Pensacola, Florida."

"Wow! Do you think I could see the beach while I'm here?"

I get out and grab her pink zebra print bag. Jazz would have loved this. Reprimanding myself, I shake those thoughts away and lead her up the concrete steps. "Yeah. I don't see why not. It's warm enough so we could definitely go swimming."

She squeals loudly while she jumps up gives me a hug. Mom answers the door and introduces herself and Grace. Symone is full of laughter and affection and quickly has Mom eating out of her hand. I was a little worried about my mom's reaction to her with their past, but she knows how much this means to me. Talk is still limited because as well as she's doing with Symone I don't think she's ready to talk about anything regarding Dad, which is completely cool with all of us. Grace lets Symone swing in her hammock swing she received from Jazz for Christmas, but after a few minutes she gets in Symone's lap. Their laughter is heard from down the hall, and I laugh because it's contagious. My two little sisters playing and laughing together has made up for all the torment I felt over the last few weeks when I found out the truth

"She's just wonderful, Mason," Mom says while washing dishes. She hands each one to me to dry with practiced hands. We've always done this together since we never had a whole lot of time with her work schedule. Every second with her is cherished, even doing the dishes.

“Yeah, she sure is. And great with Grace too. She’s coming with me to school tomorrow for a tour. She might actually apply to South. She has a great GPA and tons of extracurricular activities to add to her resume. She’s also in the running for Valedictorian.”

“That would be great for you. And I know Grace would love it. Just listen to her laugh. I don’t think she’s laughed this much since Jazz was around.” Her eyes widen and she turns to me. “I’m sorry, Mason. I didn’t mean to say that. It just slipped out.”

Jazz. Her name has been coming up a lot lately and I have an urge to see her, but I swallow it down with the lump in my throat. I’ll worry about that later. Tonight I want to enjoy my family so I shrug it off. “It’s fine.

“Can I ask what happened? I mean, I know I wasn’t always welcoming toward her, but she did make you happy. And if you find someone to make you feel that way, you need to hold on to it. Because if you don’t, someone else will. Or it may be too late when you finally realize it.”

Nodding my head without a word, I kiss her cheek. I don’t know what to say or think right now. Picturing Jazz with someone else is like stabbing me in the chest with a dull, rusty knife. And not just kissing someone else, but her marrying someone else, being happy with them and growing old. The other guy waiting at the altar while she walks down the aisle. Her having another last name besides mine. Should I just sweep it all under the rug and forgive her regardless of what happened? And what if it was all a mistake? Would she even want me back after what I said and did that night?

Keeping myself distracted, I decide to take the trash to the dumpster outside. When I exit the apartment I see a drunk and stumbling Chanda leaning on the railing to help hold her up. She looks ready to fall over and

I'm positive alcohol isn't the only thing floating in her system. She must hear the door shut behind me because she looks at my face.

"Mason! Come here, babe. I missed you." Her voice is loud enough to wake the dead, so I sit my trash down and walk toward her.

The closer I get the stronger the smell of hard liquor is. Why must she continuously do this to herself? "Where the hell have you been?"

"Eh! You know. Here and there." She pulls a cigarette out of the pocket of her black, leather mini skirt. "Where'd you go? You just left me."

"I had family issues that are none of your business." I can tell she's not listening because her eyes won't focus on anything while her body sways. I grab her cigarette and toss it in the grass before she can burn herself.

"Hey! What the fuck, Mason?" She tries to shove me but only manages to weakly throw herself in my arms. "Mmmmm. You smell nice." She inhales my neck as I hold her up.

"I'm sure anything smells better than you right now. Let's get you upstairs." I lead her to my door but decide to just take her to her own apartment. I don't need Symone to see this and decide not to visit in the future. Her door is unlocked and luckily her dad is passed out in his recliner so I don't have to endure his yelling. After I lay her down on the small bed in her room, she blinks open her eyes and sits up unsteadily.

"I always knew you'd come back to me. You always have been my hero and one day you're gonna take me away." She flings her arms out and hits one on the wall behind her. "Shit, that hurt!" Her words are slurred and she continues to sway. I should leave but I really want her phone. "Are you going to get me out of here?"

She's making no sense which is not surprising. I ignore her questions. "Can I see your phone?"

She falls back down on her pillow and shrugs her shoulders. "Sure. But you already know my number, baby." She reaches in her pocket and pulls it out before her eyes start to close again. God I hope she doesn't OD tonight.

Taking it from from her limp fingers, I flip it open and go straight to photos. I see a lot of her with different people at clubs. Her snorting cocaine and kissing a few people, but no Jazz. Before I let frustration set in, I go to her text messages and look for my name. When I click on it I finally find what I've been looking for. I feel my legs start to shake as I stare at the picture so I sit on the floor before I fall. The image looks totally different when viewing it with a clear mind. I see Professor Wallace leaving, but Jazz has her arms crossed. Something I didn't take time to see before. I know this is her angry stance. Flipping to the other pictures I never took the time to view, I see one of her face. Her beautiful face that looks scared and pissed at the same time. Her eyes are wide and her cheeks red with anger. I feel like pure shit. She didn't want him there. She didn't cheat on me. She didn't hurt me like I thought. But I hurt her and I'm not sure I can fix the damage I caused but I'm damn sure going to try, not only for her but for our little girl.

Chapter Twenty-Three

Jazz

"Mmmmm! That feels so nice." My voice comes out in a moan that can't be helped. I feel the pressure of a hand on my foot as it continues to work its way up my calf muscle. The soft, leather chair vibrates on my neck and back to further relax my tense muscles and erase my stress. "Tru, this was a wonderful idea. Thanks, chica. You really know how to treat a woman."

"Don't thank me. Thank your brother." She yelps so I look in her direction. "Sorry. I'm very ticklish," she tells the little lady doing her pedicure. When she looks at me in the other massage chair, I notice how happy she looks today. Her hair is in a high pony tail with long waves that still manage to reach her breasts, and the purple and white polka dot halter dress is beautiful on her.

"That color you picked out is going to look so good with what you're wearing. Of course I could never pull off purple so I stick with pink."

"No. You choose to stick with pink, but you'd totally rock any color. Even vomit or diarrhea green."

"Eww!" I laugh and over exaggerate. "Maybe so, but since I'm having a girl I'll stick with pink. She'll grow to love it just as much as I do."

"Can I just say that I absolutely love the name you picked? Finlee is so original and has star quality. How did you come up with it?"

The lady puts on my little foot thingies so I won't mess up the hard work she did on my toes. "I honestly don't remember. I've always liked the name Finn because it's so different. I just spelled it differently and added a feminine touch." I walk over to the dryer and Trudy follows. I hope what I'm about to say doesn't offend her or make her upset, but it's something I really want to do. "I actually picked out the middle name too."

When I don't continue right away she looks up from her phone. "Really? What is it? And why do you look nervous?"

"Well … her name will be Finlee Breanne, in memory of your son Brian." I watch her mouth drop open and her green eyes widen. "Is that okay? I didn't want to offend you, but it's something I've really been thinking about and really want to do. It even has a nice ring to it."

She stands up and walks over to me. My rambling stops because I really don't know if she's going to knock the shit out of me or hug me. I mean, I don't think she would but have you seen her right hook? Tru Ali all the way. Instead of the KO, she stands me up and gives me the tightest hug I've ever received. And that's saying something. When she pulls away she's smiling with watery eyes.

"That is a beautiful name and I feel honored you'd do that for me. Thank you."

"Aww, sweets. Thank you for coming into our lives. We love you and you're going to be the best auntie ever for Princess Finlee."

She laughs and wipes her eyes. "Princess, huh?

"Damn right bitch. Because I'm the queen."

We drive back to campus to get my car after we leave the salon. I'm feeling fresh with my new toes and wax job. My belly is so big for being eight months pregnant that shaving is definitely out of the picture. I don't need to accidentally nick the goods, right? Even though no one is around to enjoy it, the doctor will appreciate it.

Tru heads to her afternoon class while I decide to walk around. Being alone in my apartment is not fun and really depressing. I've really been thinking about moving home, but the nursery is perfect for Finlee so I really want to stay there for a while and get some use out of it. Mason did a great job putting all the furniture together—the dresser, the changing table, everything except for the crib. Every day he was with me helping to get things ready for the baby or at his mom's helping with Grace. I was usually with him when he was there. We never did anything in front of Grace and we barely even kissed. He was very strict about that and I respected him more for it. So how did he have time to date or fool around with Chanda if he was so devoted to me? Or sleep with her for that matter? Things just don't add up.

Sitting under one of the largest oaks on campus, I continue to try and work things out in my mind. I miss him and in the deepest part of me I know he cares for me. Maybe he was so disgusted with what I had done that he just acted out. I feel my emotions getting the best of me but it just can't be helped anymore. My throat clogs and burns, but I swallow it back not wanting to cry again. I should be done with the waterworks already.

"Funny seeing you here." My heart jumps out of my chest and I scream from the unfamiliar voice. "Shit! What the hell? You almost gave me a heart attack." When I see Bo sitting beside me I start to laugh. Great way to switch emotional gears.

"Sorry. You looked so serious sitting here all alone. Thought I could make you laugh, and look..." he touches my cheek "...I succeeded." He smiles and I notice a cute dimple on his cheek, but I still feel nothing for this good looking guy. Nadda. Zilch.

"Well, thank you but you really didn't need to almost make me pee on myself to get me to smile. Just produce a chocolate bar and some beef jerky. You'll see me smile while inhaling it. Lately I've been bringing David to shame."

"Oh really! So a way to make you happy is to feed you? Hmmm ..." He taps his chin while he thinks. I watch his strong profile work, begging for some kind of effect but I only feel like a weirdo for staring. And now I'm hungry. "Why don't I take you out to get something to eat then? You can pick where and get whatever you want."

Shocked, I squeak out, "Like a date?" He nods and I feel my heart stop. I'm taken aback that this good looking guy would want to take a girl who's eight months pregnant out on a date. "Are you on drugs? Can you not see that I'm about to pop out a tiny human in a few weeks? Why on earth would a guy like you want that kind of baggage?" For some weird reason I feel pissed off at this guy. I hold up my hand before he can answer. "Is it because I'm pregnant that you think I'm an easy lay or some shit? Oh hell to the no on that! If you're hoping to take a dive in this, you can forget it and take your cute dimpled face away from me because the Jazz party closed months ago."

I stand up and start walking toward my car. What nerve some assholes have! But honestly I'm just lashing out at someone to get some of this anger out of my system. And I really need to keep Bo at a distance. Guys are bad news. When he starts to call my name I ignore it and keep walking. Then I hear a familiar laugh break through my inner ramblings. It causes my heart to hit my stomach and my feet to stop. Turning around I see him. Mason.

All the emotions I've tried to bury all these weeks come rushing back and the air leaves my lungs. He looks so happy. Smiling and laughing. I've missed that sound so much, and I want to be why he's smiling again. When we make eye contact for the first time in over a month I feel like we just saw each other this morning. I feel like nothing has changed between us and we're still best friends and lovers. His vanishes as his expression morphs from happiness to shock. Then a small smile starts to lift his lips and my feet want to go toward him to have him hold me and tell me it was all a lie. A bad dream. Then my nightmare becomes a reality again when I see her. A thin and tall beauty queen with her fiery red hair and long legs. She jumps on his back like it's normal and wraps them around his waist while laughing. They look so happy it causes me to see red. He politely sets her down and starts to walk toward me, but I can't deal with him being with someone else. Turning away, I start to speed walk away from him before he sees the tears and sees me break again like I didn't want. Now, instead of picturing Chanda and him together, I get to picture him with someone else. Someone who's a perfect beauty and actually good enough for him.

Feeling a sharp pain in my chest, I take a deep breath trying to calm down. I start to feel disoriented and lost so I shake my head trying to get myself in order. I need to get away. The dizziness won't go away, though, and shaking my head only makes it worse. I feel sick and want to vomit so I try to cover my mouth with my hand but I can't lift it. My body is heavy and weak all of a sudden and I'm scared. My heart rate continues to escalate and my head feels so heavy it's hard to hold up. I'm terrified but unable to stop what's happening to me. Everything is spinning so fast that I reach out to steady myself but nothing is there. Spots form and soon my vision fades in and out. I can barely make out faces hovering above me, all worried and screaming, but I can't hear anything they're saying. Only the sound of my heart beating at high-speed reaches my ears, only the sound of it breaking. Again.

The next thing I see when I open my eyes is a searing light that has my eyes screaming for relief, "Shit!" My throat is dry and scratchy. I'm positive from the heat coming out of my mouth that my breath is killer too. What the hell? My voice sounds like it did when I spoke for the first time a few weeks ago. I was just talking to … to … hell if I know. But I know I was definitely talking. I'll worry about that later. First thing I need to do is find the friggin' light switch and turn it off and then get some water.

I try to reach out but hear movement beside me. "Hold on, Jazz. Don't move." Tru's voice is close and then I feel her touch on my hand. "I'm going to grab Jax and tell the doctor you're awake." She leaves and I feel the coldness of where her hand was just a moment ago. In fact my whole body feels cold and shaky.

What did she mean doctor? Then I hear the familiar beeping and some not so familiar scratching noises. Inhaling deep I smell the familiar scent of disinfectant and immediately know I'm in the hospital. Now I'm scared.

Slowly, I try to open my eyes again and after a few attempts I succeed. I see the ominous IV pole with its clear tube hooked up somewhere in my flesh and the heart monitor with its colorful wires leading to the horrible sticky pads that adhere to my chest. I hate those bastards. Out of all the painful things I've had to endure throughout my hospital visits, those things are what bother me the most. Have you ever had to pull them off? They're like leaches to your sensitive skin and hurt like a bitch coming off.

I feel my heart pick up and the familiar burn in my throat. I'm scared and angry that I'm here. Again. After all the years of taking precautions and trying to avoid ending up here under these circumstances, I've failed. I've allowed my emotions to take over and almost lost not only my life but my daughter's. Then I remember Finlee. Panic accompanies my anger and I reach over with all my strength and touch my still swollen belly. When her active movements set in I start to calm and take deep breaths to slow my heart rate. Whatever happened must not have been too bad if they didn't take her, right?

The door opens and Jax rushes in with my parents on his tail. When he grabs my hand and kisses my cheek I see his lip is busted and swollen. "What happened?" Before anyone can answer we are interrupted when the door opens again.

I watch as an older nurse with grey hair and kind eyes walks in with a syringe full of something. "What's that?"

"It's just something to keep you relaxed while you're awake. The doctor wants to try a different method instead of the previous way." She cleans the valve on my IV tubing before she sticks the syringe in and presses the plunger. Immediately, I feel warmth start to spread up my arm. We wait for her to leave before Jax answers my previous question.

"Your oxygen level dropped very fast and you passed out. You were rushed here and quickly sedated and put on some much needed oxygen." He moves to the foot of the bed so Mom can take the chair beside me.

"Um … thanks for the info, but I was actually asking about your lip." Even though he's just answered my next question, I exhale loudly. "No wonder I feel like shit. Oops!" I glance at my parents. Cussing in front of them is something I have always tried to avoid.

Mom just smiles and wipes her teary eyes. "You can say whatever you want. I'm just glad you're awake. I've been so worried all week."

"What?" My voice rises and my throat burns as the words push their way out. "Week? I've been here for a week?"

Dad sits on the foot of my bed wearing his serious expression. "They put you under and hooked you up to a ventilator in an effort to get your levels up and avoid delivery until the baby's lungs are more developed. They've given you steroid shots and antibiotics are being provided through your IV. The doctors feel it's best to do a cesarean tomorrow or the next day so they can go ahead and put the new valve in. Apparently the old one gave out and started leaking way more than usual so they've kept you calm with sedation but decided to wake you up and explain everything to you before we take you back to the OR. Also, you need to remember that after this new valve is in place, you need to continuously take medication to prevent a blood clot from forming." He pats my leg and looks at me with the look of a reassured dad. "Everything will be fine. I know it's against a doctor's protocol to say that, but the team working on you and my granddaughter are very good, so I don't want you worrying any more than you should."

"Thanks, Daddy," I whisper and feel relief. He winks but I still see the shimmer of tears in his eyes.

Soon the doctor and nurse come in and explain the procedure to me. It turns out that I will be getting a mechanical valve instead of a biological one like before. That's why I'll be on blood thinners daily. They also explain that I can have more children in the future, but I really need to plan the pregnancy appropriately so they can better care for me. *News flash, people. I wasn't planning on getting pregnant.*

Everyone kisses me goodbye and leaves, everyone but Tru. She's sitting beside me biting her nails. "Are you okay? I know this has to be hard for you, but I promise anytime you want to keep Finlee you can. She is going to love you so much."

Looking at me she smiles. "Promise. I can keep her some nights?" I nod my head and see her worry is still there. "Look. I need to talk to you and I really don't want to do it now but you need to know how Jax got his busted lip."

"Um, okay?" I push up with my elbows gingerly to sit straighter and wait.

"Someone is here and refuses to leave. Someone who explained everything to all of us. Someone who loves you so much he busted your brother's lip when he tried to keep him away from you." She takes a deep breath before she continues. "Mason has been by your side every day, Jazz. He hasn't been home or to class. I've been forcing him to eat and drink to keep himself healthy. He refuses to leave the hospital or even this room until he knows you're okay."

The thought of him with the redhead has my inner bitch coming out. Even though the thought of him being here causes my insides to melt, I won't admit it. I shrug and act like I really don't give a shit. "Well I'm sure his new girlfriend won't be too happy about that."

"Well, Jazz, the thing is the girl who was with him that day is actually his sister." I look at her like she's lost her mind. "I know it's crazy and hard to believe, but she is his sister. They have the exact same eyes."

"I don't understand. How is it possible?"

Then she tells me of the day I fell apart. Apparently he fell apart too. His mom's constant lies over the years piss me off and my heart breaks for the boy who grew up without a father who truly wanted him. My tears stop long enough to imagine me ripping out Chanda's black evil heart for spreading lies when she has no idea what went on in my apartment that day. How that dickhead has threatened to take my child away and ruin my life. When Tru tells me about Symone and how she is so much like me, I feel happy again because he found his missing family, even though depressing circumstances are the reason that made it happen.

"Wow! Mason will never meet his dad. That is so sad." I feel so bad for him and have an urge to hold him and make it better. He now has so many people that love him and want him in their lives. Little does he know that I want him in mine too.

Chapter Twenty-Four

Mason

I see her standing only one hundred feet away from me and my body ignites. Maybe it's from nerves or excitement. At the moment I can't tell, but I'm ready to find out if she's willing to forgive me or not. After a few steps forward, I notice I'm still the same distance away from her as I was a moment ago. I try a second time but have the same result. Fuck! I feel frustration set in so I throw down my bag and start to run toward her. Running is something I never do, but I know I should be gaining some distance. I'm still in the same spot where I started. Turning in a circle, I run my hand through my hair while trying to figure out how to get to Jazz. Maybe she can come to me.

I turn around, ready to yell her name, but she's no longer standing. Her form is lying on the grass and I can't tell if she's dead or alive. My heart leaves my body as fear sets in. I start to run again, but the distance between us refuses to shrink no matter how long my legs move. People are all around the campus but no one seems to notice the love of my life lying in a heap on the ground, not even the people walking passed her prone form.

"Someone help her. Can't you see her?" I yell as loud as my lungs allow but nobody listens. They continue on their way like we're invisible. "Help! Please help her."

I see David walking my way so I yell at him, but he just continues to talk to the girl he's walking with. When he gets close I reach out, desperate to make contact so I can shake some sense into his dumbass, but my hand can't hold him. It feels like a force is pushing it away from his body. He doesn't flinch or break stride while I let out a scream full of frustration.

"Shit! Why won't you help her? Why won't anyone help her?" My desperation and fear causes tears to form. My chest burns and I just want to get to Jazz. My heart constricts knowing she's hurt and I have no way of stopping the pain. So I run. I run so hard my legs feel like jelly. But I refuse to stop until I reach her. "Jazz!" I yell, but no matter how hard I run or how loud I yell, she stays down, not moving and far away. "Jazz!"

My body jerks and my eyes snap open. I see the white walls of the hospital that have become my home this week and exhale with relief while my heart slows. It was just a dream. Rubbing my hands up and down my face, I flinch when I brush the cut above my eye. Jax has a mean punch, but he still couldn't stop me from getting to Jazz last week. He would have had to kill me. He still gives me "go to Hell" looks and I can't blame him. I feel like kicking my own ass after the disgusting words I told Jazz that night. But luckily they listened to my reasons and having Symone with me helped, as well as Dad's obituary in my wallet. Everyone else has accepted my apologies, but they don't matter. Only one person does and I just pray she will see me.

"Mason?" Tru's voice reaches my ears so I turn and see her leaving Jazz's room. Jax walks over and grabs her hand. "You can go in now, but the doctors gave her something to relax.

"That doesn't mean you can get her worked up either." Jax waits for my nod before he leads her away.

Taking a deep breath, I open the large, brown door to her room. When I make it past the privacy curtain I see her. My heart warms and even though she just woke up from being sedated for a week, she is still beautiful. Her hair is in disarray and surrounds her pillow with its golden strands. Her eyes are red and I see some cloudiness in the blue, probably from the medication she was given. The wires and monitors that are watching her and the baby's heartbeats and oxygen levels surround the bed and side table. She looks so small sitting there with plastic tubing on her face and nose, but not delicate and weak. She looks like the fighter she is. A fighter who's determined and strong, ready to take on anything and anyone. Including me.

I remain where I'm at while she appraises me with her eyes. It's her call if she wants me close, but after the nightmare I just had it's very hard. I want to run and touch her to prove to myself she's truly okay and awake.

"Hey." I place my hands in the pockets of my jeans that seriously need a wash.

"Hey." Her voice is soft and husky, and you can tell it hasn't been used in a while.

It still has an effect on my body, though. Not just my male anatomy either, but also my heart that speeds up, my brain that pictures our most intimate moments together, my sweaty hands that are desperate to reach out and touch what's supposed to be mine, and my feet that are needing to take me closer.

She must get the hint that I'm waiting on her approval because she points to the chair by the bed and tells me to sit.

Careful not to pull out any of the wires by accident, I sit and look at her. Now that she's ready to talk, I'm ready to tell her what I've wanted to say ever since I found out the truth.

"I'm sorry. I'm so fucking sorry, Jazz. The words I told you that night weren't true and said in anger. So much shit happened that night and I lashed out ready to get away from all the lies." I grab her small hand gently to avoid the IV. "After we left the doctor, I knew he was the father. And I was fine with it, but then I received a phone call that changed everything I had ever believed and known in my life."

She intertwines our fingers and I feel as though I can breathe for the first time in over a month. "I know everything, Mason. You don't need to explain." She wipes a tear from under her eye with the other hand. "I won't lie and say the words didn't hurt. In fact, the memory of that night still rips me open, but I understand. After what your mom lied about and your dad having an affair, and not to mention the picture Chanda sent you, I probably would have done the same thing." She looks at me and I see love shining in her eyes again. "I've missed you so much. Not just this..." she squeezes my hand she's holding "...but I've really missed my best friend. The person who always knew a way to make me smile and feel better. I had no one to do your job. And I was miserable."

Standing up, I lean down ready to kiss her lips but she turns her face away and I get her cheek. “Too soon?” I ask, trying to hide my disappointment.

“No, but I have the worst morning breath ever, so until I can brush my teeth these dry, chapped lips are off limits.”

“Oh really? I don’t think so, woman. I haven’t kissed you in over a month, so you need to get over it.” Before she can argue I grab her chin and turn her face toward mine. “I love you.”

Then I kiss her. When my lips first make contact, she remains stubborn and keeps them closed. I kiss one corner then the other before I lick the seam of her plump lips. On the second lick I take her bottom one in my mouth and suck. “Mmm! Still perfect.” She opens like I knew she would and I thrust my tongue in. Caressing her tongue softly, I hear a husky purr rumble from her throat. My hand leaves her chin and goes to her pulse loving the fast beat, but then the reason she’s in here hits me. I pull away swiftly. “Shit, I’m so sorry, baby. Are you okay?”

She looks fine, only flushed. “Um … yeah! Why wouldn’t I be?”

I scratch my head, too agitated and desperate to calm down. I don’t want to over react. “Your pulse and heartbeat was fast. I didn’t know if that was bad for you.”

“Come here.” She crooks her finger at me and I see her feisty side start to come alive again. I stand close to the bed again. “Closer.” Bending over she reaches up and runs her fingers through my hair, causing chills to surface before they settle on the base of my neck. “The only thing bad for me is you not loving me or you trying to leave me. So don’t you ever pull that shit again? Because we’re yours and I would never hurt you.” She pulls me down close and I feel her breath on my lips. Her eyes stare into mine and the sky I love and missed is back. "Got it?" I nod, speechless, before she kisses me with a month's worth of kisses all rolled into one.

Waiting is something I've learned to hate this past week. The second thing I've learned is that I can't live without Jazz in my life every day. She's my everything and not knowing what's going on in the OR is killing me. My mind won't stop thinking of what could go wrong while she's in there. Not just to her but to Finlee. That little girl who's being born today is a piece of the woman I love, and over the past several months I've also fallen in love with her. I don't think of her as not being my daughter anymore, not since Jazz and I talked yesterday and we laid it all out on the table. Our past mistakes don't matter any longer. We learned from them and are hopefully moving on—together.

I talked to Grandma Ginger yesterday when she called to check on Jazz and her great granddaughter. She also wanted me to know about the reading of my dad's will. When she told me of a savings account of my dad's he left for me over the past twenty years I almost fainted. I have never had that much money before in my life and it doesn't feel real. She plans on flying down after Jazz is settled in and recovered to give me the paperwork. Before I could tell Jazz the news, it was time for her to be wheeled back and so I pushed it aside, but I plan on helping out any way I can and hopefully she won't argue.

Feeling a hand land on my shoulder as I make another pass in front of the Coleman family, I look and see Jeremiah. Scanning his facial features I see the tiredness but not fear. I should take that as a good sign and calm the hell down, but I can't. Not until she's in my arms again.

"Son, she's going to be fine. I have complete confidence in the team working on her and the baby." I nod my head because no words will form. I still don't feel better. "I also want you to know that a father isn't someone who helps produce a child. It's the person who loves that child and raises them as his own. Believe me, I know firsthand." The door suddenly opens and Dr. Parnell walks out. "Doctor Coleman?" Everyone stands waiting for news. "Everything on my end went beautifully. You have a four pound three ounce little girl who has some of the loudest lungs I've ever heard on someone so tiny."

The women speak with excitement over the news, and I even have a smile on my face, but I need to know how my other girl is. "And what about Jazz?"

She looks at me with a serious expression. "As far as I know everything was going as planned, but that's all I can say. My specialty is delivering babies. But everyone working on her are some of the best and have done this several times."

We shake hands even though my nerves are still on edge. "Thank you."

"Do you want to see your daughter?" Of course the doctor has no clue about the truth and still thinks of me as the father. I glance at the Colemans who are all staring at me with expectancy. Even Jax's attitude has calmed, and I think Tru is the main reason for that.

Turning back to the doctor, I nod my head. “Yes, sir. How many can come?”

“Only two at a time. They have her in the NICU at the moment doing tests, but I believe she’ll be fine and will soon be in the nursery.”

I turn toward the woman who raised Jazz. The person who taught her how to love openly, but to never let people run over her. “Mrs. Coleman? Would you like to come with me?” Looking at Jazz’s mom, I see the excitement build and she smiles brightly. Her hair is coming out of her ponytail and she’s not wearing makeup, but she doesn’t care.

“I’d love to.” She grabs my elbow and we make our way back to my little girl.

Chapter Twenty-Five

Jazz

I'm so excited to be going home today and away from this friggin' hospital. Staring at its boring walls and smelling its disinfectant aroma gets old after the first day, and I've been here for two weeks. Thank goodness I don't remember the first week because I know I would have had cabin fever. What I'm really excited about is getting to hold my princess whenever I want to and not having to worry about the doctor telling me to rest all the time. And when I say that, I mean it. And it wasn't just the doctor doing it. It was my mom, Trudy, and even Miss Brenda. So today is the day I can go home with my baby. Finlee Breanne Reed.

People might think I'm cray cray for putting Mason as the father on the birth certificate, but I don't care. We are officially together and officially a happy family. “Isn’t that right, Princess? Mommy and Daddy love you so much.” My heart melts and skips a few beats looking at Finlee in my arms while she’s wrapped in a soft pink and white blanket. Even though she’s gained half a pound in one week, she’s still tiny. Her small, pink hat encases her head full of brown hair and the mittens Jax bought her cover her ten fingers. They’re pink with the words “Future Knockout” embroidered in white on the tops. I could stare at her all day.

“You ready?” Mason comes in from loading all the flowers and balloons into his truck. He assures me we’ll all fit even though I still have my doubts. Trudy and Jax already took one load and headed to my apartment to get everything in order for our arrival. Mom and Dad left yesterday because life called, but I plan on going to see them in a few weeks. McKenzie is dying to get her hands on her niece and loves the fact she’s ten and an aunt. Cohen was disappointed I didn’t have a boy for him to play with and told me to have one next time. I just shook my head and laughed.

“So ready. You have no idea.”

He sits the car seat down and takes Finlee from my arms. “Hey, sweet pea.” Watching him kiss her head and gently put her in her seat, I fall in love with him all over again. This feeling always makes me wonder why I fought it for so long.

“I love you, Mason Alexander Reed. Thank you for loving us.” The need to tell him how much he means to me overwhelms me while happiness encompasses my whole soul. My soul mate. That is what he is. Someone engraved in me so deep that without him I’d be lost and searching.

He glances up from looking at Finlee and gives me a smile. “I love you too, Jasmine Marie Coleman.”

He walks my way and I'm taken back to the first time his confidence surfaced. His stride is so sexy and I can't wait for the day I can jump him like a chimpanzee and have wild monkey sex. He comes down to my level and looks me in the eye. Since I'm sitting in a wheelchair, he's on his knees, but I love him this close. He takes my face in one hand and holds me. "You are so beautiful and even more so now. I didn't think that was possible until after you gave me a beautiful daughter." When his lips touch mine and rub gently back and forth, warmth spreads from my core to my skin. I know we need to stop before it gets too out of control, but as his tongue mates with mine, stopping is the last thing on my mind. Luckily he has more will power than I do and is able to slow the kiss down. He pulls away and looks down at my feet sitting in the wheelchair foot pedals.

After a minute of calming his breathing, he still remains looking down. "You okay?" I let my fingers slide in his silky hair and love the feel of it running across my open palm.

"Yeah, but I want to ask you a serious question. Okay?" He looks straight into my eyes with nervousness. Nodding my head, I swallow while I wait for his question. Not gonna lie, I'm kind of scared because I can't deal with another breakup.

"You know I'm not good with talking or putting words together, but I love you and Finlee more than anyone or anything in this world. And I want you to know I'd do anything to protect you both until the day I die. These past few weeks have taught me that I don't want to be without you for one more day. So I want to ask you..." he takes a deep breath but never breaks eye contact "...if you'd change your name to Jasmine Marie Reed and become my wife."

My heart speeds up from either nerves or excitement. I'm not really sure. This is a huge ass step in life, but it's one I want to take. Even though we just officially started dating again, it doesn't change anything. Our whole relationship has been different and nontraditional, so why not have a nontraditional engagement to boot. Besides, I know that I'll never love someone like I do him. He's become my best friend over the last year and we know everything about one another. My answer is easy.

"Yes."

His eyes widen with surprise. "Yes?"

Now the waterworks start, I'm too elated to give a damn about my freshly applied makeup. "Yes. I'd love to be your wife." He still looks in shock and hasn't moved. I don't even think he's blinked. "Hello! Aren't you supposed to kiss me now or something?"

Shaking his head, he smiles and finally blinks his thick black lashes. "Oh yeah!" Wrapping both hands in my hair he places his lips over mine. "I promise I'll get you the best ring out there." His whispered words against my lips are nice, but I don't care about a ring. As long as I have him and Finlee in my life material things aren't important. Besides, I know his money is tight.

My thoughts vanish as he seals our engagement with a kiss that causes my insides to curl together and ignite with heat. *Dear Lawd sweet baby Jesus!* My man can kiss and make me squirm, especially when his mouth leaves my mouth and travels slowly to my ear. His breathing causes me to cross my legs and wish for privacy and a time machine to get the next four weeks over with. "I love you, future Miss Jasmine Reed."

Before I can answer and beg him to do something I know I'm not ready for, Finlee's cries blast out my eardrum. Taking a breath, he stands and looks at me with a wink. "That's our cue to get the hell home I guess." I wait for Mason to pull the truck around, but what he drives up isn't his usual ride. It's a white Chevy Traverse with all the bells and whistles. Confused, I wait until Finlee and I are buckled in before I ask about it. He tells me it's a rental and wanted to see if I liked it. It's fine with just enough space for all of us and then some. It has black leather interior and a third row seat.

"It's fine. In fact it has me thinking my car isn't a good idea for a baby. I might actually need something bigger. Something with four doors."

"Well then we can go together to get two vehicles." I see his brow furrow in concentration. He's going so slow I don't think I'll ever get home. "You don't have to drive like my great grandpa, ya know. And are you thinking of getting rid of your truck?" I don't know if it has enough of a trade in value, but I won't say that.

"Yeah. There's something I've been meaning to talk to you about but too many people have been around." He glances in my direction. "It seems my dad had a savings account he put a few hundred dollars in every week for the last twenty years. And in his will he left it all to me."

Once again I'm rendered speechless. "Holy shit balls!" Well maybe not. I cover my mouth and peek at Finlee in the backseat. Looking at the mirror, her reflection shows her smiling in her sleep. Money seems to make her happy. Or maybe it's Mommy's potty mouth. "Wow. I'm so happy for you, Mason."

"Yeah. I was in shock too and don't know what to do with all that money. Gigi is coming down to visit and bring the paperwork to get it transferred once you feel okay."

"Really?"

I've been intrigued about his lost family since day one and can't wait to meet them, even Symone—the redheaded beauty queen. After discussing our soon to be guest, and when to tell everyone about the engagement, we arrive home. Slowly, I make my way up the steps while Mason carries Finlee and her heavy ass car seat. Once inside I just about jump out of my skin when everyone yells "welcome home." I even see Mom and Dad. Sneaky bastards. Of course the noise causes Finlee to wake up, but it's okay because everyone wants a chance to hold her. She must be a drama queen like me. My party is not only a welcome home bash, but also a baby shower. It's full of laughter and gifts. I feel so blessed to have all these wonderful people in my life. Watching Tru hold Finlee and Jax sitting beside her with his arm draped over her shoulders protectively, I melt. They definitely need to give Finlee a cousin, and soon too.

Mason's mom even loves on Finlee and dotes on her like a true grandmother. I walk over to her and give her a hug. "Thanks for coming. It means so much to me."

"Oh, honey. Thank you for loving my son and letting us be a part of this child's life." She hands Finlee to me and I happily take her. My arms feel better when she's there. "Thank you for forgiving me for what I did to him. Everyone makes mistakes in life. Some obviously leave larger wounds than others. But you need to figure out a way to heal them so they don't ruin your entire life. Luckily my son's forgiveness has helped mine to heal. And your forgiveness of him has helped heal his." She wipes away a tear. "I pray

Mason helps yours to heal as well. Because you need to be whole to care for this precious little girl."

She walks away but her words stay with me the rest of the day. Without hesitation I can say that my wounds and confidence are healed because of Mason. He is the balm to help me see that I am beautiful on the inside and out no matter my past mistakes. And I like this feeling. A lot.

Mason and I announced our engagement while everyone is at the apartment. And to my surprise everyone is happy, even Jax. Soon after that people start to leave and thank goodness because I can't wait to get a shower and lie in my own bed, with Mason of course.

Before my parents make their exit, Dad pulls me and Mason to the side. He gives me a hug. "Congrats, baby girl."

"Thanks, Daddy." I feel like there's something else he wants to say so I wait and brace myself.

I don't have to wait too long. "Well, Jazz, you know how I have a private detective looking into the professor?" I nod my head. "It seems that you were the only one or he's really been careful. We haven't found anything on him besides a heated argument with his wife."

My heart drops. I was really hoping that we could find something to blackmail his ass if he ever made anymore threats. Unfortunately, that doesn't look like it's going to happen. "So what now?" I feel Mason pull me to his side and kiss my head. Calmness starts to seep in immediately.

Dad takes a deep breath and shakes his head. “Now all we do is wait. I really don’t think he’ll push the issue because he has too much to lose.”

Walking my dad to the door, I fight to conceal my worries, but I can’t shake the bad feeling setting in my gut.

Chapter Twenty-Six

Mason

I look over at Jazz as I pull into the car dealership and see her biting her nails. Again. "Stop worrying. Grandma said she'd call if she needed anything."

Today is really the first time Jazz has been away from Fin since she was born, and it's showing in her nervous mannerisms. I can imagine how she feels. My first day back to classes was killer. I'd constantly text to see if they were okay. Jazz ended up sending me pictures of the two of them throughout the day and it helped, except for one picture she took while changing. She swears she didn't mean to take it, but I know her game. She knows I have Barney balls right now. They're called Barney balls because they have completely passed the point of blue and are now purple. It's a danger zone for any and every pair of pants I own. Masturbating just isn't the same. Sleeping with her every night and feeling her ass against me or waking up see her breast pop out to feed Finlee doesn't help either.

Grandma Ginger has been down for three days and quickly fell in love with my family. Jazz loves her just as much. They both love to shop and plan on a huge Finlee spree before she flies out next week. We took care of the funds that were left to me and now we're looking for a new ride. My next big purchase is a ring, and Tru is helping me with that. I've only asked that it has pink in it.

Placing her hand in her lap, she looks in my direction with a pout. "But what if I didn't leave enough milk? Or what if she gets scared?"

"Believe me there is plenty of milk in the freezer and Tru even has some in hers. You've produced enough to feed her for a full year. And she won't be scared because she loves Grandma." I park and get out, taking her hand after she meets me in front, and we start to walk and browse the selection.

"I know. But I can't help it."

"Well why don't we find a car and then instead of sitting down for lunch we grab a pizza and go home instead?"

I see her smile and watch as she relaxes. After looking at several vehicles she settles on a silver Chevy Tahoe z71. She says she's going to put black and pink stripes down the center, and I promise not to hold it against her. I purchase a used, blue Dodge Ram four-door pickup. It has the space in the back for Fin and the power I've always wanted in a truck. Having this money is going to change our lives, but I'm not going to blow it. I've gone ahead and talked to Mom about moving into a better apartment or possibly a house. She's still hesitant and says that the money is mine and not to spend it on her, but she's sacrificed to provide for Grace and me all these years I want to help. After talking to her a bit more and mentioning how she should move closer to Finlee I think I've been able to convince her.

After signing the papers and taking the keys, we order a pizza and head home. We don't see anyone around when we walk through the door, but then we hear her in the back. She's singing a song that's vaguely familiar but I don't know where I've heard it. The nursery door is open a crack and we see them cuddled in the rocking chair before walking in.

"Hey, Gigi. We brought pizza."

She looks up with her soft, grey eyes surrounded with laugh lines. The auburn hair surrounding her aged face isn't common for someone else in their seventies. "Pizza? That's one of my favorites. But, honey, I thought you two were going out to eat."

"I couldn't wait to get home." Jazz walks in and kisses Gigi on the cheek before she takes Finlee in her arms. I love watching them together. The love I see shining through her sky blue eyes is something every child should see when they look at their mother. Finlee's eyes are luckily going to be the same color as Jazz's and not like Professor fuckhead. "I didn't want to miss anything. Like what if she rolled over or something like that and I wasn't here?"

I laugh at my crazy fiancée. "She's too little to roll over. The only thing new she'll be doing is working on another disgusting poop diaper. And maybe a new facial expression."

“See? I don’t want to miss it. The faces she makes are so stinkin’ cute. I just want to eat her up.” She starts to talk in baby gibberish to Finlee. “Say ‘Daddy, Mommy can’t miss my new faces. I’m just too pretty.’”

“What about the poop diapers? Are you saying you don’t want to miss that too?” I ask, walking to stand beside her while she plays with Fin. I reach out and touch one of her chubby baby cheeks, and I’m still amazed how soft her skin is, just like her mommy.

“Believe it or not yes. But it’s your facial expressions I like then. When you see the surprise in her diaper you make the funniest face. It looks like a duck with a scrunched nose and puckered lips.” She imitates the face and looks ridiculous. I still kiss her puckered lips.

“Oh, I have seen that face. Mason, it is hilarious. And when you add the sound effects of gagging, that really tops it.” Gigi is laughing right along with Jazz. I wouldn’t be surprised if Fin started too.

“Well those sound effects aren’t fake. I’m actually gagging just from the look of it. Thank God it doesn’t stink. Then I’d be in real trouble.”

All of us walk into the living room and eat pizza while watching some of Jazz’s favorite reality television shows. Fin lies in her bouncer seat and lets the vibrations soothe her to sleep. when I feel my phone vibrate, I look and see it’s Chanda. I haven’t heard from her since I confronted her about the pictures. I’m surprised she’s calling after our heated argument.

She had told me that I looked upset and that was why she went to Jazz’s apartment to confront her. She noticed the door open and the Professor leaving. Even though it sounded innocent, I told her to stay out of my business and to stop with all the sexual insinuations she’d been throwing at me.

I debate on answering it or not and decide to let her leave a voicemail instead. I end up deleting it because I don't need any of her drama. She probably wants another ride because some loser she picked up in a bar left her again. When will she learn?

Jazz takes our plates and walks in the kitchen. Afterward she comes over and lies on the couch beside me, placing her head on my lap. I let my fingers run through the golden strands. I don't know what were watching, so I just concentrate on her breathing. Soon it evens out and I know she's fallen to sleep.

"I'm going to head back to the hotel. I have a brunch date with your mom around ten and I don't want to be late." Gigi stands and starts to gather her things. She and Mom together tomorrow should be interesting. They haven't seen each other since Dad left Mom. Gigi always thought we didn't want anything to do with Dad or anyone in his family. I'm kind of worried for my mom because Gigi isn't one to hold her tongue, but Mom made her own bed.

After she leaves I take Jazz in my arms and carry her to our room to lay her in our bed. Placing the covers over her small body, I kiss her lips. "I love you, baby."

Me moving in just kind of happened. I never asked and she never asked, but I haven't left. I guess I'll get my things from the frat house and move them here later.

Staring at her relaxed features, I notice how innocent she looks. The lighting illuminates her long blonde hair as it's strewn across the deep brown pillowcase. She mumbles something about pudding and rolls over, which ruins the angelic vision. Laughing, I walk back to Finlee who's wide awake and making some really cute expressions while wiggling her tiny body.

"Hey, beautiful. You ready for a new diaper and some milk?" I pick her up and carry her on my shoulder back to her room.

After I'm done and heating some milk, my phone starts vibrating again. Looking down I see Chanda's name pop up. Again. What the hell is her problem? I quickly deny the call and continue to get my girl ready for bed. A few minutes later I hear a knock on the door before yelling on the other side. "Shit!" I put Finlee in her crib and walk to the door, ready to blast whoever is on the other side. I pause at the sight of Chanda standing there with a busted lip and black eye.

"What the hell happened?"

She doesn't look drunk or like she's been out all night. In fact she's in her work uniform. Her makeup is smeared and her hair is in disarray. Someone obviously beat the hell out of her.

"My dad. He was drunk and wanted all of the tips I made tonight." I lead her inside and sit her at the dining room table before fixing her a bag of ice. She flinches when I put the ice pack on her eye. "Of course I didn't make a lot tonight and he had a fit." She crumbles before my eyes. "I'm sorry for bothering you so late, but I didn't know where to go. Your mom is too close to him and I just wanted to get as far away from him as possible so I didn't wake her."

"You need to go to the police." Looking up, Jazz walks in with rumpled hair and sleepy eyes. My heart stops for a second seeing her stand there. Is she going to be mad about Chanda being in here with me? Does she think something is going on between us? But her eyes reach mine and I know she doesn't. She walks over and wraps her arms around my waist reassuringly. "You can't let him get away with this. Nobody should have the right to treat anyone like that."

"Oh what the hell do you know? You and your perfect fucking life with your perfect family."

My back stiffens but Jazz steps forward before I can. "Listen here, Chanda. I'm sorry you got the shit beat out of you tonight, but this is my home and I won't have you talk to me like that. I'm happy to help you in any way possible, but I will be shown respect and so will my family. And if I'm not, I'll kick your ass myself."

Chanda looks just as surprised as me with Jazz's fierce words. I've heard some stories of her attitude when her feathers are ruffled, but I've never seen it with my own eyes.

Jazz ignores Chanda's look of surprise and continues. "Now like I said before, you can get cleaned up and I'll grab you some clothes, but I really think you should call the police and press charges. It's your call."

We wait in silence while Chanda battles with her decision. After a few minutes she decides to just forget the whole incident and go to bed. I know it's her own flesh and blood, but getting beat like that isn't right. I keep my mouth shut because I know it will only land on deaf ears.

The next morning I wake to Jazz feeding Finlee beside me. Looking at the clock I see it's only five so I have a few hours to rest before class.

"Mornin', beautiful." Stretching, I move closer to her warmth. "Sorry, I mean *beautifuls*." Finlee looks to be asleep but every so often her sucking will start again.

"Mornin' to you too, but I swear after she eats my ass is going back to sleep. This child has been stuck to my boobs all night." She looks down at Finlee while I feel my dick stiffen from the sight and her words. "Thank God. She's out."

"She's one lucky girl," I whisper with envy as I watch Jazz walk out to put Fin back in her crib. I rub my palm over my length and hiss from how sensitive it is. Man, I hate jerking off, but until Jazz is fully healed, I'm riding solo. In a huff I lie down and cover my eyes with my arm. I hear the door shut and then feel the bed dip.

"Well, one of my babies is taken care of. Now it's time for the other." Her voice is husky and breathless. I see her looking at my tented boxers. Sitting up, I cover it. I don't want her to think she has to do anything early. "Sorry."

Her hands land on mine. "Don't." She brings her eyes to mine and scoots only and inch away from me. Her warmth mixed in with her scent has my dick getting harder. Add her lust filled eyes … well then you've got me about to explode in my shorts.

"I'm going to go get—" I don't finish because her mouth is on mine and I fall back into the pillows. A growl erupts when she sucks my tongue in her mouth. Before I can return the favor her lips are on my chin, my neck, and then she's scraping my nipple.

"Geez, I have missed this." She straddles my lap and I let out a noise I can't describe. I think I purred or something.

“Fuck!” She thrusts her hips against my length and I feel every millimeter of movement. Even through her panties and my boxers I feel the shock waves grabbing my balls and running down my legs. “Dammit, baby. We got to stop!” God knows I don’t want to, but I don’t want to hurt her. I know the first time we actually have sex again it’s going to be rough and fast. I’ll do slow, maybe by the third or fourth round.

“Yes we can.” Her voice is muffled because she has yet to bring her face from my chest. “Be still. Let me do this for you.”

“Do what?”

She doesn’t answer. She looks at me through fallen strands of gold as she works her way down to my belly button. When she gets farther down to where my boxers meet my skin, her pink tongue licks from side to side. My breathing comes out in fast pants because I know her intentions.

She sits up and pushes her hair out of her face. “Lift your hips.” Like a robot, I do and her finger grabs the edge of my boxers gently before she forcefully moves in and rips my boxers down. My dick springs out like a flag waving in the air saying “I surrender.” And I do. I surrender to this beautiful girl that captured my heart with one look and threw the key away when she kissed me.

“You’re gorgeous.” Her eyes leave my length and stare into mine. Her words catch me off guard. No one has ever considered me anything other than cute, nobody but her.

Holding my stare, her hand comes up. She then sticks her index finger in her sweet, warm mouth and sucks it while showing me her pink tongue swirling around. The image of her doing that to me has my hips thrusting with need. “You like that?”

“Yes,” I say, growling. She smiles and instead of giving me what I want, she sucks each finger slowly and with care. Little minx. After a few minutes the torture is finally over. Or so I think. Just then she licks her palm up and down several times while my breathing causes our own personal concert. If I could fuck her I would, but since it’s still off limits, I ball my fist in the sheets before I grab her and impale her fragile body.

After her palm is wet, she lets is slowly wrap around my dick and again I thrust up. I’m desperate to ease this need. I watch as her head lowers, and then I feel her mouth encase my tip and slowly moves down. I’m so sensitive I know I won’t last long. When her tongue rubs my spot with just enough pressure, my body loses control. Reaching up, I grab two fistfuls of her hair while my dick fucks her mouth. Hell, maybe it’s her mouth fucking my dick. I can’t tell and she doesn’t let up, and the noises she’s making sound like she’s really enjoying it. In fact, she even sucks harder. When I’m close, but not ready for it to end, I feel her free hand join in and caresses my balls. After that I lose the battle.

“Holy shit.” The words leave my mouth right before I let go.

Breathless, I lie there stunned. Then I feel her body crawl up mine again and she lays her head on my chest. “I love you.” She kisses above my heart.

When I can finally speak, I tell her I love her too, but her breathing has evened out and she’s already asleep.

Chapter Twenty-Seven

Jazz

Lounging around in some shorts and a tee, I click through the channels looking for something to watch other than Baby Einstein. Fin is addicted to classical music and rock. I've tried several times to see if she'll stop crying with country, but every time I push play or switch it to CMT she gets louder. But give the child some Slipknot or Chevelle and she's intently listening. Two months old or not, the child knows what she likes.

Looking at my phone I see Mason will be home before the storm hits. Tonight he had a call to help the auditorium's sound system because it wasn't working right. Fall semester is starting in a few weeks and everything has to be perfect to welcome the new students. Tru's dance team is performing, and since Elle was accepted into the Joffrey Ballet Company she won't be here next year. Jamal is actually the new captain and maybe Tru can be co-captain. She's practically a junior with all the advance classes she takes.

After a very interesting rerun of The Vampire Diaries—team Damon baby—I hear a soft knock on the door. Nerves set in because everyone is busy tonight. When I get to the door I look in the peep hole and see Oliver's wife or ex-wife. What the hell? Taking a deep breath, I ready myself to open the door. Is she a friend or foe? I'm not sure but hiding behind this door won't give me an answer. I can tell she's just as nervous looking in her brown eyes framed in glasses. And she's not alone either. Two little girls with brown hair and brown eyes stand beside her. One looks to be McKenzie's age and the other might be six. I see Oliver all over the oldest, and she looks at me like I'm the Devil. I can't really blame her if she knows the story.

"Sorry to disturb you, Jasmine, but my girls wanted to meet their sister."

Caught off guard, I look at her with wide eyes. "Um …"

Should I deny that Finlee is their sister and stick with the story about Mason being the dad? But there's really only one answer to that question. No. I would want to know if my biological mother had another child, if there was another child with my DNA walking around somewhere. And looking at the younger girl's excited eyes, I know it's the right choice.

"Sure. Come on in."

I follow them in and shut the door, wondering if there is another reason for the visit. "So are you girls thirsty?"

"Where are my manners? Addison, Marilyn, come introduce yourself to Jasmine." They both walk over and stand in front of me with two opposite expressions.

The youngest sticks out her hand. I see the dirty fingernails and know this one is a tomboy but definitely a beauty. "Hi! My name is Addison Rose Wallace, but everyone calls me Addie. I like to fish and hit boys and my favorite color is blue. Sort of like your eyes. They're very pretty."

"Thank you." Her words produce a smile from her mom and me. I take her tiny hand and shake it. "Nice to meet you, Addie." She just smiles and goes on to look at the pictures on the wall. Most are of Finlee, but there are a few of all three of us.

Marilynn stands still with her arms crossed. She doesn't like me a bit and it shows. After her mom clears her throat she huffs out a dramatic sigh. "My name is Marilynn Grace. You obviously know my last name and the other stuff about me is none of your business." She turns and walks away.

"Young lady, you come back here and apologize. Now!" Allison's voice is stern but Marilynn doesn't seem affected and continues to ignore her mother.

Giving up, Allison turns my way looking regretful and apologizes. I don't know why, because the child has every right not to like me, and I can't blame her. With her parents' divorce and the new baby sister that's not her mom's, well any eleven year old can connect the dots.

Shaking my head, I turn my attention back to the hysterical mother. "No, it's fine. I was that age once and attitude is an everyday expression for them." About that time Fin wakes up and gives everyone a startle. She is all lungs. "Hold on." I walk in the nursery unaware of tiny feet behind me.

“This room is amazing.”

After I pick up Fin I watch Addison take in the room while spinning in circles. “Thank you.” Placing Fin on the changing table, I freshen her up and she calms right down. “You’re such a big girl.”

“She so, so, so cute. Can I hold her? Please?”

“Addie, stop begging. Besides she’s so tiny.” Allison walks closer and gets a good look. “Was she early?”

“Yes, but only by four weeks. She just takes after me in stature I guess.”

“And my dad.” Marilynn stands outside the door sneering.

“Marilynn, you are this close to getting grounded. And I mean no phone, TV, or iPod. Got it?” This threat only receives a shrug and a view of her back as she walks away. “That child has been driving me crazy. I just don’t know what to do.” Her voice is starting to sound thick and I see moisture build in her eyes. I believe it’s time to talk and figure out why she’s here and what’s next. I really want Mason beside me so hopefully he will hurry.

After getting Finlee fed and settled in her bouncy seat, I take Allison into the dining area to talk. This way the kids are visible, but hopefully they won’t here what’s being said.

The almost tears are gone, so her voice is higher. “I’ve been wanting to come see you ever since that day we first met. I knew instantly who you were when he sat by me and saw you and your friend kissing. Jealousy was clear as day. I mean, I’ve been with the man for over a decade so I kind of know him. But the guy you were with he was so sure the baby was his and he seemed so in love with you I wanted to find out if my suspicions were wrong. For his sake. I was already filing papers because of Oliver's past affairs." My eyes widen with the news.

"Oh yes, he's been cheating on me for years, and I should have left him years ago but didn't. I loved him from the first time I saw him at the country club. He noticed me and not many men did back then. But what I later realized is it wasn't me he noticed it was my status and last name. My family comes from a long history of Mobile money. He won my parents over and of course me. He was so suave, but underneath he was a snake. I paid for his schooling and his car. When he constantly went on trips to conventions a few years back, I knew something was going on then. I didn't want to believe it. We had just had Addie and I didn't want to lose him and break up my family. And he has been a phenomenal father to the girls. That was another reason it took me so long to file the papers."

She tucks some stray brown hair behind her ear while I visualize the story she's telling me. "After a few years of this I became depressed. So bad I got hooked on prescription pain medication. Luckily my family was there to get me out and made me see I was better than Oliver. Better than I gave myself credit for. So I've been building a case against him for about a year now and he was recently served his papers. He doesn't want to sign them, though, because if he loses me he loses his money. I know your family has money as well. Correct?" I nod my head while my brain tries to digest everything she's telling me. "Well, he's probably going to try to get you back. Especially now that you're not a student."

"Well you don't need to worry about that. There's no way I'd even think about getting back with him." I look at the woman whose family is broken and angry because of mistakes I've made. I've forgiven myself these past months and I just hope she can forgive me too. "I'm truly sorry you're going through this. I promise on my life I had no idea he was married or had children." I grab her hand desperate for her to believe me. "The signs were there, but I was too naïve to notice. I'm sorry for hurting you like this."

The tears sneak out from her eyes. "Don't worry. I forgive you and I figured with the way we talked that day at the doctor's office, and from your expression when you saw him sitting there, you had no idea. Besides this isn't his first affair. But it will be the last one he has while he's with me."

We talk for a little while longer while the girls fawn over Finlee. They love her name and from the looks of it, her as well. Even Marilynn has smiled every once in a while. After they leave I take Fin and go lie in bed. I'm mentally exhausted and now the rain has come. I let the patter of rain on the windowpane and Fin's breathing lull me to a restless sleep.

"Okay, girls. Let's get perky. You're both on duty tonight." Glancing at my cleavage, I admire its fullness and the way the coral fabric hugs them tightly. Tonight is my first official date with Mason. Needing some alone time, we have his mom and Grace babysitting at our place. Tru's working and Ryan's band Lyrical Obsession is supposed to be on fire. I haven't seen them play since New Year's all those months ago, and even then they sounded good. Tru states they have brought major business and Ms. Janet, the owner, is thrilled.

Mason is ready and waiting in the living room with everyone else while I make some last minute changes to my accessories. My belief of a guy waiting for his date still stands, even if they live with each other. I really haven't dressed up this much since before I became pregnant. The outfit I'm wearing is a short, strapless cocktail dress with an empire waist. The top is coral satin and the bottom is black tulle. The sash travels around my waist and forms a bow in the back. It's very pretty and something I bought especially for this special occasion. Tonight is the night to listen to Marvin Gaye and get it on. I squeeze my thighs together in anticipation of what the night holds for us.

Besides the amazing sex to come, we are also celebrating. Allison came by last week with news her divorce was finalized. She also took the evidence of Oliver's many affairs with female students to the board at South and he lost his job last week. The police are checking the ages of each girl to make sure no statutory rape charges will be filed. She said he showed up at her house pissed beyond belief and cussed her and the girls out for turning their back on him or some shit like that. She had to call the cops and after a few threats spewed from his mouth, she also got a restraining order on him. After that he left and hasn't been seen or heard from.

Running my hands through my hair, I watch the curls bounce before they fall into place. Then my heart stops when I hear Finlee screaming in pain. My inner sex goddess is replaced by Super Mom immediately. Running out the door I reach everyone huddled around Grace and Finlee. "What happened?"

Mason is kneeling and talking softly to his sister. "Grace tried to give her the bottle back and it …"

I bend down and check on Fin while I wait for him to finish. “You okay, Princess?” Looking up and down her tiny body I see no marks or blood so I calm down. After kissing Grace’s head, I stand and turn toward Mason. He’s standing in front of me with his mouth hanging open and wide eyes.

“Are you okay?” I ask innocently. He likes what he’s staring at and I like the look he’s giving me. His eyes have darkened and I see his nostrils flare with each breath, but I like playing games with him so I run one hand slowly from my neck down to my breast and let it linger. “Do I have something on me?”

His throat constricts before he shakes his head. When his eyes finally leave my breasts and reach my eyes, he arches his brow and smirks. Busted! “You’re something else. You know that?”

I walk over and wrap my arms around his waist. He smells so good and looks so sexy in jeans and the plaid button down shirt. I can see a white tee under it because it’s loosely buttoned. I can’t wait to strip him bare. Looking up I smile. “I know. But I don’t mind being an unusual person. Just as long as I’m your unusual person.”

He kisses my glossed lips. “Forever.” The warmth of his words has me liquefying in his arms.

After a wonderful dinner together we head to Jay Jay’s. I’m happy to be out with Mason but at the same time I want to just go home to Finlee. But knowing how much we need this, I decide to stay out for a little while longer. Walking inside after not going out for so long feels strange, but that feeling quickly fades as my friends surround us for the night. The conversations held are enough to make me blush and that is no easy feat. Between sexual positions and Jamal's male on male conversations I'm starting to feel flushed. It's been a long thirteen weeks.

Mason gets up to grab another round, and I see Cory but Ryan isn't with her and hasn't been for most of the night. Looking around, I see him and he's dancing with another girl. She's definitely not as pretty as Cory, but she's still working Ryan on the dance floor. I thought they were together because they'd been kissing when we first arrived. Concerned, I scoot over to my friend ready to kick some ass if she tells me to.

"Hey, sexy. Is everything okay?"

She stares at me and her expression. I notice she isn't upset. In fact, she looks happy judging by the smile she gives me. I can't tell if it's fake or not. "Sure, lil' momma. Why wouldn't it be?"

How can she not see him grinding on a girl only twenty feet away? "Did you and Ryan break it off or get into a fight? If not then why the hell is he humping some chick over there?" My voice rises from anger, but she only smiles more and then has the nerve to laugh at me. "What is so funny? I'm seriously about to nut-punch the asshole."

She grabs my arm as I start to stand. "Hold up, mighty midget. I see him and it's totally fine. We're only sleeping together. Nothing more, so he can bump and grind on her all he wants."

I sit back down and turn in her direction. "So you're only friends with benefits?" She nods and takes a drink of her Long Island iced tea.

The image of Mason dancing with some random girl pops in my head and catches me by surprise. My heart hurts from it. How would I have been able to do it? How could I just sit here and watch him flirt with another girl? My eyes widen while I look around the room for him. Knowing what the consequences could have been if we actually went through with it—if I stayed blind to my feelings. I wouldn't have him beside me like I do. He could be off with someone else and eventually leave me for an actual relationship.

"How do you keep your feelings from invading? How can you watch them together? I couldn't do it."

"Well no shit! You and Mason are like yin and yang. Polar opposites, but together you two fit perfectly and make something intricate and beautiful. But that mushy shit isn't for me. Not yet anyway. So instead of a cold rubber vibrator to get me howling, I was offered a warm, talented dick. And to top it off he has a mouth that likes his dessert anywhere and everywhere." She looks at the two and scrunches her brow. "But I think it's time to move on and from the humping going on with those two, I think he realizes it too." She smiles and turns toward me, but keeps her eyes cast past my head. She acts like ending things with him is so easy. "And I think I found someone too. Excuse me. I found my possible meal for the night." I watch her barely covered ass sashay over to a guy with his back turned toward me. She accidentally bumps into him and says something that has him laughing. *Go, Cory!* When he turns I see it's Bo. I haven't seen him since the day I passed out. From what Tru said he was warned to back off by Mason, but Mason swears he politely told him that we're back together.

Turning back around I notice Mason is still gone and isn't at the bar. No one seems to know where he is so I start to walk around the crowded room. I'm offered drinks and asked to dance several times but decline both. Since I'm breastfeeding and on a blood thinner I have to watch my alcohol consumption. No sense in bleeding to death from a scratch or giving my infant daughter a buzz. A few minutes pass and still no Mason. I see Ryan walking past me. I grab his arm to stop him.

"Have you seen Mason?" I yell over the crowd and he only smiles and walks to the stage. Dick.

I decide to go back to the table to get away from the hyper mob that's coming out to the dance floor for the show. With my back turned, I hear the microphone screeching through the speakers but ignore it and continue on my way. Then I hear my name being said and unless there is another Jazz here tonight I know it's meant for me.

Chapter Twenty-Eight

Mason

This is it. "Jazz? Can you come up on stage please?" I hear Lyric call her name and watch from the side as she turns around with wide eyes. Everyone gets quiet and looks behind them for the person who's being called on. The woman I love.

She points to her chest. "Me?" Then I walk out to the front of the stage. When she sees me her confused face scrunches up and she looks so dang cute.

After she makes her way up, I grab her small left hand and take the microphone from Lyric. "I know this is unexpected and out of character for me. You know I hate bringing attention to myself, but this is something I need to do. And I need to do it in front of the world. Since the world is busy, these fine people here tonight will do." I look at the hundreds of faces in the crowd. "Is this okay with everyone?" I hear a lot of "fuck yeahs" and whistling. When they calm down I once again face my confused fiancée. Ryan walks over and hands me the ring. The ring I had made just for her with its many diamonds encased in white gold. All the diamonds surround one special one that's pink and square.

Feeling it in my hand, I take a deep breath and get on my knee. Ryan holds the mic between Jazz and so my words are heard for everyone to hear. "Jasmine Marie Coleman, I fell in love with you the first time I saw your smiling face on a photograph. And when I met you in person I knew you were too good for me, but I also knew you were meant for me. You've watched me dance and didn't laugh. You built me back up when I was at my lowest. And you healed me when I was broken. I want to make you just as whole and happy as you have made me. And I promise to dedicate the rest of my life to do just that. So with that being said, will you prove to these people that you love me and become my wife?"

Tears that started after I got down on my knee keep her speechless so she nods her head. When I push the ring on her tiny finger, I feel relief. It fits perfectly.

Home is not an option tonight. Tonight calls for a stay at the best hotel in town so we have no interruptions. Tonight is also about being officially engaged and showing her the best night of her life. I knew we were already engaged, but I wanted an official proposal with witnesses … and to show everyone that the sexiest woman I know will be my wife.

When she notices we're headed in the opposite direction of home, I tell her my plans for our night alone. Before she can freak out about staying away all night, we make a call to Mom and she tells us the girls are asleep and everything is fine. I know she still worries, and I do to, but tonight I want her all to myself. Mom is great with the baby and has been around more since she quit her job at the convenience store. I had deposited some money in her account to help her out for a while and when she refused it I told her it was an advance for the future babysitting jobs I'll be asking of her.

I grab our bag and grunt from the weight before grabbing Jazz's hand and making our way to check in. Since I really didn't know what girl stuff was needed for a night away, I went to Tru. When she handed it to me I was surprised by the weight. All I had put in there were clothes for tomorrow and my toothbrush. Now it feels like a few bricks were packed.

After we get our key, we head upstairs to the honeymoon suite on the floor below the penthouse. Her eyes widened when the clerk told us which room we'd be staying in, but spoiling her is my mission in life. The closer we get to our room the more nervous I start to feel and I don't know why. I mean sex isn't new to the two of us, but it has been a long time. Deep down I'm terrified of hurting her. She's been through so much already, and I don't want her to go through anymore heart surgeries … or any surgery for that matter.

"Hey, what's wrong?" She takes the key from me and enters it into the reader.

Before we walk in I stop her. "Are you sure about this?" Her eyes widen and I know the words come out wrong. "I mean, are you sure you're well enough? I don't want to hurt you."

"Shit, Mason. You scared the hell out of me." She exhales and then grabs my cheeks. "I'm fine and the doctor did clear me. I can get as freaky as I want. And believe me I plan on getting super freaky with you."

She brings my face to hers and our lips touch. I wrap my arms around her waist and pull her to my body. I'm sure she can feel my erection through my jeans, but I need more. Her words of getting super freaky have me ready and my nerves are gone. She isn't one to hold back if she's hurting, so until she tells me to stop, I'll keep going. I let my hands slowly travel down her back to her round ass before I lift her up to straddle my body. The heat between her legs is warm against my stomach, and when she grinds against me I know it's time to go in.

Pushing the door open with my back, I walk backwards until I hit something. Opening my eyes, I see it's a marble countertop. Perfect! Spinning around, I reluctantly place her on it before I back away. I see her flushed cheeks, swollen lips, and dilated pupils. A strong urge to pound my chest overtakes me. Because I, Mason Fuckin' Reed, can turn this beautiful woman on. But I resist it and distract myself with the task at hand.

"Be right back." I kiss her lips gently before I go grab our bag and shut the door. When I go to close it, however, I see an older couple staring. By the smirks they're wearing I'd bet they just witnessed our whole show. "Evening." I nod politely. They just smile but the gentleman pinches the lady's ass. I hear her laugh while the door closes behind me and I make my way back to Jazz. "I hope when we're in our nineties we'll still be getting it on like the couple who just got a free show in the hallway."

She watches me intently and runs her fingers through her hair. The ring catches the light and I smile. It's perfect on her. "Really? Well if they wanted a real show, then they should've stuck around." Her voice is breathy and definitely enough to put dirty thoughts in a saint's mind.

I slowly make my way to stand between her legs, where my body belongs. "Oh yeah?"

She bites her bottom lip and nods. Bending her knees up, she flattens her feet on the counter and I watch her legs spread open wide while she leans back on her elbows. My eyes automatically look down. Holy shit! She's bare and beautiful. And oh so fucking wet.

"Lie back, baby."

She does what I say before I hit my knees and bring her ass to the edge of the counter. She smells intoxicating when I get close to her core. I slowly run my tongue around her folds and barely touch her clit with my tongue, but she jumps regardless.

I grab her bare feet and place them gently on my shoulders. "Hold on."

Then I dive in—licking, sucking, and nibbling. Anything my mouth is capable of I perform it on her. "Fuck, you're good."

The tangy sweetness of her juices on my tongue has me straining against my jeans. When her hand reaches for my hair I know she's close. So close. Bringing my finger up, I push it in her pussy for only a second before I take it out and slowly rub it over her anus.

She loses it after that. "Oh fuck. Fuck. Fuck!" Her screams and moans cause my hips to thrust toward the cabinets in front of me. My body belongs to her and knows it wants to be deep in her warmth. Her voice is like a mating call, and my dick is ready.

Standing, I unbutton my jeans and have them down and somewhere across the room in record time. I bet Superman isn't that fast. Grabbing her hips, I look into her eyes and dive in. A loud growl rumbles up from out of nowhere in time with her moan, but my body is on automatic. She sits up and wraps her arms around my neck as I sink into her over and over again. When I go to kiss her it's difficult and uncoordinated. I'm fucking her so hard our mouths can't keep contact with one another for more than a second. I stare at her flushed face as she pants hard enough to cool my heated skin.

"Perfect. You're so damn perfect." She smiles and does something that squeezes my dick like a vise. And I lose the battle, but damn I won the war.

We head straight to Finlee's room once we arrive home the next morning. She's sound asleep but Jazz picks her up and cradles her close, ready to make up for lost time.

"I missed you, Princess." Watching the two is amazing. The knowledge that they're mine hits me and I smile.

Jazz sits and starts to nurse, so I go and talk to my mom who's feeding Grace breakfast. "Good morning."

Mom takes a seat with her cup of coffee. "Morning, son. How did last night go?"

My smile is immediate. “Well she said yes. What more could I ask for?”

Her arched brow tells me she wants details so I tell her. I don’t remember the exact words I said last night because my nerves were so messed up, but I do remember her face. I’m saved when Jazz comes in and joins the conversation. She of course remembers what I said word for word. When Jazz shows her the ring I see the approval in Mom’s eyes.

After breakfast Mom starts getting ready to leave but Grace is staying with us since she has a shift later tonight. Chanda has been staying with a friend somewhere and hasn’t been seen.

“No word from anyone at work?”

Mom shakes her head as she grabs her purse. “Nothing. I know she needs the money, so I don’t know why she’d just quit all the sudden.” Walking over she places a kiss on each of us before she leaves. She quickly knocks after I’ve shut the door. “Sorry, honey. I forgot to give you this. One of the neighbors said it was left in their mail by accident.” She passes me an envelope addressed to Jazz then walks out a second time.

Walking into the dining room I take a seat by Grace and lay the letter on the table. “Here, babe. You got a letter.” She stares at it for a few seconds with wide eyes before her eyes look up at mine. Her face pales and she shakes her head. “What is it?” I stand and go kneel by her chair. “What’s wrong?”

She takes a deep breath before she answers on a whisper. “Oliver. That’s Oliver’s handwriting.”

Taking it, I rip it open.

Dear Jasmine,

I hope this letter finds you well enough to understand what I'm about to say. I have contacted a lawyer and plan on having a DNA test done. You should be receiving a subpoena soon and I expect you to cooperate. I'm sure you're already aware that my employment has been terminated by now. But I plan on fighting the allegations tooth and nail. When I do have employment again, I also plan on gaining custody of my children. All three of them.

You might be wondering how. Well you just have to wait and find out.

Sincerely,

Oliver M. Wallace PhD.

Anger and outrage don't describe my feelings at the moment. All I want to do is hit something. Hard. But then I see Jazz take the letter from my hands. After she reads she looks up at me with terror in her blue depths.

"He's going to try to take my baby?" I catch her before she hits the ground. "He can't have her. Dammit! He can't."

I sit on the floor with her small body curled in my lap crying. "Hey. Look at me." Grabbing her wet cheeks, I turn her to face me. "He won't take her from you. I promise you. I won't let him. Got it." She takes a shuddering breath and nods her head. We sit there in each other's arms for I don't know how long. My brain is stuck on the promise I made her, and I've never been one to break a promise. And this one I will keep, even if I have to kill the motherfucker myself.

A few days after the letter's arrival, we get the expectant subpoena he promised. It gives us the name of the clinic with appointment time and case number. It also provides a court date for the results to be read, but we already know what it will say, and knowing the truth doesn't change the fact that in my heart Finlee Breanne Reed is my daughter. Deep down I was really hoping it was a bluff, but he seems adamant about pursuing this. Jazz called Allison and she hadn't received a letter at the time, but the next day it came and said something similar to ours. She has her lawyer looking into it, and they both believe it's a bluff, but the guy has balls.

Walking into the courtroom we keep our attention on the judge and not the asshole on the left. For someone I used to admire in the classroom he has truly become someone I despise in the real world. Don't get me wrong, I wouldn't mind him being in Fin's life because every child should know their dad, but trying for full custody when the mother is a hardworking and loving person? That's just cruel and selfish. And if he truly wanted her in his life then why not come by and try to see her. We haven't heard a word from the guy besides the letter. I have a feeling there is an ulterior motive for all the theatrics and not just the children. I just don't know what yet.

After the judge calls order we all stand while the bailiff brings the yellow manila envelope over and places it in the judge's hands. Jazz reaches for my hand and puts a death grip on it. She is so scared I can feel her body shaking. Dropping her hand, I place my arm on her small shoulders and hold her close, needing to take that fear away. I kiss her temple and look behind us. Tru and Jax are a few rows back with Finlee. We weren't going to bring her but Jazz didn't want to be away from her for too long, so they came for support and to kick the shit out of the guy if needed.

The judge opens the envelope and takes out the papers. "Mr. Oliver Morris Wallace. It seems you are the father of three month old Finlee Breanne Reed. Congratulations." He hits the gavel and dismisses us all.

"Thank you, Charles. Sorry, Judge Steiner." Oliver smiles like a snake and rubs his palms together. "Now I want to meet my daughter." He makes his way over to where we're standing.

Tru and Jax are already by us and Jazz has Fin wrapped in her arms. I kiss her tear stained cheek. "Hey. We'll make this work. He has nothing on you. It takes some really heavy shit for a mother to lose her children."

"Oh don't be too sure, Mr. Reed. Now pass me my child." Oliver reaches out and after a moment of hesitation Jazz gives her over. He looks down and scrutinizes everything. "Oh she's perfect. The only thing that needs to change is the name. Really what kind of name is Finlee? And we'll definitely need to fix the last name. I mean she looks just like me and no child of mine will have any other name than Wallace."

I take a deep breath before I knock the shit out of the bastard. Jax must notice because he shakes his head. But I also see the anger he's also holding back. Not causing a scene is harder than I thought.

"Finlee is a great name. So it's not changing. You might be the biological father and you can be in her life, but you can't just barge in three months later and act like you give a shit. And you definitely won't dictate what I choose to call my daughter." She sticks her arms out when Fin wakes up from the commotion and starts to cry. "Now give her to me. I need to nurse her."

He hands her back and glares at her menacingly before I step in and give him a look that says "back the fuck off."

"Well I got news. She's my child and I will have a say in her life. So stop being a dramatic child per usual." He walks away but looks over his shoulder. "Oh and expect to hear from my lawyer very soon. I really don't think you're fit and healthy enough to care for a child, and I'm sure Charles will agree with me."

"You son of a—" Jax's arm is around my waist holding me back.

"Not the place, man. Not the place."

The bailiff's watching us and straightens his shoulders, ready to come over if he sees fit. I take a deep breath and shake off Jax's hold even though I'm far from calm. "I'm good." My eyes stay trained on the dick in a pressed suit as he walks away.

Chapter Twenty-Nine

Jazz

After the paternity reading we decide a weekend at the beach is needed. So after packing half the nursery up, because I freaked about leaving something, we head to Mom and Dad's. When I step out of my Tahoe, I see my parents sitting together on the white steps of the front porch. I immediately run to them and let the tears fall. With the warmth of their bodies surrounding me, and the sensation of salty wind in my hair, I feel like a child again. Sometimes even adults need their parents when they're scared or having a shitty day. I still think my dad is a super hero who will kill the bad guy and my mom is Mary Poppins with the best medicine to make it all better.

When I finish Mason grabs my hand and we all head inside. After the first hour I know the normalcy is exactly what I've needed. My nerves are much better after seeing everyone, and I really can't help but laugh at Cohen. He is still crushing on Tru and continues to keep Jax away as much as possible. He's a sly little booger, and Jax can't blame anyone but himself. He did teach him everything he knows. Suave Cohen even went as far as to bring her a ring from a quarter machine that he had wrapped up with a bow. After he placed it on her finger and she thanked him, he looked at Jax and told him that he could still be in the wedding. I can't help but smile and it's been constant. I love my family and without them I don't know where I'd be.

Even my sixteen-year-old brother Drew stays home instead of going out with his entourage of friends. He says I'm more important and he wants to be here in case "the wasted fuck" shows up. Hitting him in the shoulder like a good big sister, I tell him to watch his mouth. But he sees my smile. Knowing Mason and I aren't alone in all this makes it better in a way. It gives me hope that no matter what Oliver says or threatens to do, I will not lose the family that has formed over the past year. He hasn't seen the Colemans in action when it comes to fighting for our loved ones, but he's about too.

David comes up Saturday and the guys go surfing. Mason wasn't going to go because he's worried about me, but he needs some guy time. I ask David to get him out there and make him have fun. Being David, he makes a bet with Mason that skateboarding doesn't take as much skill as surfing and then it's on. It's funny to watch my man's macho side come out.

After packing up, Dad asks to speak with us in his office before we head home. Walking through the door brings back Thanksgiving Day memories and I can't believe how things have changed in the past ten months.

Dad sits at his desk and dials a number while on speakerphone. When the person answers I know immediately its Dr. Whitney. "Hello, Jeremiah. I got your message earlier and I'm glad you called. Is Jasmine able to hear me?"

"I'm here, Doctor Whitney. And so is Mason."

"Good. Well I hope you're okay with your dad calling me and informing me of the situation. I'm so sorry you're having to deal with this, but I want you to understand that in any case, heart issues or not, taking a child away from the mother is a difficult task. She basically has to be deemed mentally ill, have an unstable home, neglect the child, and a number of other situations that don't count for you. But there is one I'll let your father discuss. You are healthy and there are no health issues that will affect you raising your child. So with that said I'll see you for your follow-up in a few weeks and I'm sure all of this will blow over."

His words have really helped me with my insecurities of my heart issue, the one thing that has always haunted me in a way. "Thank you doctor, Whitney." After the phone disconnects, I sit heavily on the couch and exhale loudly.

"Feel better?" Mason sits to my left and wraps me in his arms. Nodding into his shoulder, I inhale his comforting scent that reminds me of home. "Good, but remember your dad needs to talk to us."

"Thanks, Mason. I wanted to—" The door opens and Mom walks in with Finlee. After she hands her to me she stands beside Dad.

"Have you told them yet?"

"Not yet. But I'm glad you're here." He kisses her temple before he turns his attention back to us. "Okay. There is an issue that may or may not be a reason for this guy to try for custody." Sitting up, I give him my full attention. "A judge likes to see a stable home life for a child, and yours could be deemed unstable depending on the judge."

"What? How is our home unstable?" My heart rate picks up as my calmness starts to disappear. And honestly I'm a little insulted.

"It's not unstable by today's standards, but didn't you say he was friends with this judge?" Mason and I nod in unison. "Then he could see the image of you two living together out of wedlock as unstable and use it against you."

"But we're engaged. Doesn't that count?" Mason squeezes the hand that rests on his knee.

"Like I said before, it depends on the judge. And I have a feeling if he actually wants to take you to court for any reason he'll try to get a judge he's close with."

Mason releases my hand and leans his elbows on his knees with an exhale. I can't help but reach over with my free hand and rub his muscular back. "So what should we do? I don't want to move out and leave Jazz and Fin unprotected."

Observing Mom and Dad, I see them look at one another and feel like they are reading each other's mind. I hope one day Mason and I have that type of connection.

“What your father and I think is that you two should get married. Soon.”

My mouth hangs open with shock. “Soon? How soon?” I peek at Mason, who is sporting a small smile along his profile. He must see me staring because he looks my way and winks. I return it happily.

Mom starts to glow as she faces us. “You could go to the courthouse any day during the week and get it done. But I would love to have a little gathering afterward or even a small wedding. Oliver won’t do anything until he gets another job and builds a case so we have time to plan a little something. And if you two give me a month I can seriously whip up a ceremony here on the beach.”

Wow! Talk about the unexpected subject. I have to admit they have a point, and we are already engaged and living together. I want to be sure this is something Mason wants before jumping up and down with wedding excitement. Even planning a small, intimate one is exhilarating.

“Can you two give us a few minutes to talk about this before we give an answer?”

They agree and make their exit, but I have a feeling they’re not far past the door, especially Mom. She has been going nonstop about wedding ideas since she found out I was engaged. A date was never set because of all the shit Oliver started. He’s a pain in my ass and I refuse to let him ruin my happiness with his annoying intimidation.

“What do you think?” I can tell Mason’s nervous. His voice always adopts a small quiver and some words become high pitched. It’s one reason why I love him. Tingles start to radiate up my arm, and I place Fin on my shoulder. “Honestly, the whole subject caught me by surprise. I know we’re engaged and plan on marriage, but I also know you're wanting to get further in school." Standing, I bounce her and think of my next words. I've never sugar coated anything so I'll just be honest. "But I want to marry you." I stop and look in his direction. "I'd do it today if I could. I'll do it tomorrow if you want to. But I won't force you to rush into anything you're not ready for. Just know whenever you are ready I'll be ready."

He stands and walks in front of me, staring down. The sunlight coming in the window causes his eyes to turn the most beautiful shade of green I've ever seen. It always surprises me how they can look brown in the shade and emerald in the light. With dark lashes surrounding them, the contrast is indescribable. He reaches up and touches my cheek. I feel the callus of his thumb rub gently and my pulse picks up, not only with a desire that heats me to my core, but with love so real it heals every wound I've ever had and will have in my life. It makes me whole and complete.

"I'd have married you a year ago. I'd have married you yesterday. And I'll definitely marry you tomorrow or any day after that." He kisses Fin's head. "You two are my world and I need my world to live. So you tell me when and I'll be there."

Call me selfish, but I want to hear him say it again. "Really? You'd marry me tomorrow?"

"Really. If you want we can go straight to the courthouse and do it."

"Would you care if I wanted a teeny tiny wedding?"

"Nope. I wouldn't care if you wanted the biggest wedding of all weddings. As long as you're happy."

"Well you are in luck, babe. Because I only want a small one here, on the water, where I grew up. Where you made the stupidest decision last Thanksgiving that turned out to be the best decision in disguise. And I want Gigi and your whole family to come and stay on the beach. We can look into renting a house for them. Is that okay?"

"Like I said before, we can do anything that makes you happy."

Ideas start popping in my head of colors, dresses, and even food. I smile mischievously. He has no idea what he just got into. Or maybe he does and that's why he loves me.

Mom discovering Pinterest for wedding ideas is a bad idea, considering we only have four weeks until the ceremony. Announcing the news to people is exciting and surreal because the more I say it, the more real it becomes. This time next month I will be Jasmine Reed. It's not going to be a huge ceremony or anything, and the wedding party only consists of my close friends. Tru will be my maid of honor, while Cory and Symone my only two bridesmaids. Kenzie is a little upset when she isn't chosen, but I tell her she has to be a flower girl with Fin and hold her while rolling down the dock/pier. That brings an immediate smile to her face like I knew it would. She loves her niece. Mr. Cohen will be the ring bearer, but instead of walking he wants to drive his Jeep. I tell Mom not just no, but "hell no." He'll drive off once he spots a pretty girl on the beach. She only laughed and I know my argument went ignored. Of course Mason chooses Jax as his best man with Ryan and David as his groomsmen. I worry about Cory, figuring she'd be upset about walking with Ryan down the aisle, but she swears she's fine with it. And she's even bringing Bo as her date. It seems they have really hit it off and I'm surprised. But I really have no right to be. I mean, look at Mason and me. Total opposites. Maybe country boy Bo and rock chick Cory will end up with a happily ever after.

The main color really doesn't surprise anyone. Pink of course. But not just any pink, hot pink mixed with a silver-grey and black to give it an elegant appearance. Because the day will be elegant and the best day of my life.

As the days pass with busy planning and schedules for food tastings and fittings, no word is heard from Oliver. I'm grateful but still surprised. And as much as I tell myself not to worry, a bad feeling remains in my gut and refuses to leave. I refuse to think about it today because Mom, Tru, Cory, and I are going to pick out dresses. I am so excited and nervous.

"What if I can't find a dress that gives me my moment?" I ask while pulling into the Bridal Boutique.

Cory looks at me like I'm stupid. "What moment? When you say I do or when Mason makes you scream his name in three different languages? You know what they say about the quiet ones, right? They make you holler the loudest." She wiggles her groomed brows and I can't help but laugh.

"No, you horny dork. The moment when I see myself in the dress and I know it's the one. Like on those bridal gown shows. What if all those chicks on TLC are paid to cry and have somebody poke them in the eye and my expectations are too high so I love a dress but refuse to get it because I don't cry? And what if I go back for that dress and it's gone. What do I do then?"

Mom places her arm on my knee to get me to stop rambling and calm my nerves. "It's not fake, sweetheart. You'll get your moment. And if the dress isn't here then we'll go somewhere else. Remember your aunt Sophie is a seamstress and will add or subtract anything you want. She's been dying to help out."

My aunt used to own her own boutique in New Orleans that sold hand sewn dresses for women and children. She would always make me some of the cutest clothes when I was little, and I'm planning on getting her to make Fin some as well. She lost the shop when Katrina hit and everything was ruined. After that she decided to move closer to Mom. She's been contemplating on opening another one, but it hasn't happened yet.

Feeling better, we make our way in the shop and notice the continuous racks of color coordinated dresses in different styles and fabrics. "I don't see the wedding dresses," I say but get no reply.

Looking around I see Tru's wide eyes taking in all the racks of clothes. When she pulls out a price tag they become even wider before she drops it and turns away. She's so funny when it comes to spending money. Jax has tried multiple times to get her to go shopping for herself, but she always buys him something instead. Not me. I absolutely love to shop.

And from the looks of it Cory does too. "Hell yeah, Jazz! Look at this one." She holds up a black dress that's backless and has a cut out for a bare midriff. "This is hot. Add some fishnet tights and thigh high slut boots and you wouldn't be the only one getting some that night."

"Nope. Not going to have a dominatrix for a bridesmaid. And especially with my grandparents there." She reluctantly places it back.

I spot Mom speaking with an older lady behind the counter. She looks to be in her early sixties and is dressed for business in a skirt suit of teal. It looks great with her salt and pepper hair. The lady pours each of us some champagne before walking over.

"Good morning, Miss Coleman." She hands me my glass. "I hope you're ready to find your dream dress today. Shall we head upstairs to the white room?" After I nod she regally walks ahead and leads us into a friggin' wedding dress emporium.

It's the holy grail of dressing rooms, and I hope Heaven looks just this way. It's a room with white couches and chairs along the walls that are decorated with colorful throw pillows. Each couch has a colorful table with a white centerpiece in the middle and chocolate kisses in a white bowl. Fan-fucking-tastic! Taking a candy out of one, I notice the walls are adorned in the most beautiful black and white wedding photographs and intricate mirrors. She leads us to an area with a white platform surrounded almost completely by mirrors. The only two exceptions are the sitting area for my party and an archway that I presume leads to the dresses.

After everyone's seated she leads me to the dressing area where we start talking. I find out her name is Gail and her mother opened the shop years ago. She and her daughters run it now and from the looks of it, business is booming. After she asks me some very detailed questions regarding my colors, venue, and what I would like in my dress, I start the tedious task of trying on dress after dress after dress. After several hours of no luck, I start to feel defeated and a possible nervous breakdown coming on. Then Gail brings out one more. It's a white princess style gown that's sleeveless with a straight neckline. The bodice is embellished with jewels and the bottom is made of beautiful layered taffeta. It has a white sash that can be dyed to any color around the waist and creates a bow that falls along my left hipbone. After I'm zipped up and see myself in the mirror, Gail places a jeweled tiara on my head to add to the effect. And what do you know? I have my moment.

A few days later I'm back at home getting Fin ready for her checkup with her pediatrician while Mason is in class, and I hear a knock on the door. Picking her up off my bed, I walk to the front and look in the peephole. The person on the other side is a complete surprise to see after all these weeks of no word. I debate on even opening it, but I know Mason would want me to.

Chanda stands on the other side, but she doesn't look the same as she did the last time she showed up. Instead of the busted lip and black eyes, she looks good, happy even. Her hair has grown out past her ears and she's not running around half naked. She's wearing some khaki capris and a plaid button down. "Hey, Jasmine. Sorry to bother you. Is Mason here?"

I still don't like his name coming out of her mouth, but I know they used to be good friends. "No, he isn't. He's in class and won't be back for a few hours."

"Good. I really wanted to talk to you. Can I come in?"

Surprised and wary, I think about it. She seems harmless and actually nice, so why the hell not? "Sure. Come on in." I lead her into the living area and place Fin in her pack 'n play that sits against the wall. "Mason and his mom have been worried sick about you. Where'd you disappear too anyway?" I sit across from her on the couch.

She smiles and shrugs. "Well, I needed to get away so I moved in with a friend. But that went to shit …" She stops and covers her mouth. "Sorry. Didn't mean to cuss in front of the little one. What's her name?"

"Finlee. And it's fine. She doesn't repeat words yet."

"Oh, that's a nice name. Different. Well, anyways, I ended up meeting someone. He helped me see that I'm more than the life I was living and could do better. I'm even enrolling into a GED program."

"Wow, Chanda. That's great. Mason and Brenda will be happy to hear that." An awkward silence falls between us. We've never been friends, so I really don't know what to say to the girl. Might as well get to why she's here. "So what did you want to talk to me about?"

She nervously tucks her hair behind her ear. "Well, I wanted to apologize for being a major bitch to you in the past. It's just Mason has always been my way out of this shitty life I have. I knew he'd do amazing things one day and would get out of the low class hole we grew up in. And I wanted out. And I thought he'd always be in love with me and take me with him. He was my future ... until I met this other guy of course." She smiles but it seems forced. "So since I'm in a better place I wanted to say thank you. Thank you for loving Mason like he deserves and not using him like I was. Oh and congratulations on the upcoming wedding."

The girl in front of me is saying the right words, but I can't fight the feeling she doesn't mean them, that they're practiced. Maybe it's because she has caused Mason and me so much drama throughout our relationship that

I'm not ready to believe her. My phone ringing from down the hall and breaks through my musings.

"Shit! I'll be right back." Back in my room I spot it on my bed and see it's Mason. "Hey you."

"Hey, baby. How are my girls?" I'll never get tired of his voice or the way it can change from sweet to feral in a second. Thoughts of last night surface, but I quickly shake it off. *Not the time for a replay.* I close my bedroom door so Chanda can't hear our conversation. Apartment walls are thin. When I tell him of my visitor in the living room he sounds just as surprised that she's here. He's really stunned when I tell him about her apology for being a bitch to me and what she did. I don't want to let her take up our whole conversation, so I change the subject to tonight's plans with Jax and Tru. We try to get together a couple times a week and have game night or go to the movies if Brenda can watch Fin. After we hang up I head back in the living room.

I start down the hall and notice Chanda is no longer on the couch where I left her. "Sorry about that." But only silence greets me and trepidation takes root. Spinning around frantically, I don't see her anywhere in the living room or the kitchen area. "Chanda?" I call, but no one answers, not even Fin's usual gurgling. Fear takes over my whole body and my stomach drops with each second that passes. Everything slows down and I can hear only my heart hammering in my head. Running as fast as possible to Fin, I notice she's no longer there and my whole world collapses.

Chapter Thirty

Mason

Sitting at my uncomfortable desk, I stare at my test, ready to finish and get home. This surprise quiz is the last thing I want to be doing. And it shows in my answers, or lack of. I've only written my name at the top of my paper. Man, oh man! Jazz in the shower last night is really what's on my mind, not molecular levels of different species. Unfortunately I have another class after this one, so it will be a while before I can get a replay of her on her knees with water cascading down he blonde hair. Feeling the vibration of my phone, I jump and quickly silence it before the instructor hears. As soon as I do it starts up again.

"Mr. Reed, is there a problem?" The instructor is a short round man, who I think colors his greying beard with possible shoe polish. I swear every time he wipes his face some comes off, but he is smart when it comes to scientific shit.

Looking up from the papers in front of me, I watch as he holds out his hand. "Bring it here. You can get it back after the—"

The door slams open and Jax runs in wearing a fearful expression. "Mason. We need to go. Now."

"Excuse me, sir. You can't just barge into—"

"I can and I just did," Jax yells so loud the class jumps.

My heart rate spikes and I yank my bag off the floor, not caring if shit falls out. "What's wrong? Is it Jazz?"

He shakes his head. "It's Fin. She's been kidnapped."

I hear everyone's deep inhalation of breath just as mine escapes my lungs. Fear and anger war in my body while I pass him and run toward my truck. My mind is on Jazz and my little girl so I end up going the wrong way. "Mason. I'll drive." We run to his Jeep and I notice Tru's in the back crying.

"What the hell happened?" My voice is low because of the burn clogging my throat, but I fight it. Tears will only blur my vision and cause me to seem weak. And I know Jazz needs me to be strong.

"Chanda came over and Jazz says when she walked back into the living room she was gone. So was Fin." Jax speeds through traffic with his hazard lights on, but no speed is fast enough. It won't change what happened or get Fin back any quicker.

After a second his words register in my head. "Chanda? What? Why would she take Fin?" That fucking bitch! How could someone take a child and not just a random person, but someone I've known for years? But the answer doesn't change anything. All that matters is getting my daughter back. Then I'll make that bitch pay.

Later that night we're still no closer to finding answers or Fin. Police have been in and out all day asking questions, and the whole time I've had to watch Jazz relive every second Chanda was here and the second she knew Fin was gone. It has broken me and left me feeling powerless. I've tried to hold her several times, but she can't be still. She's restless and keeps looking at the clock. With every hour that passes the further Fin could be getting away from us and the chances of us finding her lessen. To think that just this morning I fed her while she played with my finger. I kissed her head of soft brown hair and told her I loved her. And now she's gone.

After the police finally leave for the night silence engulfs the apartment. Everyone is here, including my mom and her parents. Drew is keeping the little kids at Jax's apartment, and until we have more answers we won't tell them what's going on. Cory and Ryan showed up an hour or so ago and are sitting in the living room lost in their own thoughts with everyone else. It's weird seeing everyone together and not laughing. But tonight there's only grief, fear, and a shitload of anger.

"She's probably hungry." Jazz's voice is a sad whisper. She stands looking out the window so I go to her, wanting to do something, anything for her. "She has no food. She doesn't have any diapers or her favorite blanket. What if she's cold? How will she get warm?"

My heart breaks a little more with each question that leaves her mouth. I wrap my arms around her waist and let her lean against me, wanting to absorb her grief. "Shhh, don't do this to yourself, baby."

She pulls away irritably and starts pacing the room while everyone watches in silence. "Why, Mason? Why shouldn't I?" Her voice is loud, broken, and angered. "She's my daughter and some bitch you brought into our lives took her. So why shouldn't I be concerned for her? Chanda doesn't know a thing about Fin. She's just a selfish bitch who is money hungry and desperate. I have no idea what she'll do to her? She could sell Fin on the black market just for her next fix for all I know. And I can't stop her. I'm her mother and I should have protected her better." She stops pacing and looks at me with so much turmoil written on her face that my soul hurts. Clara gets up and gently touches her shoulder, but she yanks it away. "Don't. Don't comfort me. I deserve what I'm feeling. I don't deserve anyone's sympathy or concern. Why should I get any when she's probably scared and can't tell anyone what she wants or needs?" She takes a shuddering breath but only crumbles more. "Because of me she's gone. Because of me not trusting my gut she's missing. And there's not a fucking thing I can do about it."

Having enough of her feeling responsible for what happened, I walk over and grab her into a hug. She fights me and tries to escape my hold but I refuse this time. "You listen to me. We'll get her back. I'll hunt that bitch down and get our daughter back. I promise." Kissing her head, I feel her yield and latch on to me. Her cries are my fuel to make this right. "I love you so damn much. I'm getting her back." Looking at Clara, I nod my head. She comes and takes Jazz from me as I grab my keys off the table. Fuck the cops telling us to stay home. I run to my truck and get in. Before I can crank it I see Jax, Ryan, and David get in. "Y'all don't need to come."

"Fuck yeah we do. That bitch took our niece and we're getting her back." We hit the streets daring any motherfucker to stop us.

An hour later we pull into a hole-in-the-wall bar where supposedly Chanda likes to hang out. Ryan called Lyric and asked him if he's seen her. According to Lyric she hasn't been there in a few weeks, but one can only hope she shows up tonight. Of course she wouldn't bring Fin with her so she'd have to leave her with someone else. And right now I'm warring with myself which one I'd prefer. Chanda is obviously working with someone else and has a fucking death wish. I was raised not to hit women, but it's going to take everything in me to stop myself when I see her.

Walking in, I'm assaulted with a heavy whiff of liquor, cigarettes, and marijuana. The four of us get stared down and pushed while looking through the rough crowd. Ryan seems to actually know people here so he's hollering continuously in someone's ear. I keep my eyes trained on the swarm of faces, and I really want to stand on a table or some shit to get a better look. The smoke filled room makes it difficult to see everyone's face. I know there's a stage somewhere because Ryan said Lyric used to play here acoustically and it's where they formed Lyrical Obsessions. I can see why. Their music is dark and angry, exactly how I feel tonight.

"I got something," Ryan hollers to Jax, David, and me before he makes his way to some pool tables stuck in the back. When he nears one with three guys playing a game, he speeds up his steps. Then he grabs the long ponytail of one of the guy's and slams his head against table. Ryan wears a savage sneer as he holds the guy's face into the wood. "Hey, Zitshit. Long time no see, you fucking pussy." He yanks him up and turns him to face us but keeps a hold on his collar so he's still in the guy's face.

I go on alert and my back straightens, ready for someone to jump me at any moment. I'm not a fighter at heart, but tonight I'll fuck up anyone who wants a round. Until my daughter is back safe with Jazz, I'll take on this whole bar if I need to.

The guy must see something feral in Ryan's eyes because he throws his arms up in surrender. That or he's seen Ryan fight before. He even tells his friends to back up with a shake of his head when they try to interfere.

"What the fuck man?" His pupils look dilated and sunken into his ashen skin. The red acne covering his cheeks is the only color on his face while his jeans are faded and hang low showcasing his underwear.

"My friends and I got a few questions and we want answers. Got it?" The guy nods. "Where's your friend Chanda been lately? And don't think about lying either because Lyric is on his way. And you know what that means for you and your boys, right?" His eyes widen and his face pales when Lyric's name is mentioned. "Now where is she?"

"I—I don't know, man. She disappeared a few weeks ago. I've been looking for her myself because that bitch owes me money."

Ryan lets him go and looks at his clenched fist. "Not the right answer." He punches him so hard the guy spits out a tooth.

"Excuse me, son. You causing trouble here?" Looking behind me I see an older man with a long grey beard holding a twelve gauge shotgun in his large hands. This is the first time I notice the audience surrounding the dead silence and us. The guy approaches, ready to intervene, but stops when Lyric walks through the crowd that parts with every step he takes. It's like he's some kind of god, a god who's tatted up and wearing a backwards cap.

He touches the guy's shoulder just one time and waits for him to put the gun back behind the bar. Then he approaches Ryan and only the sound of his boots are heard along the worn, wooden floor. He nods to Ryan to move and then takes his place. The guy holds his busted mouth and looks like he's about to shit his pants as Lyric stands facing him. I look at Jax and David and see the same question on their faces. What the fuck is going on?

"So, Z, I heard you've been selling bad shit on my streets again. That correct?" Lyric stands calmly looking at his fingernails, like he's discussing the weather or some shit. "And I really wouldn't lie about it if I were you." The guy swallows hard and you can see beads of sweat build up on his forehead, but he remains silent. "Well, I'll tell you what. You tell Ryan what he wants to know and I'll let you by this time. If you don't tell him…" he smiles with cold eyes and places his arm around Z's shoulders "...well, if you don't tell him I'm going to cut out your tongue and use it as an example for your fucking cohorts since you don't like talking these days anyway. Sound like a deal?"

Everyone stands in silence while waiting to see what happens next. Fortunately the guy decides to talk. When he says "blacked out Escalade" I know exactly whom Chanda's working with and who has Fin. I'm helpless because I have no idea where to find them. Thankfully, I know who will.

As we make our way back to my truck I tell the guys what I suspect before I call Jazz to check on her and get the number I need. Clara's voice isn't what I was expecting. "How is she?"

“She’s asleep right now. Her father gave her something to help calm her down. Shortly after you all left that asshole professor showed up.”

Her words have me slamming the door as I get in the drivers seat. *Fuck! Why did I leave her?* “What did he say?” He has balls to show up after taking Fin. My hatred for that fucker is really makes me have murder on the brain. Visions of punching the guy are interrupted when I hear a scratching on the other line before Mr. Coleman comes on the line.

“Mason, did you find anything?

“Yes and No. I was calling to get a number out of Jazz’s phone. It’s Allison. Oliver’s ex-wife. What did he say to her?”

As everyone loads into the truck I can’t help but tap the steering wheel, desperate to get rid my anxiousness. I listen as he explains how that asshole yelled how a good mother wouldn’t lose her child and he will be talking to his lawyer soon. Pulling out on the road I let the tires squeal and burn ready to find the fucker.

“Don’t worry. My fist shut him up before he left.”

Yeah right! Telling me not to worry is a lost cause. I can’t help but worry about Fin and Jazz. “Thanks, Jeremiah. But shit! I wish I was there.”

“I know. But I handled it and you’re doing what needs to be done. Here, I found the number. But why call her at three in the morning?”

“No time to explain, but I’ll call you back as soon as I can.” We end our call after he gives me Allison’s number. I anxiously call her but she doesn’t answer. I press redial and on the third try she finally picks up. “Allison, it’s Mason. I need to know where Oliver is staying?”

Her voice is gruff and you can tell she just woke up. “Huh? Oh my God, Mason, did you get Fin back? And why do you want to know where he lives? Especially at this time?”

“Because I’m pretty sure he took Fin.” I hear her inhale sharply but luckily she doesn’t ask any questions.

After she gives me the information, I hang up and we head to our destination. It’s about an hours drive away in the middle of nowhere, but the more I drive the farther it seems. Hearing a beep, I look down and see I’m almost out of fuel.

“Shit!” The guys are in the back with tonight’s commotion at the bar as the topic of conversation. Ryan won’t tell us what the hell went down tonight no matter how much David begs. And honestly, I really don’t want to know. Whoever Lyric Devereux is, I don’t want to mess with him.

After pulling into the gas station I step out and open the gas tank door only to see a folded piece of paper fall on the ground. Picking it up before I forget, I start the pump and then unfold the letter. Nothing could prepare me for what it says.

Mason,

I don’t know when you’ll find this but I hope it’s soon. Oliver has a family wanting Finlee unless you can pay more than their offer of one hundred thousand dollars. He’s well aware of Jazz’s trust fund as well as your new funds. Bring the money to the address written on the bottom before three days time and she’s all yours. If you show up without the money, then she’s gone.

P.S. Don't be stupid and call the cops. Fin and I are somewhere you won't find us if you do. Plus the family is really looking forward to adopting a child like her. You know. To help out a single mother like myself.

Chanda

"Fuck!" I yell and slam my fist on the side of my truck. I hear and feel the crunch in my knuckles, but the physical pain is nothing compared to how I am emotionally. The guys come around and David grabs the letter out of my swelling hand. I can't answer the questions they are asking because my fury is suffocating me. All I picture is finding the two pieces of shit and torturing them before I go home with Fin. What kind of a person can sell their own daughter?

"Whoa, dude. Listen to this, Jax." David reads the letter aloud, but I try not to hear the words again.

Covering my ears, I squat down to catch my breath and think. I can't go to the bank and get the money out until in the morning. Hell! I don't even know if they'll give it to me. That is a lot for one transaction. I start to pace as the guys talk, but right now I can't listen to them. I wanted to get Fin back and have Jazz wake up to her, but that's not going to happen. I'll have to wait and get the money first thing in the morning.

"Mason we need to get your hand looked at and go to the cops." Jax's words have my head coming up in alarm.

"No cops. Didn't you read the note? They'll give her to only God knows who." I look at my right hand and see the swelling and bruising that's already forming. "I'll just put ice on it. It's not a big deal. I need to be at the bank when they open." Standing up, I move to get in the truck, but Ryan stops me.

"Man, you need to go to the hospital and get it looked at. You know the drill. Besides the bank doesn't open for five hours. You'll be out of the ER by then. So give me your damn keys. I'm driving." Reluctantly, I hand over my keys and let them take me to the hospital.

Jax stays with me while Ryan and David head back to my apartment. After being called to the back, I'm diagnosed with a boxer's fracture and they put my hand in a splint. I continuously look at the clock and check on Jazz while waiting for discharge. When I'm finally released, Jax and I walk out and see David. "Where's Ryan?"

"He said he had something to do but he'd be back soon." I once again look at the clock and see it's only seven in the morning. Shit! I still have two hours. David drives in silence to the apartment while I try to think of what to tell Jazz. Disappointment is not what I want to see on her face this morning. I want to find my girls together like every morning. "David, where's the note? I want to make sure I keep it with me."

He digs in his pocket. "Here you go. Ryan had it."

I slowly open it up, dreading reading the words again. I want the address imprinted into my brain so I don't forget where I need to go. When the paper unfolds, it's not the note from Chanda. This one is from Ryan and I'm once again wondering what the fuck is going on.

Mason,

Fin will be back before banks open. Lyric knows people so I gave him the address on the note. He might be a scary motherfucker, but he doesn't believe in kidnapping. Oliver will be disappearing for a while, but Chanda will be locked up for kidnapping. You shouldn't have to worry about either one for a long time. This never happened so burn this ASAP. Got it?

Ryan

Before I know it we're back and the parking lot is once again surrounded with police as well as News stations. Jumping out, I race through the crowd needing to get to Jazz. After I finally make it up the steps I see my apartment door is open. Getting closer I see police and EMTs checking out Jazz as she sits on a stool. She has tears running down her face and I start to panic. "Jazz! Are you okay?" Racing to her side, I stop when I'm standing a foot away. I step closer cautiously; scared that what I'm seeing is an illusion. When I'm right beside her Jazz looks up smiling happily, and I fall to my knees when my legs give out. My eyes fall from her face to the bundle in her lap. It the most beautiful sight I've ever seen: my beautiful Fin asleep in Jazz's arms—where she belongs.

Epilogue

Jazz

"A toast to Mr. and Mrs. Reed." The crowd goes crazy after Ryan's speech on Jay Jay's stage. With those words I hold Mason a little tighter. Even though we've been married a week, I will never get tired of hearing them. I'm officially Mrs. Jasmine Marie Reed. Holding out my left hand, I admire the matching white gold band with pink diamonds that sits alongside my astonishing engagement ring. My man knows me so well. I feel like the luckiest girl in the world. It may not have been love at first sight, but I know it's forever for us. He's my other half and my soul mate, but most of all he's my hero. He's been there for me through everything. And not just me, but Fin as well. Speaking of Fin, I feel a vibration in my pocket and know Brenda has sent me another picture of the girls together. My anxiety from her kidnapping is still an everyday issue, but we manage and I'm positive it'll get better.

It's been a month since she was taken and a month since Chanda turned herself in. When she was asked in court why she did it, she never gave an answer. I don't care though. As long as Fin's back in my arms, I couldn't give two shits if there was a reason or not. She's lucky that bars separate her from me because it would not be pretty.

Mason's mom is keeping the kids tonight at our place while we're out. Leaving her has been difficult for me, but tonight is a special party thrown by our friends since we never planned a honeymoon. I really can't do more than that. One night away from Fin is pushing my limits, and I know Mason feels the same way. Maybe one day we will have an actual trip with just the two of us, but just not today.

The day he walked in and saw Fin in my arms he cried in front of me for the first time. I never thought a man's tears would cause me to fall in love with him all over again, or for that love to be ten times stronger, but it did. It confirmed how much Fin means to him. How much we mean to him. To know he's been up all night looking for her was so self-sacrificing. I never asked what he went through that night and he never told me. Reliving that day and night is something I never want to do, so the less said the better.

"Hey. Why the tears?" Mason wipes my cheek with his thumb as we sit at our table listening to our friends.

"Nothing bad. I'm just happy." I smile up at him, admiring his shaggy hair and the way it falls the across his forehead and the dark green of his eyes. Well they actually look brown in this lighting, but I know the truth. I know him. “I love you, my husband.” His smile widens, displaying his cute dimples.

“I love you too, my wife. Want to dance?” He grabs my hand off the table and leads me to the crowded dance floor.

“Wait you two.” I look and see Tru and Cory blocking our path.

“Why? Mason was about to show me his moves, and besides, I love this song.” Bruno Mars’ *Treasure* is playing and I can’t wait to reenact our first night dancing. Mason looked so out of place and even when I danced close to him, he still wouldn’t touch me. The memory causes another smile to form.

“Because Jax is talking to the DJ. I have a song for you two. I think it fits and Cory agrees.”

“Okay, why can’t we dance to both?” Mason asks them.

“Because I want a video of you two dancing together. I want to video the whole thing from beginning to end. So you need to wait. We didn’t really get one at the wedding because you two kept Fin the whole time. And your first dance looks more like a game of Ring Around the Rosy.”

We concede and wait until we get the okay. Cory is right. The whole wedding Fin was within arm’s reach. My separation anxiety is strange but everyone understands, even Mason. I’m hopeful it will get better because I want to enjoy my husband without a sleeping infant in the same room. I want to get loud and rowdy like the last time we stayed at a hotel together. I did get some amazing toys from Cory as a wedding present and I’m eager to try them. Definitely tonight.

When the song starts with a beautiful piano melody, we make our way through the crowd and settle in the middle. Mason pulls me close and as the song's words pour through the speakers I know it's perfect for the two of us. "What is this?" I ask Mason.

"John Legend's *All of Me*." He starts to sing in my ear and shivers run down to my toes and back up my skull.

It's beautiful and his voice is surprisingly soulful and so unexpected. My heart is full of this man who loves me with my scars and all. This man who has healed me with his love and devotion to make me happy. I close my eyes and just take in the feel of him wrapped around me. Take in his scent as it surrounds me and makes me feel at home. Take in the words that he sings to me that fit how I feel about him. All of me loves all of him. Forever.

After we dance to a few more songs, slow and fast, we head back to our friends who are laughing and hollering. Ryan is necking some chick that I'm positive was just kissing David. I see another bimbo in David's lap and know he definitely doesn't care. Rolling my eyes, I sit beside Cory who is still with Bo. They actually go out on dates, and when I asked her about it she told me to drop it so I did. I still see how she watches Ryan. I might not be good with book smarts, but I know when someone is jealous. And she is the definition of jealous. Just ask the straw that's mangled in her hand. Tru is off tonight and she sits comfortably in my brother's lap with her arms wrapped around his neck. Jax isn't drinking because he wants Tru to act like her age for once. Even though she's only had two shots, you can tell she's pretty tipsy and I can't wait to see her on the dance floor again. Sitting beside Ryan is Lyric. He just stares at everyone who walks our way, like he's always on alert or something. He doesn't drink but smokes like a freight train. He never smiles and barely talks unless it's to Ryan. His eyes land on mine and I feel my heart drop but cover it with a smile before I turn my attention to something else. I don't let many people frighten me, but he scares the shit out of me. He looks like the most delicious thing to grace this earth with his lip ring and backwards cap he usually wears, but he's not sociable. He's cold and that is too bad. He would totally have chicks all over him if he'd smile every once in a while. They usually stay away because of his dark look, unless he pulls one into his lap and then she's the chosen one for the night and squeals like a fucking pig. Ugh!

Luckily I don't have to look at him for much longer and Cory doesn't have to continue the straw massacre of the century because the band makes their way to the stage. Ryan's on drums, Lyric is lead guitarist and vocals, and a guy named Jimbo is bassist. Ryan says he's a fill-in until they find someone else. I hope they do soon because the guy doesn't fit Lyrical Obsessions rock style at all. The crowd gathers at the front of the stage, but my party stays where we are. Well, except Ryan's bimbo. She follows just like a groupie.

They start and I immediately recognize the song because Fin loves Chevelle. Plus Envy is her favorite song on the Hats Off to the Bull album. We all stand but since I'm short I stand on my chair to get a better view. Lyric's whole demeanor changes on stage. He actually talks and works the audience almost like a lover. The girls scream and he strokes the microphone stand like it's his dick, and I'm not going to lie. HAWT! I'm so into the performance I don't notice the whistles and stares coming from behind me. Then I see David's eyes plastered to something or someone toward the bar.

"Fuck, she's hot." His bimbo hits his shoulder and pouts, but his eyes are trained on another so he ignores it.

I turn around and see who has his attention and she is hot. She's tall and slim with black shorts that kiss her ass cheeks and a white tank top displaying bright red lips on the fabric. In fact I think she's braless. The red lips match her fire engine red hair that's straight as a board and flows down her back. The upper part of her arms are colored with half-sleeves of tattoos and it makes her even sexier. I really love her black knee-high boots with red ribbon lacing in the back, which forms a bow at the top. I watch her as she makes her way to the bar and Janet walks out to hug her, but soon they are in an argument. What the hell? Nobody has ever argued with Janet and got away with it.

"Okay. I haven't been with a woman in a while and swore that dick was so much better. But with her I'd definitely give it a go."

Startled, I look at Cory. "You've been with a girl? Oh hell! Never mind. I don't want to know." My attention is once again brought to the firecracker that is done raising Hell with Janet and is now making her way up the stage. And she looks pissed. She gets up there and the music stops before she yanks the mic from Lyric. *Oh shit!* He looks pissed too.

The audience is a mixture of catcalls and boos from the interruption, but she just gives them the finger. "Tell me one fucking thing and I'll leave. Who the Fuck is riding the black 88' Harley FXRS and is parked in the staff parking?" Her voice is familiar but I know I've never seen her before. This girl is like a redheaded sexed up Kat Von D.

Lyric walks over and grabs another mic from the bassist. He stares at the redhead with enough anger to set her on fire. "Me."

Her angered eyes squint before she stares him down while slowly walking closer toward him. I feel a shake on my shoulder and look down to find Trudy. "Yeah?"

"Do you know who that is?"

I shake my head and turn back before she can answer. This shit's getting good. You can feel tension in the air and it's almost electric. When they are close and staring at one another all Hell breaks loose. The girl rears back and punches Lyric right in the mouth before she jumps off the stage and shoves past people, vanishing out of sight. Lyric stands there rubbing his jaw, watching her disappear into the crowd looking just as bewildered as everyone else. However, his look is more savage.

People are screaming and chaos is everywhere, but Trudy is still beside me trying to tell me something so I give her my full attention. "Who was that?"

Before she can answer Janet walks up and looks at Trudy and me. "Blaire's back. And the girl is fucking pissed."

The End

Acknowledgements

Thank you, God, for all the blessings

Thank you, Jordan, for being an awesome supporter and the love of my life. Thank you, Bethani, for being my little princess and making me smile when you're around. And thank you to my future adopted son or daughter. I can't wait to meet you.

Mari and Juliana with Keepin' it Real Book Blog, thank you for becoming awesome friends and pimps for the stories I write. ❤ you both.

Abby and Lisa with Abby's Book Blog, thank y'all for keeping me encouraged and making me laugh on several occasions. Xoxox

Jammie Cook, my sweet assistant that has really been a life saver and someone special to me, thank you.

Bethany and HEA Bookshelf Blogger. Such sweet ladies and love to pimp Indie Authors. Thank you.

Thank you, Max with The Polished Pen, for making Editing so much fun. You are so awesome.

Bella Bookaholic, Emma Readbooks, Patricia with A Literary Perusal, and many, many, many more Bloggers. Thank You All and I Love You.

Authors are my Rock Stars. \m/

R.D. Cole lives in lower Alabama with her husband and little girl. She is looking into adoption to help her family grow and loves animals. She has seven dogs that are spoiled and would take in every stray if she could. Her husband eventually put his foot down. She loves to read, write, paint, and dance, but also loves to go muddin' with her friends on Team Mayhem. She believes in God, family, and friends.

Website:

http://www.authorrdcole.com/

Facebook:

https://www.facebook.com/r.d.coleauthor

Titles by R.D. Cole

The Learning Series

Learning to Live (Book 1)

Learning to Heal (Book 2)

Learning to Forgive (Book 3 coming soon!)

Learning to Stand (Book 4 coming soon!)

New Series

Pretty Country (Book 1)

TOUCH ME (TOUCH, #1)

t. h. snyder

PROLOGUE

SUNDAY SEPTEMBER 2, 2012

At this very moment I'm sitting on the back of a Harley, which could very well be stolen, setting off into the sunset with an amazing guy. His strong muscular form is driving and the vibrations of the motor send shivers through our bodies.

I recall the past few years I'd spent with my ex-boyfriend, Marc. I close my eyes and rest my chin on this man's back. It's easy to remember the heartache and the pain of loneliness. I can still sense the tears I shed for Marc. My ex never cared for me the way I loved him. I was in love with Marc for years; he played my family and me for fools. Marc stole my heart and stomped on it the day I found him in bed with my best friend Natalie. That day I lost Marc and I lost a huge part of me as well. I told myself I wouldn't give my heart to another man again.

The wind ripping through us feels cool against my body and it's tangling through my thick, wavy, brown hair. I scan my eyes looking down along his powerfully built chest and see my arms wrapped around his waist for fear that I may fall. The mere thought of falling in love scared me for too long.

My eyes move over his broad left shoulder and I catch a glimpse of my reflection in the side mirror. The twinkle in my big-brown eyes and the smile across my face bring out an emotion as if I'm a little girl just waking up Christmas morning.

I have a sense of freedom that I haven't experienced in a long time. I never imagined emotions this strong would consume me again.

The past few weeks are nothing I ever imagined. This man in front of me is the one who allows me to be me. He loves me for the person I am, not the woman he wants me to be.

CHAPTER 1

SATURDAY AUGUST 11, 2012

CHAR

"Shit, ouch, double shit!" I bounce across the living room on my left foot, stubbing my toe for the hundredth time. Ugh, when the hell is Chloe going to send for the rest of her shit?

My sister promised the movers would be here yesterday to move out the last of her non-essential things from my small one-bedroom apartment.

Surprise, the movers never showed or worse she never scheduled them to come.

As a single 24 year old female, I don't need much living space; I do however prefer things have their place in my little world and these boxes do not deserve a spot here.

My apartment is indeed small. It's really all I need for me. I have everything decorated the way I want it and my place is cozy. It has a modern flare to it with my wall décor, curtains, and the few pieces I have scattered around. The furnishings are a slightly used leather couch and chair in the living room which makes it extra comfy and a giant sleigh bed in the bedroom. The place comes together quite well, except for the cardboard boxes I want out.

I don't know why I even bother getting angry. I love my sister, I do, but her lack of consideration for others amazes me sometimes.

Chloe is my older sister, the one I always cover when she can't figure a way out of a jam. Chloe is older than me by two years, but I always thought I was the more responsible sibling.

Ugh, to hell with her. I'm not going to dwell on the drama, at least not for the next five seconds. Then the pain of my toe smacks me in the brain, "Ouch!"

Chloe got an amazing job, the chance of a lifetime for her. Since the offer, she has relocated herself across the country from Boston to Los Angeles. She can pursue her dream career as a sports analyst for ESPN and to be honest, I'm proud of her.

In addition to these damn boxes, Chloe also left a wee bit of man drama here to keep in line. His name is Derrick Peters, and he is madly in love with my sister. Chloe and Derrick have been dating since they were in eleventh grade.

I know that one day they will find themselves back together and get married, but for this moment he is once again waiting for her.

This isn't the first time these two have attempted a long distance relationship.

I remember the day our mom and dad took my sister to New York University (NYU). I thought he was going to lose his mind. Derrick sat on the front porch as the car pulled out of the driveway and didn't move for the remainder of the night. He was a hot mess that I couldn't stand. Derrick was Chloe's problem to take care of, not mine.

Here we are, six years later facing the same Chloe and Derrick drama. The wonderful kid sister I am to Chloe and best friend to Derrick, I keep him occupied and make sure he doesn't get into trouble.

RILEY

"Dude, where's the hammer?" Derrick asks as I walk in the front door.

"Well, hello to you too Derrick." I answer in a cocky tone.

Even though Derrick and I met a few weeks ago, we've built a bond of friendship as though we've known each another longer.

"I sure as hell don't know what you're talking about. Aren't you using the hammer dude, its right there? Besides take a break from being Mr. Fix-It and grab some of this shit so it goes in the right spots this time."

"I'm just trying to finish off a couple of things Chloe and I had planned when we bought this house. Now since she has picked up and moved straight cross country, I have to finish what we started." Derrick says in a pissed off tone.

Damn Derrick, what the hell was this guy doing to his house? He's been a real mess since I met him a few weeks ago. I moved here to avoid drama, not live with it again. After my parent's death and my sister's refusal to talk to me, I don't see a need to surround myself with people who are crazy.

I busted my ass for six years after college helping dad build up the contracting business. We were damn good too. It's amazing how one week and a bastard for a brother-in-law can ruin your life; taking hard work and dreams away.

The abrupt decision to move from North Carolina to Massachusetts may have been a dumb idea. With no family left and losing my job I figured hell why not. After all, I'm a huge Red Sox fan.

Thank god I was lucky when I came up to visit the city of Boston a few weeks ago. I met with Derrick after seeing an ad on Craig's List for a roommate. He had a place to live that cost little in rent, allows me to keep my dog and is in a small town not too far from the city limits. It was a perfect fit to start my new life.

So I moved in a few days ago.

Without a real plan or career direction, I packed up my loft apartment, loaded up the Durango, and hit the road with Manny my bulldog.

After Derrick and I bring the bags into the house, I start to put shit away. Now that everything is in its place, I decide to help Derrick find the tools he needs for the latest house project.

Derrick appears to be a smart man. He's a junior partner at a prestigious law firm, but to be honest I don't know how handy he is in the home renovation department. From what I gather, he is trying to upgrade his new house little by little. Good thing he has a craftsman and building contractor living under the same roof.

After we found the tools Derrick was looking for, I decide to take a seat on the couch. I watch as he attempts to hang a set of shelves next to the TV. The man doesn't seem to be struggling, so I figure why bother offering my help.

I ignore him and the offbeat hammering, kick up my feet, scratch Manny behind the ears, and turn on the tube. The Red Sox are playing the Phillies, not a chance in hell the team will lose this game. Come to think of it, I need to get my ass to Fenway to watch the team play in person. Hell yea, adding that to my Boston to-do bucket list.

The decision to move was good; a change of scenery was what I need. Derrick and I mesh well; we're two peas in a pod. The house gives enough room to have privacy when needed and Manny is happy to have a huge backyard to run and be a dog.

Things were starting to work out. Life is good...for now.

www.ingramcontent.com/pod-product-compliance
Lightning Source LLC
LaVergne TN
LVHW020702110826
845149LV00012B/2082

* 9 7 8 0 9 9 1 2 8 9 4 1 7 *